boyracers

alan bissett

Polygon

FT
Pbk

First published in 2001 by Polygon
Revised edition published in 2002; reprinted in 2005;
this revised edition published in 2011 by Polygon, an imprint of Birlinn Ltd

West Newington House
10 Newington Road
Edinburgh
EH9 1QS

www.polygonbooks.co.uk

ISBN 978 1 84697 178 5

British Library Cataloguing-in-Publication Data
A catalogue record for this book is available on request from the British Library.

Typeset by Hewer Text UK Ltd, Edinburgh
Printed and bound by Clays Ltd, Bungay, Suffolk

for the lads who were there

Colin Armstrong
Allan Mann
Thomas Tobias

heddy haw

like rebel angels, bright, restless, sensually attuned to the flux and flow of mortal Falkirk, Belinda our chariot, our spirit guide, the wind rushing up and past her face thrust out like some wido Helen of Troy. The low growl of Belinda's undercarriage as Dolby shifts her into fifth and our mad singing at the dusk – mine, Brian's, Dolby's, Frannie's – Hallglen receding like stars at warp speed cos it's Friday, seven-thirty, time for Top of the Pops, and tramps like us, baby, we were born to run. The Glen Brae carrying us down down into the belly of the town, where houses are big and where one day we'll live, playing pool and drinking cocktails, in a champagne supernova in the sky, where a woman, a rich woman, is bending down to weed her garden and her arse flashes up in the air, then is gone. We whistle, like a release, like the end of a shift. Frannie, in the back seat next to me, telling another work story, his Rangers shift giggling with him, talking about some guy in Tesco who has the nickname Ace of Spads.

'Ace of *Spades*, ye mean?' Dolby says.

'Naw,' Frannie's like, 'Ace of *Spads*. He gets drunk wan night ower in Spain an asks this guy tay tattoo Ace of Spades on his face. Big Motorhead fan, ken?'

'I like him awready,' Brian says.

'So the Spaniard can hardly speak English, let alone write it, and this drunk Scotsman's no makin much sense.' Frannie snorts, kicking the back of Dolby's seat, knocking the wee plastic Han Solo off his place on the dashboard. 'I mean, can ye imagine it – no only gon intay yer work wi Ace of fuckin Spads tattooed across yer mug, but it's no even spelt right?'

Brian's phone plays The Good, the Bad and the Ugly theme somewhere under the maps and Mars bars and Eagles CDs and whirlpool-fitting requisition forms, muffled by the roar of Belinda's engine passing from

1

FALKIRK DISTRICT to STIRLINGSHIRE, Dolby trying to teach me the laws of physics with an Irn-Bru can, Frannie slobbering over a fish supper, dripping its vinegary smell, and there's streetlights, millions of streetlights, passing like tiny orange fish in the ocean.

A Stirling ned, as we pass through Bannockburn, senses our Falkirkness through the walls of the car. He unfolds his Tommy Hilfiger arms from his Tommy Hilfiger chest, throws a coin at us. It hits the bus shelter across the road. Brian's for stopping the car and going back, but Frannie's not giving a shit, not really, his cheeks full as a hamster's and wet cod slipping onto his Rangers top – 'faaaack!' – it slides a slow snail trail.

Dolby holds up the Irn-Bru can like a teacher. 'Right,' he begins again. 'Now this can is currently travellin at' – the speedometer – 'sixty-six miles per hour.'

'Sixty-six?' Frannie goes, trying to clean the grease from his top with some Barrs lemonade and an AA map of Saltcoats. 'That aw?'

'Whaur the fuck's that phone?' Brian's tutting, turning to me. 'Have you got it, runt?'

'Now if I wis tay drop this can,' Dolby explains, 'it wid land . . . thus.'

He lets the can go. It drops straight down.

'Brian Mann here,' Brian answers gruffly, finding his phone.

'By why does it no land in the back seat ay the car?' I say, confused, wishing I hadn't spent four years of Physics lessons gazing at the back of Tyra Mackenzie's lovely head and hoping I don't end up in a job at the Grangemouth refinery, where someone's life might somehow depend on my knowledge of the effects of speed on an Irn-Bru can. 'The car's movin forwards while the Irn-Bru's still in the air,' I say, 'I dinnay understand it.'

'Is it cosay the theory ay relativity?' Frannie asks, between gulps of fish supper.

Dolby shoots him a withering glance. 'Got fuck all tay dae wi the theory ay relativity, ya dick. It's cos the can is travellin at the same speed as the car.'

'But no while it's in the air,' I say, 'No while it's fallin.'

His face creases. 'How's that likes?'

'Cos it's no touchin the car.'

'Eh? Whit?' Dolby says, 'Alvin, this Irn-Bru is travellin at sixty-six miles per hour whether touchin the fuckin car or no.'

Brian runs his thumb along his stubble almost hard enough for it to catch fire. 'Aye,' he grunts into his phone. 'Naw.'

and we know it's somethin to do with Smiths (the pub) (where he's a barman) (having just turned nineteen) (cos he's Brian the fuckin Mann and he takes shit off nobody) (except 'burds') (except 'Catholic burds especially') (because 'it just feels durtier wi Catholic burds, Alvin, I dunno why').

'Anywey,' Frannie coughs, lobbing the remains of his fish supper out into the Dunipace waste, 'guess who I wis oot wi last night.'

'Oot wi oot wi,' Dolby says, 'or *oot wi* oot wi?'

'Oot wi oot wi.'

'*Oot wi* oot wi?'

'Listen,' he emphasises, 'I wis just oot wi her, awright?'

'Aw.' Dolby's face falls. 'Who?'

'Scarlet.'

'Who?'

'Scarlet,' Frannie repeats, raking through the pile of Dolby's CDs which lie scattered: Muse, Foo Fighters, Moby, Cream (that's Eric Clapton's Cream, not the nightclub), the Gladiator soundtrack and Eminem. Dolby? Playing hip-hop? He surely must've bought it thinking it was Boney M.

The Irn-Bru can. How it falls in a moving car. My confused Homer Simpson-ness. It'll come to me.

3

'Aw *Scarlet* Scarlet?' Dolby beams. 'Niiiice. Heddy haw.'

Brian is nodding into his phone, serious. I can actually hear the sound of his thumb rasping across his stubble. 'Aye,' he grunts again. 'Naw.'

'So whit did Scarlet havetay say?'

'Mainly "take yer hand affay there".'

petrol. Pit-stop. Crisps, chocolate, juice stop. Me, Frannie and Brian clamber in to pay for it like a three-headed monster, Frannie straight up at the counter, handing over his patter with the cash to the girl serving. 'Could you tell us how to get to Abadeeeeeen from heah?' he says, in an accent so ridiculously posh she has to twig, but no. The girl gives us directions as best she can, even though Aberdeen is in, like, a whole different dimension from Falkirk. Then Frannie's comedy withers in the main attraction which is Brian Mann, movie hero. Clint Eastwood in a shirt from Burtons in the High Street. He strides up to the counter, spurs clicking, and the girl's eyes flick on and a smile curves round her mouth, as he silently hands her his Curly Wurly. How could she know that this smouldering rock of a man was born with stillborn charm. He recently tried to chat up a girl in Rosie's with the line, 'You're a Catholic, aren't ye? Aye, I can always tell.'

I buy a can of Cherry Coke. 'For poofs, that stuff,' says Brian, stamping three glass bottles of Irn-Bru on the counter, which will probably be gone within the hour.

In the forecourt, that sharp tang of petrol making me feel queasy, Frannie glows. 'She fancied me. See that wee honey? I lightened her day right up.'

'Heddy haw,' goes Brian.

I glance back at the girl. She's arranging the counter. She looks about as inspired as paper.

4

Back in the car. Belinda hums with satisfaction. 'Whaur next?'

'Maddiston.'

'Glasgow.'

'Cairo!'

Dolby starts a debate with me about the new Stephen King novel, while Frannie and Brian, the Ibrox twins, cut across with Rangers news, which means I only hear, 'He's good with ghosts, but shite with aliens,' before, 'Advocaat's the maaaan,' and 'twelve million on one player!' and 'reckon we've got a shot at Europe' all pile on top. Then it's the chiming riff of U2's Where The Streets Have No Name, Frannie's favourite song, and Karaoke Colin, his dreaded pub alter-ego, takes over

I wantay run

I wantay hiiiiiiide

I wantay tear doon the waaaaaaws that haud me insiiiiiiiide

I wantay reach oooooot and touch the

Traffic lights at red.

later, a smooth feeling on the rise into Bonnybridge, the UFO capital of Scotland. We spot a few aliens lingering at bus-stops, bored outside chip-shops, Frannie stubbing his finger against the car window, going, 'There's Yoda . . . and she's Greedo . . . and she's . . . ooh Princess Leia.' Frannie has a habit of rating women as Star Wars characters, even if he's been with far more Jabba the Hutts than Princess Leias.

'Whit about her?' I say, pointing at a tracksuit with pony-tail.

'Her?' he goes. 'Ugh. Darth Vader when he took his helmet aff.'

Then he starts on us. Brian, imposing, hairy, is Chewbacca. Dolby is Obi Wan. Naturally, grinning, Frannie awards himself Han Solo.

'I suppose since I'm the youngest,' I pipe up from the back, 'I'm Luke Skywalker.'

'Naw, Alvin,' Frannie laughs, hurling a twisted crisp-packet at me. 'You're an Ewok.'

> Whaur the streets have nay name
> Whaur the streets have naaaaaay naaaaame

right enough, Brian consumes the three bottles of Irn-Bru, burping happily, as Frannie's phone goes all Christina Aguilera on our asses, and Dolby's pulling Belinda over so we can pish.

Frannie slouches over his own splish. 'Just heard. Celtic beat Aberdeen 3–0.' He shakes it despondently.

I look down the road. About a hundred yards away there's an old couple having a picnic on a fold-down table. Old and gentle. Maybe seen a war or two together, maybe even still in love. Cars whizz past them. The husband carefully spreads onto pieces of bread, while his wife pours from a flask of tea. 'Hey!' Brian shouts. 'George and Mildred?' The wife looks up to see Dolby and Brian shaking urine from their dicks. Brian points at their picnic. 'Sortay thing's *that* tay be daein at the sideay the road eh?'

We cruise past and they stare dumbly at us like tortoises. 'Fuckin noddies,' Brian's muttering, 'I hate auld folk.' He stabs Led Zeppelin into the stereo and his head does a frustrated, funky peck.

Dolby's eyes widen in the rear-view mirror, furious. He's just noticed what I'm wearing. 'How many times have I telt ye, Alvin, get that stupit baseball cap aff.'

'Why?'

'Cos ye make us look like boyracers.'

'Are we no boyracers?'

6

Both Brian and Dolby turn to me. The air gathers menacingly. 'Are we *fuck*,' Brian almost spits, the word curling from his mouth to land on my Matrix t-shirt. I look to Frannie for back-up but his thumb is tapping at his phone, which he shows me and which says the Rangers score.

God's Eleven 0
Hibs 2

'D'ye see any birds in here wi bad perms?' Brian demands.

'Are there stickers on the windays that say On a Mission?' Dolby.

'Are there Buckfast bottles clinkin in the back?' Brian again.

'Naw.'

'Well, take that fuckin thing aff and stop actin yer age.' Brian turns back round and starts singing the wrong words, off-key, to Whole Lotta Love.

'Boyracers,' Dolby moans. 'Typical schoolie.'

Frannie snaps shut his phone, dripping exasperation, and stuffs it away and runs a hand through his hair and goes, 'Whit we talkin about?'

'The, eh, *head-gear* that schoolies and losers wear.'

'Aw right,' Frannie tuts. 'The runt at it again?'

after we leave Falkirk's skanky parts, summoned back into the tan-stocking finery of the sandstone houses, sex begins building up a head of steam under the bonnet. We talk about women and underwear, women in underwear, finally, women *out* of underwear, as we imagine rich wives hanging sheer knickers on washing-lines that flex above fresh, well-trimmed grass. Frannie regales us again with Elaine, legendary section manager who plucked his cherry when he was about, oh,

7

Alvin's age, and they look at me as if it's me alone who's keeping them from entry to the palace of love. 'That's your problem, Alvin,' Brian says. 'You wantay get yer dick oot them books and intay some wee schoolies.'

'They aw go for aulder guys,' I moan, then clench shut my eyes as I realise the bait I've just dangled, which – 'whoooaah' – they clamp onto, hungrily. 'Get them roon here!'/'Gie them ower tay me!'/'I'll show them an aulder guy!' (god almighty). I'm afraid to report, however, that even if Brian has the Mann With No Name physique, the finesse was stolen and shared out between the other two. Frannie, for example, since Elaine, has been known to satisfy the urges of many a frustrated wife between shelf-stacking in Tesco's, and can you really blame some overworked woman of 35, 40, for listening to a horny 19 year-old who tells them how pretty they are, that their man and kids don't appreciate them, christ, they lap the Franster up in there. Every Tesco's Christmas party, Brian and Dolby lose him after five minutes to a quick one with some wookie round the back.

Falkirk town centre. The nightclub doors flung open and a tempo pounding out like jungle drums and the young – drawn from sleepy shires by chart rhythms, block-rockin beats, the call of the wild. Lipstick smoothed over lips, t-shirts unfurled down chests, tights wriggled up thighs, while shaving cuts absorb the splash and sting and

> The Force, Luke is what gives a Jedi his power. An energy field
> created by all living things. It surrounds us and penetrates us,
> and binds the galaxy together with

8

the other sex's body. Midriffs, torsos, necks. The word Dolce, the word Gabanna. Low, slow whistling from Frannie, that becomes

there's not a team like the Glasgow Rangers

Tesco's, as we ooze past, bleeds its red letters down the windscreen. Frannie prays to the place that pays his wages and Brian slaps him – 'fuck off' – slaps him again – 'ya dick'. John Cusack, Renee Zellweger, the Cruiser exuding mik-white grins in the window of Blockbuster. 'Who's read American Psycho?' I say, but we park, disembark, with the laughter of females at dusk, with the Lads switched to automatic, pulled along in the tractor-beam of nice arses towards

Rosie's nightclub.

At the head of the queue are six bouncers. Six pairs of eyes to try and sneak beneath. Dolby turns to me. 'You bring fake ID?'

'Em.'

'Naw?'

'Naw.'

Dolby and Brian shake their heads, weary cops saddled with a rookie. 'Right, well, here's the plan.' We merge into the queue. Frannie has changed from his Rangers shirt into a Top Man shirt.

I recognise the two girls in front of us from school, 15 year-olds trying desperately to look 18. One of them starts adjusting her barely-there chest. 'Tell ye whit I says tay her, Emma,' she seethes, in her mother's voice, 'Make a fuckin choice, I says. Ye canny like Destiny's Child and the Sugababes equally.'

'Fuckin outtay order,' her pal agrees.

'Alvin,' Dolby commands, 'stick close tay us. The bouncer might assume yer the same age.' I shuffle into position. 'If he asks for ID whit should ye dae?'

9

'Pretend tay search for it?'

'And why will ye no find it?'

'Must've left it in ma other jacket. Sir.'

'Good. Dinnay call him sir. He'll probably no go for it, but it's better than just shruggin and lookin like a knob.' Dolby's tone suggest I'm often shrugging and looking like a knob. 'Fake date ay birth?'

I reel it off, smart.

He nods, without much confidence, checking me up and down. Shoes shined black. Shirt almost stapled into place. Hair slick and stiff with gel. I don't feel very old. I feel that over-groomed, stuffed way you do on the morning of a cousin's wedding.

'Have ye shaved?' Brian growls.

'Aye. Twice.'

I peer through the club window. Alvin through the looking-glass. My reflected face looms ghostly in front of me, and for a second I am dislocated, hovering with the pretty faces, listening to chat-up lines from immaculate blondes over the sound of Basement Jaxx/Armand Van Helden/Geri Halliwell. Drinks glowing a Mediterranean neon, live lived in knife-like prime, while I

Stand outside.

In the grey Falkirkness.

Frannie has let in workmates from Tesco's, there are grumbles from the rest of the queue. He does his MC bit – 'Andy, Mark, this is the Lads. Brian Mann, fellow teddy bear. Heddy haw.' They shake hands fraternally. 'This is Dolby, he works at Whirlpools Direct.'

Dolby taps cracks in the pavement with his shoe.

'And the wee yin here . . . this is the runt.'

The pair nod at me, unimpressed, before commencing the Ibrox chat with Brian and Frannie – 'aye, there's definitely a split in the dressing-room likes' – and the queue shunts up.

10

Falkirk cinema across the road is showing Scary Movie. Dolby is chatting up the girls in front of us. They turn over their accents, stroke their 15 year-old curls and sigh 'Work? Oh, well I work for an uh . . . management consultancy firm in Edinburgh.' Q: How can you tell someone in Falkirk is lying about their job? A: It's in Edinburgh. Seriously, have you ever met anyone in Edinburgh – batting their eyelashes, patting their ringlets – who admitted to working in Falkirk? Dolby-Wan Kenobi's gesticulating to these schoolies, 'Canny believe you've no even read an X-Men comic!'

One of them laughs, high and piano-like. 'You're so funny.'

The bouncer leans his meaty head out like a truck-driver in traffic. I duck, fearful, then try to position my shoulders that sort of Liam Gallagher way so that I look older, harder, cooler, but my shirt feels far too tight on me for it.

The queue shuffles up.

A gaggle of girls roams past in pinks and lilacs and my stomach starts flopping like a fish on a deck.

'Y'awright there, Alvin?' Frannie frowns. 'Look a wee bit pale.'

'I'm fine,' I swallow, 'too much Irn-Bru.'

'Too much Irn-Bru,' a Tesco boy splutters, 'aw, the wee man.'

I imagine that, inside, Daft Punk segues into Radiohead and Thom Yorke starts wailing about jumping in the river with black-eyed angels. The floor empties in protest, until the DJ panics and sticks on some dance choon that goes 'Ooa-*ooa* Ooa-*ooa*' and the place goes barmy. But for a brief moment there . . .

'Ye've never seen the film Gregory's Girl?' Dolby is choked, crimson.

One of the girls pats the others hand and says, 'Isn't he funny?'

'Have ye seen Alien?'

'Naw.'

'Are ye alive?'

Why are they still laughing? I'm wondering where the hell I'm going wrong with lassies. All along the queue people are tapping at phones, reading texts, grinning, tapping, reading, squawking, raucous, then a random, hip-hop snatch of thoughts:

How did the Cruiser feel about the world seeing Nicole Kidman's tits in Eyes Wide Shut?

Will the government shut down Falkirk as a non-profit-making industry?

What if the Cruiser and Nicole, right, were just walking down the street, right, and I just walked up to them and asked, 'Can I see your tits?' Would they let me?

Date of birth. Date of birth.

'So you've read Stephen King?' Dolby's urging. 'Clive Barker? Enid fuckin Blyton?'

We are four people away from the head of the queue now. Three. Three steps to heaven. I can feel the music trembling in the base of my teeth. The Lads. Look cool. As gods.

Would the Cruiser and Nicole let me, do you think? See Nicole's tits? But, like, what difference does it make just cos she's in a film? What difference does it make? These questions keep me awake at night. Phones ringing semi-tone chart hits, digital love arriving up and down the queue, the Lads' patter, girls, and I sometimes wonder if it's really truly genuinely alright for someone of my generation to *not* take drugs. I mean, will it stop me from getting a job in the future?

The bouncer, eyes like flints and his smile a tiny razor-cut, turns away two hopefuls (older than me) with a malevolent, 'Backtay the nursery, boys.'

Has anybody noticed I'm wearing a girls' deodorant? (Dove)

Does Dad really believe that Mum's coming back?

Is Dolby stuck at Whirlpool's Direct forever?

Could Spider-Man kick Batman's ass, since Batman has no super-powers, just a really cool outfit?

Why doesn't Tyra Mackenzie fancy me, for fucksakes.

'There must be a law against it.' Brian is discussing Wonderbras with the Tesco's boys.

'False advertisin,' says Frannie.

Dolby will not give up on his crusade to educate these schoolies. 'Whit about Hellraiser?' he demands.

'The Old Firm should join the English Premiership,' says Brian, and everyone mutters, agreeing. 'Scotland's deid for Rangers.'

The Chemical Brothers kick into life and Rosie's howls and stomps its bright colours and I look on, a child at Santa's grotto.

> Hey girl
> Hey boy
> Superstar DJs
> Here we go!

'You're deid, ya fat fuckin bastard!' the spurned ravers are yelping at the bouncers as they retreat, the Gap stark and black on their chests, Newmarket Street cold and loveless and eerie as a graveyard. The further away they get, the more they look like vampires. The bouncer raises a nasty smile and his middle finger.

> Hey girl
> Hey boy
> Superstar DJs

'How can ye have seen Hellraiser 4 and no the first one?'

Does my breath smell of Wrigleys?

13

Do I look like a girl?
Why doesn't Tyra Mackenzie fancy me!
Do I put too much gel in my hair?
I do, don't I?
I nervously run lines from Top Gun in my head, but the only
one I can fully remember is

you screw this up, Maverick and you'll be running a cargo
plane fulla rubber dog-shit
outta Hong Kong

the two girls breeze past the bouncers with a professional tinkle of
their fingers. 'Evenin, ladies.' Their perfume dances happily on the
air and

Here we go!

the place starts jumping. 'Movin oot tay California next this year, boys,'
Brian informs us, his determination made in Scotland, from girders.
'Wait and see.'

It is my hair gel, isn't it? What if Tyra's in there and my hair's stiff
as an Oriental sculpture, my palms slick with Asda-brand gel? What
then? What if I don't even get in? Will the Lads stop letting me hang
about with them?

this is what I call a target-rich environment

boasts the Cruiser in my head, in his pristine white navy uniform, and
I've just remembered that the Cruiser and Nicole have actually split up,
and Dolby (shit!) strolls past the bouncer (what's my date of birth!)

14

who nods his head politely, almost reverentially, then Frannie, then Brian, then (what's my date of birth!)

The bouncer stops me. His hand on my chest.

the world

slows

down

'Whit are you, son?'

His words sound machine-distorted, like a bomb threat, like Arnie in the Terminator. Vhat. Age. Uh. Yoo.

The eyes of the people in the queue. They're all itching to enter once this schoolie gets his Poundstretcher-clad arse out the way. Brian lingers, holding open the door, and beyond it are giggling, tipsily dancing beautiful ones. A guy with a roving mic and a lion's mane of blonde dreadlocks is purring at glittering party dresses. The barman throws drinks like the Cruiser in Cocktail. The Cruiser and Nicole have split up. All of this moves across me in waves, in slow, swimming-pool motion.

'18,' I say in a deep voice, then add, '19 next month.'

'Date ay birth?'

your ego's writing cheques your body can't cash

I tell him confidently.

The bouncer frowns an actual frown, with the mouth turned down at the corners. His skin is pock-marked, rough, and I imagine him stubbing out his own fags on it. A badge on his bomber jacket names him the Outlaw.

'So you're 16?' he says.

'Eh?'

He fiddles with something between his teeth, with all the bored air of a lion after a meal, and I don't believe it: I've given him my real date of birth. 'That date ay birth makes you 16 years old, son.'

I try to laugh, but it comes out as more of a choke. 'But of course I'm no 16.'

The Outlaw raises his tabloid-sized hand, ushers in two pubescent girls. They wink at him. 'Mibbe no,' he mutters, 'but ye're definitely no 18.'

Brian hears this. Nods. I watch him join Frannie and Dolby at the bar, probably mouthing, 'The runt lost it.' So I turn from the throng, braving taxis that vomit more Ben Sherman out into the street. I decide not to bother going to the pictures on my own, laughing on my own, hiding behind a box of popcorn on my own. I head for home. The music dies behind me like a whale sinking beneath the sea.

in the High Street: WH Smith, Burtons, Virgin, Boots, the Body Shop. All empty, stark and flat. Their products stand regimented as if preparing an invasion. A drunk wearing a Scotland top asks me for/demands a pound for the phone, which I give him. He puts it in his pocket and walks right past the phone booth. I stand and watch the numeral X become trapped by the hand of the steeple clock.

crashed and burned, huh Mav?

when I get in, Dad is sleeping on the couch, and Davina McCall is streetmating a rugby player with a poet in Colchester. I switch it off, knowing they won't match (who does?) then throw a cover over Dad and go to bed to read some of Stephen King's Pet Semetary, the bit where the wee boy gets killed by the truck, then fall asleep with Dark Side of the Moon playing and have a lush dream about Tyra Mackenzie and me at a Pink Floyd concert in Paris and during Great Gig in the

Sky she moans, reaches over, whispers, 'Alvin,' then gently touches my
lips with her lips and I

      slip un

           der

               to

when Mum was there. I'm very small, and I'm looking at a big Phillips
atlas on the kitchen table. Sunlight tearing at the curtains. My straw in
a glass of Orangina. Byker Grove is on the telly. Derek coming in,
going out. Home. Mum roaming the kitchen, taking things out of
cupboards, putting them back in again. The scent of her perfume. The
crinkles in the back of her blouse. The smeck sound she and Dad make
as they kiss. But I can't see her eyes. I want to see her eyes. I follow
Dad's finger on the atlas, marvelling more at the hairs on his wrist than
countries so far away they might as well be Narnia. That's America,
son. Ken whaur Mickey Mouse comes fay? And that's Russia, whaur
they wear the big overcoats.

Ra-ra Rasputin?

Eh, aye son. And see – that's Spain. Mind where yer pal went for his
holiday?

Spain, aye. Says there's swimmin-pools outside and everythin.

Aye well, we cannay afford it. Anywey. See this magic wee place
here? He taps a tiny purple head, jutting awkwardly at the top of
Britain. That's Scotland. That's whaur ye live.

I look at it. I have to lean in and squint in order to look at it.

That?

That is the finest country in the world, ma boy.

17

There is hardly room to even fit the word Scotland on it. The letters spill out into the North Sea, swimming desperately towards the Netherlands.

That?

And right in the middle . . . Dad makes a dot with his pencil on the purple head . . . that's Falkirk.

I focus on the dot, try to relate it to the vastness of EUROPE.

That's the town whaur ye live. And see if ye look right intay the centre ay that dot.

He brings out a magnifying glass, so that, if I hurt my eyes enough, I can make out the tiny ridges of pencil mark on paper. That's whaur we are the now. Me and you and Derek and yer Mum.

Then he rubs the dot out.

I wake up every Sunday to the Sex Pistols. Dad in his dressing-gown, straining his vocal chords and slashing an invisible guitar. Today it's Pretty Vacant. I drag myself from bed, a prehistoric thing rising from the sludge. Patch of sunlight outside Derek's old room. Pick up toothbrush. White slugs of paste on the tap. Bleary eyelashes. Shower water revolving into the plughole like in that scene from Psycho and

> We're so pretty, oh so pretty
> We're va-cant!

bare feet making the floorboards groan. Downstairs, Dad is arranging toast on chipped plates. He nods, gives a perfunctory 'morning' as I drip through the back pages of the Sunday Mail, find a report on the lazy Rangers defeat to Hibs, see Frannie zapping barcodes on his next shift, muttering about it. I finger some toast into my mouth and offer Dad the paper, which he refuses.

'Did I ever tell ye?' His eyes alight on the sparrows on the fence outside, and I know what's coming. 'That me and yer Mum saw Elvis Costello live?'

'Elvis Costello? When?' I have to keep sounding surprised when he mentions this.

'1979?' he muses. '1980? It was at the Maniqui.'

I dump a carton of orange juice on the breakfast bar – installed during Mum's formica phase, never removed. A nail-varnish smudge still decorates one end, a quick image of Mum spilling it, her mouth an O of horror, the Baywatch theme playing in the background.

'Elvis Costello at the Maniqui,' I marvel woodenly.

'Well, it was called Oil Can Harry's back then. Docksy's before that. But it usedtay attract a lottay big name acts. Costello, the Jam, the Buzzcocks. Nay artists that stature playin Fawkurt now.'

'Nope.' I start pulling on my Simpsons socks. 'Was he, uh, any gid?'

'Aw aye,' Dad begins, nodding like a toy dog in the back of a car on a long, long trip, 'really gid.'

'Elvis Costello in the Maniqui,' I say again, as Dad's mind and mine dance druggedly around each other. When I cross to the fridge there is a pause which seems as fraught with danger as an Arctic journey. 'The Jam as well?'

'The Jam as well.'

'*And* the Buzzcocks?'

'And the Buzzcocks.'

'Uh huh.'

'Just goes tay show.'

'Yup.'

Dad takes a pensive sip, transporting himself to the fag-end of the seventies, where he is gayly trashing some phone-boxes. I'm waiting to see if there's more of the Maniqui story to escape those coffee-tinged lips.

19

Queueing for tickets in the rain? An interrupted kiss on Mum's doorstep? But no, he is treading towards the stereo and the off-button.

> We're so pretty, oh so pretty
> We're vac

The portable kitchen TV. Ghosts flicker on its screen, slide, merge into images of a cricket match, a great white shark, an awards ceremony, Lorraine Kelly. 'Brad Pitt!' she says, gleeful as a kid, then probably 'table tennis banana prince william huddersfiel,' for all I care.

I Love My Coffee, Dad's mug declares, like a placard raised at some pro-caffeine rally.

'See you fell asleep on the couch,' I mention, for conversation's sake mainly, but Dad quickly tries to justify it.

'Aye,' he coughs, 'I was watchin a film.'

'Aw aye. Which wan?'

Dad takes a gulp of coffee, his eyes on Lorraine Kelly. 'Clash of the Titans,' he says.

'Good movie,' I say. 'Good special effects for its day.' Their wedding video is perhaps half an inch further out than the rest in the cabinet. 'I like the bit with the army ay skeletons.'

'That's Jason and the Argonauts,' he says.

I muse about the kitchen for a bit. The tap is working again. Dad is not going to the job centre today. Or the doctor's. I move the lid of the breadbin up then down, noticing tiny beige crumbs that have accumulated over months. Lorraine Kelly is saying

> and later we'll be making a picture of Ronan Keating from Boyzone using needlecraft.

Dad calls from the living room, 'So whit did you get uptay last night?'

My reflection shrugs in the mirror. 'Stayed in at Brian's,' I call back, with a composure I should've reserved for the Rosie's queue, 'Watched Saving Private Ryan. Played the Playstation.'

'You no too auld for Playstations?'

'Are you no too auld for the Sex Pistols?'

Dad comes into the kitchen, a wry little snort shuffling out from him.

monday. Schoolday. Graffiti on the bus shelter: FRANNIE + ~~GREEDO~~ ~~JABBA~~ JAR JAR BINKS. Funnily enough, I end up sitting on the bus next to a girl who looks like Carrie Fisher. Skin white as a china doll's. Hands folded neatly on her lap. I am about to try and talk to her when she leaps to her feet and shouts, 'Davie, ya fuckin knob ye,' and throws a Coke can down the bus.

The Blade Runner soundtrack in my headphones drowns out the hordes. By the time I fish out the postcard which arrived from Derek this morning I'm calm as Buddha. On the front is a red London bus. In one of the windows, Derek has drawn a stick-Alvin, carrying a book of Horror Stories. The bus runs over another stick-figure, spurting ink blood. Stick-Me is smiling merrily at this gruesome death. Derek thinks I'm warped cos I read Stephen King and listen to Dark Side of the Moon. A *lot*.

Dear Floyd-loving fuck
    All is well in the big city. London has finally been *broken*.
Hoping to grace Hash-Glen sometime soon, but until then give
Dad my best and Mrs Gibson reeeespect.
    Big D.

know that moment in films? When the boat's bobbing to a shore decked in metal, or the police helicopter descends to the roof of the jungle, or the police van draws up outside the drugs bust. The faces of the men. Mouths doing chewing. Bodies locked on rifles. Eyes steel, as little things itch in the skin then

GO GO GO

the bay door opens and they stream out into bombs and bullets and shouts and stabs and glory and death and

Anyway. See when our school bus rolls up at the gates? That's what it's like.

School's a war. All these kids from all these different homes all stuffed into uniform, a pen in their hand and a stencil set in their bag, and told to go fight the good fight. The enemy: each other. A common goal: survival. Some are shot on the first day, never to rise again. Some go in and become heroes, immortal in gold leaf on mahogany in the foyer. Dux medal. Their names we shall remember.

Look from a window onto the quadrangle, with your lesson plans and your union protection and tell me it's not a war. We arrive in first year, our eyes shining like gems, our new blazers coming down past our arms so we can 'grow into them', but by Christmas we're just doing what we can to stay alive, desperate to think of something funny to say in front of the in-crowd and

She's employed where the sun don't set

growling at the smallest in the corridor, lest we be growled at ourselves, nipping out during double French to either smoke hash or buy clothes, depending on which part of Falkirk we're from, and the whole time our whole lives are dependent on every single thing we do in class, every book we (don't) read, every exam we can('t) be arsed to turn up to, and there's politicians on the telly and they're promising us that soon every single Scot is going to have internet access in their homes. In my second year, a bottle fight erupted in the quad. Plastic bottles, right enough, but hurled with enough force to break the spectacles of any dozy sod caught beneath it. Camelon lined up one side, Hallglen lined up the other. A no man's land in between where

She's the shape of a cigarette

emptiness breathed, as barren as the Somme. Everybody finishing their cola and limeade and orange skoosh, slyly smirking at the opposition, wary of big Ronnie Melville standing like an implacable god, overlooking from a high window, eyes picking out sinners the way a hawk hunts mice. But then the bell rang and

She's the shake of a tambourine

a hundred bottles whistled into the air, spinning, aerobatic, leaving defiant grins behind. The beauty of the sight, like birds in flight, an aerial display – poised, hanging, buoyed on the momentum from teenage muscles – that same kinetic force I feel in the pit of my gut as Belinda transports us to where we can be heroes, just for one day.

I'm in fifth year. I've been searching for Private Ryan in this war for that long, stopped really caring about finding him now, stopped caring about punny-ekkies just for swinging on my chair, brand name clothes I can't afford to wear, being chair in the Debating Society, editor of the school yearbook, or even listening to the hash-heads yak stonedly about Bob Marley, OK Computer, Trainspotting, and stopped caring about quadratic equations and French past-participles and whoever Scotland's First Minister is and the only thing I can find any sort of enthusiasm for is disappearing from the babble into an eternal dream where

She's in fashion

she moves through the rarified air, hair bright as sunlight. She takes her seat beneath the Midsummer Night's Dream poster. Words in delicate script above her head, *Now fair Hippolyta, our nuptial hour draws on apace.* Her hand tanned and smooth. She leans. Her bag: Prada. Her throat, speckled and lightly undulating as she swallows. Her phone: Nokia. It plays the love song from Titanic. I imagine her asleep, moaning softly, her hand folded back on her forehead, eyelashes like thin pencil marks. Mrs Gibson is reading to us from The Great Gastby. Outside, a bee bats against the illusion of the glass, and Tyra's eyes flick over at mine, then away. A pen works lazily between her fingers. I write, and in some way it is a communion: They. Cannot. Touch. Her.

me, Frannie, Dolby and Brian in Rosie's, laughing and ordering girls off a menu. Dolby's finger runs down the list and he muses, 'Hmm, I'll have the redhead. Lightly bronzed and easy on the feminism,' and Brian goes, 'Excellent choice,' and the waiter turns to me, for some reason angry, and barks

What foul dust floated in the wake of his dreams!

Mrs Gibson skelps me on the head with her book and I jerk awake. The whole class is laughing, but Mrs Gibson's alright about it, so I mumble something about cough medicine, Miss, um, makes you drowsy. She lets me off, like a guardian angel/fairy godmother/Good Witch of the North. I glance over at Tyra, blushing. Mrs Gibson starts talking about the theme of 'Desire and the American Dream' in The Great Gatsby, somehow seeming to know fine that I was out til one in the morning, cruising car parks talking about Schwarzenegger films with the Lads and I don't care what Brian says, Predator is a much better movie than Terminator.

Tyra's eyes swim with amusement. Me and her are two of the oldest in our year: my birthday's in March, hers is in April, which I think means mentally we're both more mature. She'll be one of the first in our year to pass her driving test, get a Mazda from her parents, start driving it to school with the window down and Sixties songs playing. I used to sit beside her in Computing Studies and she would have to lend me a pen every week, which usually had her initials on it. Maybe she's attracted to me because I'm obviously, y'know, a bit of rough.

Mrs Gibson scratches something on the board about symbolism, roses meaning blood/love. Connor Livingstone, meanwhile, is staring at me, imperious and cool. Wealth oozes from him. He does not fall asleep in class. He does not cruise round car parks. He doesn't have a single spot. Since his first year at Falkirk High School he's been getting private tuition three nights a week, his future assured in the paid-millions-to-move-millions-around industry. His neck suggests rugby and when he speaks, his accent glides all the way down from Windsor Road. Probably reading Tolstoy while I was watching E.T. Still, when Mrs Gibson asks a question and Connor's hand shoots up like an excited toddler's, it's me she turns to.

'Now that you're awake, Mr Allison, how would you summarise Gatsby's character?'

I pause, aware of the eyes of Connor, Tyra, the whole class. I pat my pen against my mouth, look catalogue-model Connor up and down and say, 'He's fake. He's all surface.'

Mrs Gibson cocks her head. The class waits for her reaction, pens poised. Then she scrawls in huge letters on the board THE SURFACE IS FANTASY and everyone writes it down. Even Tyra! She floats some respect my way, as cladding falls in pieces from my heart and I scribble

> How I wish
> How I wish you were here

then draw the cover of Dark Side of the Moon on my jotter. I am a thin ray of light, refracted through Tyra. Mrs Gibson starts prowling between desks, the novel open in one hand, the other trailing like a silk scarf through the room, and whenever she reads from Gatsby she bristles with magic. She should be carrying a wand. Derek confessed once that she was the only reason he ever went to English.

The heat of the classroom. Tyra's reflection in the window. Mrs Gibson's mouth making the words

> We were content to let their tragic arguments fade with the
> city lights behind. Thirty – the promise of a decade of loneli-
> ness – but there was Jordan beside me

Belinda, the Lads

> who, unlike Daisy, was too wise to ever carry well-forgotten
> dreams from age to age. As we passed over the dark bridge

the places we might go, the girls we might meet, the patter

her wan face fell lazily against my coat's shoulders and the
formidable stroke of thirty died away with the reassuring
presence of her hand,

hope Dolby's bought the new Radiohead album

and so we drove onwards

Brian owes me a fiver

through the cooling twilight

might buy a chinky

towards

the sky, fast, lit like a huge dragonfly, the road out of Falkirk before us
and Radio 1 doing Ibiza, Sara Cox addressing the glorious San Antonio
sun setting over the sea (which would be ruined, for me, by some pixie-
like presenter sticking a microphone in my face to ask if I was 'avin it
laaaaaaaahge' but there you go) and each time she shouts the word
'Abeefa!' ravers go apeshit in the background, and there's this joke that
Frannie's telling us:

'A Rangers fan dies and goes to heaven, right, and the archangel
Gabriel is pointin out aw the Ibrox legends. Scot Symon, Davie
Cooper, Willie Waddell, Ally McCoist. Wait a minute, the guy goes,
Coisty's no deid! Naw, says Gabriel. That's God. He just thinks he's
Ally McCoist.'

Seems to me the joke says as much about the teller, with Frannie
boy giving it his best/worst Super Ally charm tonight. There's one god

here. He's in the mood, and not just for dancing, and while I try to tell Dolby about falling asleep in class, Mrs Gibson skelping me awake, Connor Livingstone sniggering at me, and all about Tyra's chest, again, Frannie keeps leaning out of the window and whistling at girls and blowing them kisses. 'Hey, hen! D'ye think I look like Han Solo? Dae ye? Whit? Aye, same back!'

Brian is on a shift at Smith's. Our chances of finding any lassies are limited without him. The Franster is trying far too hard to compensate for the Mann's absence, hoping to prove to disinterested Bainsford scrubbers that tonight he's a star, and sure enough he soon gives up and starts singing, for no reason, Sweet Caroline to every girl he sees, at the top of his voice, til one of them – perhaps called Caroline – waves, making Frannie yell, 'Heddy haw!' and Dolby beam with shame and laugh and screech into the tarmac as the lights turn

Red.

Men stumbling from the Big Bar. The most imaginative pub name in Scotland. It has a big bar. The old guys croak and groan, crossing in front of us. A line of brown tweed drapes our vision for a while. The three of us watch and are appalled. There was one night when Dolby, Brian and Frannie found all their dads in Smiths at the same time. They were sitting there at the bar, by chance cos they don't really know each other that well, anyway, the Lads joined them, and they discussed the football, music, the telly, all the shite we talk, except sitting there before us like that, they told me later, they had a vision of their future. The horror of it. They walked out of the pub as though they'd just been given six weeks to live by the doctor. I bet Falkirk never seemed so dead and wasted and dustbin lid as it did that day.

Derek in London. The Vegas-like vista from his window. The beautiful, intelligent Cosmo models in every lift, in every restaurant, while We. Are parked. Outside the Big Bar.

Frannie turns to me. His eyes are clear and hard. He jabs a finger at the pensioners. 'I swear that'll never be me. Shoot me if that's ever me.'

Dolby's fingers make a gun shape and he shoots him, like Mr Blonde in Reservoir Dogs.

Amber light. Blockbuster video on our right hand side. Tom Hanks grinning away (I've been told I look like him) (and the wee swot from the Breakfast Club) becomes elongated as – green light – Dolby starts to gather speed and unfold away from the old guys who yell at the noise from our getaway across central Scotland, making Frannie shout, 'Fuckchoo man!' like Al Pacino in Scarface/Carlito's Way as we hit the open road, a snake attacking a rat, fangs glinting, the old guys trailing behind us like grey skin cos We. Are. The. Fucking. Future.

'Runt,' Frannie says, turning to me, 'there's a night in Smith's comin up. You gonnay start getting pished wi the Lads soon?'

I'm well aware that I still have no idea at all what it must be like being drunk, or having sex – or being drunk and having sex – the booze-soaked fumbles which everyone at school seems so icky about by Monday. 'Ye dinnay look at the mantelpiece when ye're stokin the fire,' is Frannie's fat-girl escape clause. I'm in absolutely no hurry, but Frannie, for some reason, won't let it lie, as though my virginity some-how emasculates *him*. I imagine the night in Smith's: me strapped to a seat, as super-lager is poured down my throat, before being made to sing Hello Hello, We are the Billy Boys, like in some grotesque Clockwork Orange experiment.

mum stumbling across a road in a pissy Scottish town somewhere. Paisley, Penicuik, Perth

'Nup,' I tell Frannie, 'I will not be gettin pished wi the Lads.'

'No even Bacardi Breezers?'

'Certainly not.'

'Toddlers can sink Bacardi Breezers, Alvin,' Frannie sighs. 'Dolby, tell him, he listens tay you. Although fuck knows how, cos ye talk shite.'

Dolby grimaces as though being told a favourite son is gay – which I'm not – and I resent his tone a bit when he says, 'Are ye sayin ye'll never drink?'

'Never,' I insist.

'Never?'

'Never!'

'Ye can never say never.'

'Never never never! There, I said it three times.'

'Why?'

No. I'm not going to tell them about Mum. I mean, they're aware, but they don't *know* anything. But one day I might tell Dolby about the sound of that first glug of vodka, the slurredly maternal words, the day she went missing, and I came home from school to find

But I'm not telling Brian or Frannie. They'd just say, 'Get a grip and get on wi yer life,' the undercurrent being exactly what Frannie tells me now: 'Alvin, you truly are a poof.'

'Whatever, man.'

Belinda rolls on. The world rolls under her. I'm not a poof. I just don't shag. I don't see any immediate reason. Still seems like something to me elephants should do, not people, so I just pick up the copy of FHM in the back seat, which lies next to Autotrader (Dolby has ringed a Renault Megane), flick through moodily, scan the interview with the actress Denise Richards posing naked with a serpent beneath the words Eden Better Than The Real Thing and the Lads start pissing themselves at a vision of me wandering the pub, gassed on shandy, beerily asking girls what their favourite books are, but I don't care, so instead Dolby tries to bring me back in by talking about the new Clive Barker novel as Belinda floats across a rise

into Laurieston, and Frannie has already covered his face with the Rangers News and Dolby thinks the book is (but I know it isn't) a sequel to Weaveworld.

'How did the boy Barker write Weaveworld?' Dolby gasps. 'Imagine havin brought somethin like that intay the world. Imagine bein like Jakey Rowlin, or the guys that did the Matrix.'

'I totally agree,' I say, totally agreeing, even although Dolby pronounced it ma-trix rather than may-trix. 'Why dae anythin unless it's a masterpiece? Why live if ye dinnay wantay change the world wi yer thoughts?'

'If ye're gonnay record an album, make it Dark Side of the Moon.'

'If ye're gonnay write a book, write Weaveworld.'

'If ye're gonnay talk shite,' says Frannie, 'it should be the finest quality shite. Fuck are yese on aboot?'

'Listen,' I say, suddenly passionate, '*we* should dae somethin. Us. We should make a film . . . or form a band . . . or drive roon America . . . or gotay university.'

'University?' coughs Frannie. 'Fuck *that*.'

Our future is emblazoned across the sky. Weakness is not permitted, pain is discarded like litter at the roadside, as we speed forth speed forth speed forth and multiply, kings of our own world, and nobody is listening to me.

Oh.

'Has anyone seen the size ay Brian's nipples?' goes Frannie.

'I have,' says Dolby. 'Huge.'

'Like plates!'

They are very much the nipples of a pregnant woman, and don't go at all with the highly Mannly look, and soon we're singing a verse of Born To Run like cats injected with steroids by a student who missed the class on injection procedure and so doubled the dose, and as Frannie opens the sunroof to belt out the chorus, Dolby asks me, 'The name Uriel. Whit d'ye thinkay it?'

'Eh?' I say. 'As in the archangel? Out of Weaveworld?'

Dolby has a thing about archangels. He's not religious. He just has a thing about archangels. Frannie has a thing about Rangers, Brian has a thing about Clint Eastwood, Dolby has a thing about archangels. His bedroom's a weird sight, I tell you: Playboy bunnies, Pulp Fiction, South Park, and a huge print of Gabriel bearing the words Let There Be Light. Dolby was furious when Frannie drew a speech bubble on it that said, 'Naw that's God. He just likes tay pretend he's Ally McCoist.'

'As in the archangel out of Weaveworld.'

'I think Raphael's a cooler name.'

'And aw the other Ninja Turtles,' tuts Frannie, who has given up trying to fiddle with the sunroof. Angels, alternate worlds, things that go bump in the night: not Frannie's scene. His idea of Fantasy fiction would be a bed, a line of Tesco's checkout girls, and a Rangers Greats DVD playing in the corner, the crowd roaring his every move.

'Uriel,' Dolby raptures, trying out the name. 'Uriel.'

'Sounds like a fuckin washin-powder,' Frannie grunts.

'Cos,' Dolby says, lowering the music volume, 'I'm thinkin ay changin ma name. By deed poll likes.'

Silence in the car. Blur singing

> Come on come on come on
> Get through it

and there's a slight bump as Belinda flattens the corpse of a cat. Frannie say, 'Ye're changin yer name tay Uriel?'

'Forget it.'

'Or Persil? Or Daz?' The corners of Frannie's mouth rise.

'I kent you widnay understand, ya dull fuck,' Dolby broods. 'I just happen tay like it.'

'Uriel,' he sniggers. 'Or whit about Muriel? Or Urinal?' and I can see him in the queue for Rosie's already: 'Alright ladies, have ye met ma mate Urinal. Ach don't mind him, he's always pished.'

This isn't as unexpected to me as it is to Frannie. We'll be browsing the Fantasy section of a bookshop, when Dolby will turn and say, 'D'ye no think that if ye had red eyes the women would totally love it?' or be paying for petrol in some rural backwater and he'll whisper, 'These places often have strong werewolf legends,' and look about, actually *wanting* something to spring from the bushes to bite and transform him, and it's a lot to do with why I like him, to be honest.

Who doesn't have that wish?

mum and dad screaming at each other. Derek ushering me upstairs to watch Spider-Man cartoons. Dad's voice. Did ye drink it? That's aw I wantay ken. Did ye fuckin drink it? The Manthattan skyline, the web-slinging, the air soaring

'Aye awright, Frannie,' Dolby's muttering, his skin starting to hiss, before turning to me. 'Anyway, Alvin, this Connor Livinstone bastard. Whit's happenin wi him?'

I tell them about Connor's club of rich acolytes, his smirk, how he claims to have tried charlie ('Charlie who?'), his working mother (Strathclyde University), his working father (Chartered Accountant), his entirely, as it happens, working fucking family. Frannie pauses to consider this, before going all Harvey Keitel in Reservoir Dogs. 'Whatchoo wanna do,' he says, 'is break that sonofabitch in two.'

'Seriously,' I say, 'what *am* I gonnay do?'

'Seriously?' says Dolby.

'Aye.'

The car screeches to a halt outside Tyra Mackenzie's house. Her door has frosted glass panels. Marigolds, tulips, roses. The number 9 in brass.

'Ally McCoist's old shirt number,' Frannie breathes, 'it's a sign.'

Dad met Mum at a punk venue. I still can't get used to the idea of a punk venue having ever existed in Falkirk. The way Dad tells it, the motorways of Scotland were packed with safety-pinned youths trying desperately to get to Falkirk to see the Drunk Fuckpigs or something. He once told me and Derek the story, out of the blue, on a beach in Irvine or Girvan or somewhere: how he saw her for the first time, wearing her New York Dolls t-shirt. I mean, boys, no even the Pistols or the Clash? The New York Dolls! He sighed. Classy. The waves crashed against the sea in doomed battalions. A child's name was dissolved by the tide. It was getting cold. Me and Derek glancing at each other. There wis this ither guy getting ready tay talktay her, and he could see me thinkin the same thing, so the two ay us went for her at the same time. Some skinheid battered intay the poor fella, so I reached her first. He beamed proudly. It sounded like something out of Back to the Future to me. Just think, boys, he said, and then came the chilling part. If it wisnay for that youse might no be here.

There you go. Born from the failure of a drunk skinhead.

I have to be able to scare my own son shitless like this. I have to sit him on a rock on the beach at Irvine or Girvan and say, 'If my mates had never stopped outside yer Mum's door that night,' and make him too realise that through such accidents are fucked-up teens made.

Dolby and Frannie's stares try to push me from the car, up the path. 'No,' I say, thinking: Tyra Mackenzie!

Then Karaoke Colin starts murdering Sweet Caroline again and Dolby's asking, 'How wid this Connor react tay you walkin the corridor wi her?' He points. Tyra is visible, pottering near her window, and I duck out of sight.

'Nay way,' I stress, my heart both retching and in love, 'I'm no makin a fool ay myself just for entertainment.'

haaaaaauns

'Alvin, how wid he react?'

'Naw.'

touchin haaaaaauns

'How wid you react then?'

'Um well,' I say, 'probably be . . . envious.'

'*Envious*,' Dolby rolls the word around his mouth. 'Tastes gid.'

reachin oooooooot

'Shut the fuck up, Frannie. So ye gontay her door or no?'

'No.'

'Are ye a pussy?'

'Whit?'

'I said are ye a pussy or a Lad?'

'I'm a pussy.'

touchin meeeeee

'Meow.'

Touchin youuuuuu

'Frannie, give it a rest eh?'

SWEET CAROLINE
Di deh-deh-deh
GID TIMES NEVER SEEMED SAAAAAE GOOD

Dolby clamps his hand over Frannie's mouth. 'Alvin,' he urges, 'don't be the runt all yer life.'

I think: this from the man who wants to be called Uriel.

But these guys have done it, lived it. I've had no Elaine Section Manager propped up against the stock room door. I've never fitted a whirlpool. I've never even been drunk. Belinda chugs, listening, and it's almost her I feel like I can't let down, not the Lads, not even myself really. Belinda is the closest I've ever been to something with a girl's name. Without her, I'd still be staring out of my bedroom window at drizzly Hallglen roofs and fridges dumped in gardens, mumbling along to Comfortably Numb. Yet here I am, outside Trya Mackenzie's house, heart doing mad choreography, Tyra herself, perhaps, dreaming right now of a knight who will ride along on a shining steed to save her.

'Okay boys.' I breathe deeply, thinking about my parents' eyes meeting across a room of pogo-ing bodies, and say, 'I'm gonnay fuckin dae it.'

'Heddy haw!' explodes in the car like a flare. They start shaking my hand, slapping my back, as if me and Tyra's wedding date has just been announced in the society press. 'Gon the wee man,' says Frannie, 'ye'll make a Ranger yet.'

I can do this.

'To Tyra Mackenzie,' Dolby toasts, and we each raise our cans – Sprite, Irn-Bru, Cherry Coke – making a metallic clink and a ripple of laughter. Already I envisage us in Smiths, like captains of industry,

36

puffing cigars and reminiscing about the time when the bold Alvin won the heart of Falkirk's finest 16 year-old, and Brian will arrest my shoulder with a huge palm and boom, 'Bloody good show, old chap,' and then they will

Boot me from the car and drive off.

Oh shit.

I look up and down the street, inhale fumes of money. Sometimes, when the wind is blowing in the right direction, these fumes will waft through Hallglen, and we stand on our tiptoes and sniff and dream and build patios, knock walls through, in imitaton of the gods. Even the grass seems different here. The grass in Hallglen is drunk. Clean windows. Cars smooth and sleek, parked as evenly as dinner-mats. Belinda looks like she's slept with half the town, the Lads making rude gestures through her fly-encrusted windscreen.

Before me, the house of Tyra Mackenzie.

Open the gate. It doesn't even squeak. Walk forwards, firm and deliberate, and be very very sexy. The front door. The way she'll run her hand through her hair. The way she'll link her arm with mine. Everyone in the school envious (it does taste good) as we kiss like stars touching, my exaltation to the top ranks of Falkirk High, the Lads applauding, hanging on my every description of her lightly bobbing breasts and in my head I'm a smirking Cruiser and the door opens and I get sudden inspiration and sing

> You've lost that lovin feelin
> Whoah, that lovin fee–

The woman's mouth purses into an odd shape. Ivory-white knuckles clutch the door and she stares. I stutter, shutting down like machinery, and say and say

'Um . . . I'm from the Save the Kids . . . Trust.'

She smiles, her eyes shiny. Her lips go ooh and she reaches for her purse, scrabbles at some coins. I glance round, desperate for an escape route, refusing to believe that I let Ally McCoist's old shirt number into the decision-making process. 'So nice of young men to be involved with charity,' she's saying, 'not like these louts who tear up and down this street blasting that awful music.' As she looks for change I glance at the car, where the Lads are flicking their tongues at me, Exorcist-style.

'Indeed,' I croak, holding out my hand to accept her change, 'it's very rewarding.'

The lady's nodding thoughtfully, but I'm trying to see beyond her into Tyra's house.

'I hope to go to Sudesh, I mean Sudan, to um.'

The hallway has a terracotta floor. Plants. I can see the names Duke Ellington and Charlie 'Bird' Parker behind framed glass. Her Dad must be a boxing fan.

'To what?'

'Sorry?'

The woman is smiling beatifically at me. 'You're going to Sudan to what?'

'To feed the world.'

But it's not her lightly puzzled reaction to this which makes me stiffen, makes my arse-cheeks clench. 'Who is it, Mum?' Tyra calls from the top of the stairs. I reach to accept the offered change, but must've done it too fast, cos her hand draws back and she switches, in a second, from middle-class citizen helping out the needy to midde-class citizen being ripped off by scum.

'Sorry, could I just ask for some ID?'

A sick feeling expands in my stomach as Tyra approaches.

'You see, bogus operators have been known to prey in this stretch.' The woman laughs patiently/not patiently at all. 'You do have identification?'

I fumble in my pocket, my eyes sliding up past Tyra's waist, her neck, to her eyes. 'Alvin?'

'Hey, Tyra.'

'What are you doing here?' She raises a quizzical eyebrow.

Her mother turns to her. 'You know this young man?'

Tyra nods. She nods the way she writes, blinks, breathes, walks, as though every movement is the page of a magazine being turned by a breeze. 'Of course I know him. He's in my English class.'

The way she says English. Like clear, clean water. The mother looks back at me, faintly grim. I am no longer some passing chancer. My germs are in daily proximity to her daughter. She glares the way Brian would glare at a Celtic fan standing outside Ibrox for no reason. I offer a cute expression that tries to say, 'lil ole me,' but I'd be as well chatting up a squaddie with the line, 'Say, what's your favourite Narnia book?'

'You're collecting for charity?' Tyra asks, and I can't look at her without thinking of Timotei shampoo ads.

'Yes,' I smile, frozen, 'for the Save the Kids foundation.'

'Trust,' her mother corrects me.

'Trust,' I smile. 'I'm going to Saddam.'

'Sudan.'

'Sudan.'

'That's good.'

We all nod. My forehead goes up then down. The absence of sudden killer meteorites in Falkirk is a fresh concern to me.

'I'm still waiting for identification,' her mother says.

'Oh, Mum,' Tyra moans, 'it's just Alvin Allison.' She addresses me. 'Isn't it? It's just you.'

I arrange my face, aiming for Esquire magazine but coming across more like Razzle. The 'just' has just done things to me. I am not Alvin Allison, I am 'just' Alvin Allison, threatless and mystery-less. My manhood is severed with one quick 'just'.

'I can vouch for him, Mum, don't embarrass me. I think it's great what you're doing for charity, Alvin. Not many of the boys at our school have that much heart.'

Oh, if you only knew.

'Look.' The mother is regretting her harshness. 'I am sorry. It's just that one has to be careful. I've seen people casing this property.'

'Well,' I say, changing the subject at the speed of light, 'really must go. You know how it is, Tyra. Lots of disadvantaged babies to feed.'

> She's show-showing it off then
> the glitter in her lovely eyes

clamber back into Belinda, which is playing Suede, who can only get played when Brian's not here cos he thinks they're poofs, even though, according to Brian, anyone with a lisp or a limp is a poof. Frannie and Dolby are having a sigh-filled chat about Frannie's parents, their frowns gone once gear is shifted into and Belinda is coaxed towards a nearby chinky where we put Tyra's mother's money towards sweet and sour pork with fried rice and make contented eating sounds, pausing to stare through rainy windows. Frannie's parents.

> Show-show-showing it off man
> where all the people shake their money in time

What I tell the Lads about Tyra isn't what happened. That's why they're quietly eating instead of driving me to a tattooist to have me branded with the word Pussy. I tell them I asked Tyra to come to the pictures with me. 'Which film?' Dolby asks.

'Meet the Parents.'

I tell them that she seemed flattered to be asked, but that it was a big decision for her and that she was going to have to think about it. Frannie puts his hand on my shoulder, nods his pride, and says, 'Alvin, you are almost a Lad.'

Wish now that I had asked her. But at least it gets them off my case, I will not be called a poof, and in a few days I'll probably believe that I performed some kind of feat of derring-do. What actually happened was that after Tyra's mother left us to it I asked her if she'd ever read any of Stephen King's short stories. She replied that she hadn't had that particular pleasure. Did she want to borrow my copy of Pink Floyd's Dark Side of the Moon at all? No. Okay. Well. Our reporter made his excuses and left.

> Oh Dad, she's driving me mad
> Come see

I once thought I'd do the son-ly thing and ask my Dad's advice about women.

'Dinnay worry,' he'd said, 'ye've plenty time tay play the field. I didnay meet yer Mum til I was about, whit, 17.'

I'm 16.

The sun is going down and tomorrow it will come up.

I study the Lads, wondering how my life/opinions/hair will have changed by the time I reach 19. Dolby's phone beeps, the theme to Close Encounters of the Third Kind. He answers it, talks to someone called Darren about whirlpool stuff. The cape of night begins smothering the town. Dolby shuts his phone, restlessly engages the engine, pulls away

41

from the lay-by where my Sudan/Sudesh/Saddam trip has been devoured and we debate which members of Queen we would be if were Queen. Frannie is Freddie Mercury, Brian is Roger Taylor, Dolby is Brian May, I'm the one that nobody remembers and

That night I dream I'm in The Blair Witch Project.

My vision is dark, shaky, low-budget. Me, Dolby, Fran, Brian Mann, camped in the Callendar Woods with bottles of Becks for rations. Friannie's wielding his camera, going, 'Pout, baby, pout', and it's an outrageous laugh. But then there's this moaning sound, and the wind rises, and the leaves start blinking across the forest floor. The lads point to the space behind my shoulder, and Frannie drops the camera. It whirs in the still, damp leaves. I turn and

> We're so pretty, oh so pretty
> We're va-cant

'Dad!' I roar, turning over in bed and sealing the Sex Pistols from my ears. 'Keep it doon, for fucksakes!'

Sleep deprivation. Didn't they use that to torture witches? The Blair Witch? What? My dream lingers then fades, pulsing into the distance. From downstairs, I hear what sounds like crying, but could be the whine of the back door as it's opened. If it's Dad, I'm not going to him, not after his last performance after watching a Trisha special, 'When Did You See Them Last?' Pull open my eyes. Stuff accumulated on my bedside drawers like a trash mountain or an art project. Darth Vader alarm clock. A shark's tooth in a wee plastic cube. Change from the fags I bought for Dad last night, which he smoked nervously all the way through, of all things, The Runaway Bride. A copy of Stephen King's Misery, its spine cracked and veined. The poems of W.B. Yeats. Things fall apart, the centre does not hold, yeah whatever. A biography of Billy Connolly that Brian keeps demanding back, even though I borrowed it from Frannie. The sound of crying from downstairs again and Scotland's brilllliant the Big Yin grins.

on the bus to school I realise I haven't done my English essay again, though there are reasons for this: mainly Dolby paying for fish suppers all round, which we sucked up greedily in Belinda, parked round the back of the Howgate Centre. Derek has sent me another postcard, his handwriting shaky, which I am reading, listening to the soundtrack to E.T. (really good and not as slushy as it sounds in the film) and a Third Year at the back throws a ball of paper which bounces off my head and I turn and give my best Brian Mann glare, but the motley bunch of gremlins just laugh, all teeth and acne, so I move to the front of the top deck where Falkirk feels flattened beneath my power.

We pass the Royal Infirmary, where I was born. The bus passes this place every day and every day I'm reminded of my own unremarkable position in the world. Nurses come and go, unaware that I was carried there 16 years ago, and surely – perhaps? possibly? – I am worth more than this?

I must be.

Does Dolby know the release date for the first Lord of the Rings film, since this will alleviate our disappointment that James Cameron never did get round to making Spider-Man, a disappointment which gets heavier

and heavier

and heavier

Kids on the bus are screaming, stamping, rioting, laquered gently by the music from E.T. Second Year boys throw punches to the sound of Eliot's flying bike. Falkirk passes by on its way to work, its pavements grey, its buildings sunless, but its air filled for the moment with strings

43

rising towards the sky, and I reckon the world could be this easy to put right. Can't we just plug it into the soundtrack of happy movies and the homeless will find homes, gunmen will pause on triggers, warring spouses will hold hands and go to the window to see the moon eclipsed by the silhouette of a bike?

> How I wish
> How I wish you were here

the squeak of magic-marker down the window of the bus (Keebo is GAY!!!!), joints being lit on the back seat, and I am surrounded by bubbles in a lava pool. They suppurate, burst, without saying anything, and I want to rise out of my own ordinariness, do something in this world, be alive, vibrant, real, but I remember how huge that atlas looked, the one that Dad placed in front of me when I was wee, the size of all those countries with fantastical names compared to our totesy tiny one, and I am Magneto in the X-Men! And I can make the bus levitate and freak everyone out! Girls' mouths twist out of pretty shape, boys as frightened as mice in a storm, all of Falkirk trembling before me as I bombard Connor Livingstone with paper clips and Tyra pleads for me to stop, and I show mercy, which she thinks is totally cool, cos I don't have to do anything of the sort. We'll have coffee back at her place. To show her I'm still just a man.

bus passess a woman in a bus shelter. The rain drizzles down the plastic. From here she looks a bit like Mum, but also a bit like Sissy Spacek in Carrie

approaching Mrs Gibson's desk, the walk of shame. Presently, no excuses are forming for why my essay isn't in, since I'd hoped she wouldn't ask, wouldn't give us the speech about how important our Higher results are, how crucial they'll be for university admission, etc. I don't belong at university, surrounded by fifteen hundred Connor Livingstones. Brian's voice growls from my memory like a rip-cord, what he and Dolby did instead of homework: 'dog it and go fuckin fishin.'

The rest of the class files out. Essays are left on the corner of the table. Tyra places hers down, slings her pink bag onto her shoulder, makes quick eye-contact with me before Bono starts singing All I Want Is You. I plan to follow her, explain my appearance at her door last night, but Mrs Gibson's voice fixes me in place. 'Mr Allison, where is your essay?'

'Miss?'

She is leafing through the manuscripts, secretary cool. 'I don't see your homework here. Have you handed it in?'

'Um . . .' I drift to the pile and pretend to help her look for it, making Mutley noises, but when I see the essay on top – word-processed and headed © Connor J Livingston – I step back, disassociating myself from the whole system. 'Naw, miss, I havenay done it.'

Mrs Gibson shakes her head, folds her arms, looks at me as though I'm a new puppy and it's Christmas Day and all but I can't keep pissing on the kitchen floor like this. I know what she's going to say. Instead of listening, I mentally evaluate Silence of the Lambs and Se7en (result: that head in the box wins every time). 'I had this same trouble with your brother, Derek,' she says, then pauses purely for dramatic effect. 'He told me about your mother.'

Mrs Gibson holds my gaze the way a lioness carries one of her cubs – tenderly, but with teeth around them.

'Do you want to tell me why your work is continually late?'

I sigh. Things escape in the sigh which I can't chase and put back. On the blackboard is written a quotation from T.S. Eliot

Humankind cannot bear very much reality.

'Is this when ye tell me I'm university material again'

'Yes.'

I run my hand through my hair but it gets caught in all the gel. 'What if I dinny wantay gotay university?'

'Well, I'm sorry to hear that.' She is looking at the floor, disappointed. 'Can I ask why?'

Yeah, she can ask, but what do I tell her? The Lads, and how they won't be there? Connor Livingstone and how he probably will? Since the time that Derek would've had this chat with Mrs Gibson, Dad has gotten a lot worse.

I drift to the window, lean my forehead against it so that a cold glass circle forms. Outside in the quad, Timberland fights Versace, leaving dirty marks, and Timberland laughs and Versace rages at the sight of herself and Tyra walks between these warring masses like a ghost. Ringtones all over the quad, a dreamy processional anthem for her, and her hand sweeps through her blonde hair

I can't live
With or without you

'Miss.' My breath mists up the window, obscuring Tyra and the sweep of her world in a single desolate puff. The words will not come. I clench my fist and close my eyes but the pain does not go away. 'Miss, I'm findin things . . . difficult . . .'

as Belinda brakes across the gravel, then silence.

Reedy crickets. The whole of Falkirk lit up in the valley below like something from a Spielberg movie. Dolby going off on some theory

46

about the way the four of us Lads fit together, what we're doing here on planet Earth, all that post-laugh stuff. He's playing the Eagles, with their tequila sunrises and Hotel Californias and tourist-trap American shit that punters like us lap up. Central Scotland is glittering. A black sea filled with phosphorescent fish. The densest shoal is Grangemouth oil refinery. My Dad used to work in Grangemouth, when he could still find work, and I probably will too, trudging through every shift, twelve hours a day/seven days a week, but tonight it looks like a constellation, a shimmering barrier reef. The mood in the car glides like a ray, but the sky is as black and gaping as the mouth of a prehistoric shark, waiting to consume us all, Falkirk, Belinda, the Eagles. Me and Dolby are covering all the subjects we can't when Frannie and Brian are here, since they usually hijack the conversation and drag it to Ibrox.

'Is there anythin bigger than infinity?'

'Are mobile phones part of a government conspiracy?'

'Are the aliens in Invasion of the Body Snatchers *really* so evil?'

'I read somewhaur, right,' I say, 'that the aliens are supposed tay represent the Communards.'

'The commun*ists*,' Dolby corrects me.

He's a closet philosopher. And very good at physics. A clever guy. He's the only person I know who reads page two of the Daily Record, the bit with all the politics on it. He'll say things that make the other two snigger, glance at each other, go back to discussing the Old Firm semi-final (so long as Celtic hadn't won it) but sometimes he stops me in my tracks, translating Discovery Channel documentaries into my language or crystallising a moment with the philosophical words of Jean Luc Picard from the Starship Enterprise. Frannie told me once that he thought Dolby could've gone to university after school, so I decide to ask him about this now.

Dolby shrugs, looks out the window, fiddles absently with the graphic equaliser of his stereo for the start of Hotel California.

But Frannie told me the answer. Dolby dogged school whenever Brian dogged it, forgot his homework whenever Brian forgot his.

Eventually Dolby mutters, 'Ye dinnay dump yer mates.'

End of discussion. He opens another can of diet Irn-Bru and chugs sugar-free girders. 'Jesus,' he gasps, 'I wish the Eagles wid go back on tour.' This is the sound of Dolby handing in his registration for the University of Life. 'Anywey,' he intones, 'better this than studyin.' Slurps. Stares at the black maw of the sky.

'Yup.'

'Only tossers and posh fuckers at university.'

'Yup.'

Frannie joined Tesco's straight from school, became cock-of-the-walk in stock control. Brian worked his way up behind the bar at Smith's, between filling in forms for his dream emigration to the States. Dolby took the job in Whirlpools Direct, installing jacuzzis in homes he'll never get close to owning.

Now he has to know about shower heads and delivery dates.

Not physics.

Or Star Trek.

'But yer only 19,' I point out, 'ye can still go.'

He just looks at me, as if I'm offering him cash to betray a close family member.

'Ye dinnay. Dump. Yer mates.'

I don't like the way he says 'mates', as though it's an accusation, so I divert him back to the old debate about the Irn-Bru can falling in a moving car and he patiently takes me through it again and his Ghost Rider t-shirt glows on his chest. 'The Irn-Bru is in the car,' he explains, juxtaposing fizzy juice with distance over time or something, 'and if the car is daein sixty-six miles per hour, that means the Irn-Bru must be daein sixty-six miles per hour. Agreed?'

'Agreed,' I mumble, scrutinising the outside of the can. I am going to understand the mystery of its vertical descent. I am going to know *how* an object can drop in the front seat of a moving car and not land in the back seat, but like the crap bit in every episode of Friends, soon I'm saying, 'Youse three are all I've got, man.' Actually, I try to say this, but I can't. These things dare not speak their name in Scotland. Dolby talks rationally about Einstein and later also how juvenile the whole Ibiza thing is, but I can see something in him too, trying to wrench its way out, like an alien in a sci-fi movie taking over the host. He eyeballs the landscape in front of us, pretty and glittering tonight but which tomorrow will look just like Falkirk again, and the Irn-Bru can still sits there, still unexplained, still haunting me with its physics and my place in the grand scheme of the Falkirk boyracer circuit.

'See,' Dolby tries to explain, 'it's like each ay us can be seen, right, in the sortay movies we like.'

'How?'

'Think aboot whit happens when we hire a film.'

'Fuck aye.' There was one night when Frannie and Brian had a Mexican stand-off about whether or not we should rent Armageddon or There's Something About Mary. Neither of them would budge. 'Frannie always wants a comedy,' I grumble, 'and Brian always wants an action film.'

'They wantay see themselves reflected in the world.'

'But you like Sci-Fi,' I point out, 'does that no make you a bittay a geek?'

'A dreamer,' he corrects me, 'aw in the terminology.'

'So if ma favourite film is Jaws whit does that make me?'

'A geek. But the point is . . .'

49

and though he tells me what the point is, I can't quite grasp it. It's something to do with how a good video-shop should have comedy, action, fantasy *and* Jaws, and that's why we work, and he elaborates this whole Stephen-Hawking-style formula of group dynamics and opposing forces and the structure of friendships, yet still based, I think, on the video-shop analogy, and though I try to follow it, it just seems to come down to the fact that we're good as a foursome. We're going places with Going Places. Palm Springs circa 2010: the four Lads in Bermuda shorts, and girls in hula-skirts bringing phone calls from James Cameron, apologising for not doing the Spider-Man film. So while Frannie sees himself unfolding in the strike-rate of a classic Rangers forward, Brian in the cigar and grimace of Arnold Schwarzenegger, and Dolby, watching the skies, I see myself in them.

and all of those roads, all of those futures, and this one useless wafer-thin present which we zip through blasting tunes uncool to the Connor Livingstones of this world, as we make the nights ours, every day wiping tables, stacking shelves, fitting whirlpools, studying for Highers, worthwhile for the few desperate moments of escape at high-speed, the faster, the further away we drive, the more that parents, shite jobs, self-loathing, uneven Oasis albums recede in the rear-view, meaning that we can do anything, go anywhere, see anyone, *be* anyone in this pathetic little Scotland-or-something country. Like characters in a plotless movie, we race through night after night, story after story, film quote after film quote, eternity stretching before us as an open road, and *this* is the reason I gave Mrs Gibson for why my essays are late: that you can check out any time you like, but you can never leave.

'Whit dae ye suppose that song's about?' Dolby asks, finishing his Irn-Bru and shifting Belinda into gear.

'A hotel,' I shrug, 'in California?'

'Dick.'

We drive home. Back to Falkirk. Where Frannie and Brian are watching the Scotland game in Smith's, their hands flailing at a near-miss, Elvis Presley singing

> Oh I wish I was
> in a land of cotton

and everyone in a huddle, joining in, delerious at a Scotland win, a swelling shout, and it's a great feeling and I spill my Coke over Brian's new shirt and he doesn't even care

But still. It was the least exciting of all the roads we could've taken that night.

and Camelon, as anyone will tell you, is the Bosnia of Falkirk. Streets like grey labour. Chewing-gum accents and Danielles with their boyfriends and their babies. The thousand-yard stares. Camelon's bowling-alley, though, is the Narnia of Falkirk. Lights. Magic. Sound. Vision. U2 blasting out from all sides and we four walk onstage – Bono, Edge, Adam Clayton, Larry Mullen Jnr – women screaming and the stadium lights coming up and a huge swell of sound charging from us and

> It's a beautiful day!

Dolby pays for the lanes. We scatter over to the pool-hall like pool balls, Brian trying to interrupt Frannie trying to interrupt him. 'Listen, boys,' he warns, 'I'm no wantin nay carry-on the night. Ho. Yese listenin? We'll play a couple ay games ay pool, then I'll thrash Frannie on the lanes, then we'll go hame. That's it.' When there's money involved, which there is this evening, Brian takes things *seriously* seriously. 'Money won,' he reminds us, going all Paul Newman on our asses, 'is twice as sweet as money earned.' He and Frannie have a bet on tonight's bowling square-off. Brian reckons he's Champions League, even though the last time they played, Frannie beat him five games to three, then spent the rest of the evening singing Elton John songs at him for no other reason than the fact that Brian hates Elton John. The Mann was pissed then, of course, which is why he was beaten. Of course. 'Nay boozin this time,' he demands, the spirit of Elton creeping up on him, camply tinkling piano keys, 'nay chattin up birds, and nay,' he insists, '*nay* fuckin film quotes.'

The second Layla comes on the pool-room jukebox, Dolby and Frannie start pinching each other's cheeks and hugging like mobsters

> We was wiseguys, goodfellas, like you'd say to someone
> You'll like this guy, he's one of us, he's a good fella.

Brian slamming three balls in quick succession, aware of the attention we're drawing from Camelon neds. He warns Frannie and Dolby to quit their Joe Pesci 'funny how' routine, nodding to the glaring baseball-caps across the hall. 'Dose fucks?' Frannie says. 'Fuget about it. Whatsa matta witchoo? Wodda fucksda matta witchoo?'

'Quit it,' Brian mutters darkly, perhaps fearing another night in the back seat of Belinda, ground down by Frannie's a capella Rocket Man, 'ye playing this game or no?'

'Mudda fucka.' Frannie lines up his shot, swear words tripping from his tongue. Frannie should really be an adjective

> like you'd say to someone
> You'll like this guy, he's one of us, he's a frannie fella

We should all be adjectives. Film critics should be able to describe the X-Men movie by musing, 'Yes, well it's very dolby isn't it?' Or Dougie

Donnelly comment on the Old Firm game, 'It was a brian mann match for most of the first half.' Or U2 describe their new album as, 'really, the alvinest thing we've ever done.'

Every living-room in every household in the land will know exactly what they mean.

'Who da fuck is dis prick?'

'Very good, Frannie.' (growl)

'I outta have ya whacked.'

'Gie it a rest.'

Brian uncages himself on a line of balls – they ricochet with business – and Frannie, here at his franniest, leans to the girl sitting at the milk-shake counter. Ned-bird hair and tracksuit and trainers. 'Bet ye dinnay hear patter like oors very often,' he smooths.

'Naw,' she agrees, 'there's no that many dickheids come in here.'

Frannie laughs, and leaves her well alone, and we move over to the lanes: four adjectives with milkshakes. Is this because Brian specified no film quotes? Rangers-tight they may be, but Frannie can still wind Brian up like no-one else, like every time Brian's about to release the ball, Frannie goes, 'Muddafuckin asshole jerk-off!' making it spin towards the gutter. Brian can't retaliate when Frannie steps up cos Brian doesn't do impressions.

The girl who called Frannie a dickheid keeps drifting back and forth, a phantom in Fila gear, glancing flirtatiously. She's attractive in a skanky sort of way.

But, then again, here's me in a Meat Loaf t-shirt.

Dolby rests his chin in his hand, tracking her with the precision of a rifle ranger.

'Think she's interested?' I ask hopefully.

'Hm,' he muses, narrowing his eyes.

'I'm bustin your balls!' Frannie yells, as Brian veers off again into the gutter. Might as well be the next galaxy, considering how far he is from beating the Franman now, shown by his bullish neck filling with crimson, his fingers flexing, as Frannie coaxes more pins to the floor then grins.

I feel damn fine tonight. Watching Frannie and Brian joust is like watching Sammy Davis Jnr beat Lennox Lewis, and I've barely thought about the shit going on at home with Dad, or Connor, or Tyra, Derek, or F(uck) Scott Fitzgerald, or my late essays, or my Higher results, or my future disappearing before me. I am actually a long way from caring about these things now. Got my best mates, U2, Belinda parked outside and a road leading to somewhere/anywhere/everywhere. Through a coruscation of neon tubes and MTV adverts (how many kids in Scotland actually snowboard?), the sound of bowling-balls hitting wood, teenage squealing, techno techno techno techno, and Frannie doing DeNiroPacinoBrando, I slink to the toilet. On the way back, I realise I am walking behind the Fila girl. I would very much like to feel a girl.

Pick a part that's new.

'Scuse me,' I cough, tapping her shoulder. She turns and frowns and is meaner-looking than I first thought, sort of like a female vampire in a tracksuit.

'Whit,' she says, the bottom note on a piano being struck.

'See ma mate Dolby over there?' Think of something cool, funny, Hollywood. 'He fancies you.'

She looks over. With all the interest of a plate of cold spaghetti watching a lecture, she says, 'The dickheid?'

'Eh naw, that's Frannie.'

She spies Brian and her face lights up. 'That good-lookin yin?'

'Naw, no him either.' Cold spaghetti again. 'The one sittin doon.'

'Wi the Spider-Man t-shirt?'

'Aye, a really cool yin tay.'

54

She extracts a long piece of gum from her mouth and snaps at it like the crap shark in Jaws: The Revenge. 'Listen, I'm no meanin tay be cheeky or nothin. But wannay yese is wearin a Spider-Man t-shirt, wannay yese is a dickheid, and wannay yese is eh *you*.'

I look at her. I shrug. 'So ye comin over or no?'

Brian snorts at my return, and I get the impression his game hasn't improved. Frannie is performing graceful pirhouettes that culminate in a delicate smash of pins. 'That wis an awfy long pish for somebody wi such a wee dick.'

I grin smugness back at him. 'I, mister Brian Mann, have been chattin up a *lassie*.' I say the word as though it will reveal a cave worth's of treasure to them but

'Whit's the score?' Dolby says.

'Five one,' Brian mutters, sending his ball on another lost cause.

'Heddy haw,' Frannie goes, punching the air.

'Did naybody hear me?' I squeak.

There is a tap on my shoulder and I turn. Facing me is a mug I recognise from the Falkirk Herald 'Round the Courts' section. His names is Steven Cotter – Cottsy to his enemies, and there are many – and he has just tapped my shoulder. His head resembles a bowling-ball. He looks like a sports shop doomed to walk the earth, brand names plastering his body like tattoos. 'Ken wha am ur?'

I nod as though he has a gun at my head.

'Well, see that lassie ower there?'

I look over the rise of his simian shoulder to the track-suited girl, glaring malevolently, having alerted the rest of the apemen. This is starting to remind me of the Hallglen ritual which begins, *Did you swear at ma laddie?*

'Aye.'

Cottsy unfolds his spherical biceps and Olympic committees everywhere feel a tremor in the force. 'That's ma burd.'

I nod again and smile sort of weakly, and wonder if I should say something like, 'and a fine burd she is too.'

From behind me I hear, 'I've won the bet, man, pey up,' and, 'Like fuck ye won the bet. Ye let Dolby take yer third shot, which means ye didnay beat me on yer ain,' and, 'But Dolby didnay hit anythin, ya cheatin bas.'

I cannot hear, 'Look! Alvin's in trouble! We must intervene!'

Cottsy gives me the once-over and I actually shiver. His last appearance in Round the Courts was for an attack at the bowling-alley in Stirling. With an actual bowling-ball. 'Cos she says you tried tay feel her up, ya wee bastard.'

The franniest reply would be, 'Aye, I wis measurin her for a spare tyre on ma jeep.' A retort which would be very brian mann would be a smack to his ape-like face. But I have no frannerian or mannesque qualities, and so the response is, 'Is that right?'

'Ye're a cunty-bawed wee snivellin knob.'

The steel in Cottsy's voice and the threat taking off its jacket in his eyes and the way he's positioning himself. Inwardly, I throw my hand over my mouth and scream. Outwardly, I just keep saying, 'Is that right?'

Ice threading through my veins, visions of Dad and Derek and the Lads weeping over my grave and swearing a pact that Alvin's death must be avenged, and so I keep saying, 'Is that right? Is that right? Is that right?' until he grabs me and roars, 'Aye it is fuckin right!' and when next I open my eyes I see

Brian and Cottsy in a whirlwind of fists

a host of Camelon neds leaping barriers, reaching into pockets

Frannie gasping

the tracksuited vampire screaming, 'You'll get faaakin stabbed!'
a fist heading straight for my face and

in the car afterwards we're totally fleeing, Frannie on the phone, raving to some unseen pal, the streetlight sliding up towards the top of the windscreen, and Dolby's hands are on the wheel as he laughs, glances in the rear-view mirror at Brian, who's as bloody as the cover of American Psycho, but grinning wildly. 'Christ we got hammered,' Dolby sniggers, and Brian stares at the streets, lights. 'It's no so bad,' he murmurs. He sounds almost wistful, as if inhaling the scent from a window-box in Kensington. He licks blood from his upper lip and an image flashes back of him and Cottsy locked in warfare, like Gandalf and the Balrog, a storm erupting around them. The tyres screech as we turn corners, waving at girls as Dolby plays the Jurassic Park soundtrack to calm us and on the windscreen Falkirk geometries turn, sharpen. Dinosaurs clothed in orchestral music, Rangers shirts made bloody, our guardian angels crowding the car, pleading, 'For godsakes don't do this again,' and Lady Macbeth Brian keeps turning his hands, fascinated by them, how red they are. 'It's really no so bad,' he whispers to the passing night.

on the way to the hospital we stop and talk to some girls. They are dolled-up and hunting aimlessly for a party. Everyone, it seems, is hunting aimlessly for a party. One of them leans into the window and whistles at the state of Brian. 'Jesus christ, whit happened tay you?'

'Paintin,' he mutters, still delirious with adrenaline.

The least damaged of the four of us (me) arranges to meet the girls after we finish at the infirmary, but they won't show, and we're not really bothered, so instead we take hold of the road like vikings, singing Eye of the Tiger, as the fight becomes fabricated into mythical status, retold with ever-more incredible details. Brian emerges with Cottsy, two of his mates and a security guard trying to wrestle his heaving form, and we convinve ourselves that the girls were attracted to our masculine glamour, even though we fought like water-balloons, but it's only when we start singing

> I love rock n roll
> so put another dime in the jukebox baby

that I realise this is one of the best nights of my life.

'Thing is,' says Frannie, 'how the fuck did it aw start?'

But nobody knows, and I'm not going to say anything, and in Belinda we zap through Falkirk like a laser-beam, listening to Guns n Roses and Tubular Bells, the dimly-lit streets reeling and shifting with ballet-dancer grace to the sound of LA metal and the theme from The Exorcist and images appear and pop like soap-bubbles, as Frannie and Dolby argue about whether or not B&Q is a better shop than Texas unti Brian kicks sand on the fire, describing the recent Rangers win in a voice that excludes all others, but planet Earth is blue and there's nothing I can do as Dolby's Adidas-clad foot stabs Belinda's accelerator and a rumble shudders up from her bonnet and Falkirk swoops behind us, the Blockbuster window screaming and the smiles of Denzel Washington, Madonna, Kate Winslet are like fly-posters whipped from walls by our passing and that feeling hits the four of us as Guns n Roses sing take me down to the paradise city where the grass is green and the girls are pretty and Frannie yelps, 'Heddy haw!' and it doesn't get any better than this, life as one fast rush of Top of the Pops, shops, the beep of Dolby's phone as he searches for a map of somewhere, anywhere, we can go and the cells of my body are alive, singing, sharp as blades of grass

fifth gear

as Brian goes, 'the Cruiser's best movie?' and titles bat about the car
A Few Good Men Jerry Maguire Cocktail Born on the Fourth of July
The Colour of Money Interview with the Vampire but nobody says
Top Gun til I say, 'nobody said Top Gun,' and Frannie starts to tell us
about every single girl in Tesco's he ever dreamed about shaggi

The pauses are fleeting.

Life lived at breathless jet pace, but then you get older.

The rests are more frequent.

Longer.

The wallpaper becomes bearable.

Until you come back from the fridge.

Sit down in front of the TV.

Realise your day is one long continuous pause.

The world sounds like the hiss of TV interference.

The air is exhausted, breathed too often.

You've either forgotten how to move, or you can't be bothered, so
you just stay there, hunting for your life down the back of the sofa, not
sure when you saw it last.

One time I found a photo of my parents up the loft. Sometime after
Mum left/before Derek left. What was I looking for? Old Spider-Man
annuals? Doesn't matter. The torch sweeping the ghost-crowded air.
That thick pile smell, like breaking into an Egyptian tomb. Dust passing into my lungs. Teddy bears and an old video recorder and cookery
books and battery-less cars and carless batteries and sealed shoe-boxes
and a veteran, one-eyed Action Man.

amazing how one small shoebox can hold so much history, can be
grave-robbed with so little fuss

Me in a Teenage Mutant Hero Turtles t-shirt, grinning at the spectacle of a Scottish summer. Mum holding Derek, a squealing piglet in her arms. What is she wearing! Dad watching me crawl across a sheepskin rug which is still in our living room to this day. But they didn't/couldn't/I wouldn't let them seem real, those people, trapped in the flash of the past. They had far too much hope in their faces for me to admit them into this cut-and-thrust present. They had to have – surely? please? – become extinct somewhere between then and now, with their crawling babies and butter-fly smiles and what-is-she-wearing summer days dissolved to dust, floating like tiny astronauts in the loft, ground control to Major Tom.

It was a lost time.

It taught me something, that photograph. It made memory seem useless and sentimental, a thing which evolution has failed to breed from us. Then I found a picture of Mum and Dad before we were born and, jesus, when Dad lists the roll-call of bands he saw, somehow . . . I dunno . . . I always see him then the way he is now, unshaven, in his slippers, nodding appreciatively along to the Jam, while punk erupts around him. But there he was, caught in the stark blink of the camera, with a sneer, a ripped t-shirt and

mum

She looks a bit like Debbie Harry, eyes piercing out of the picture like blue daggers, danger and glamour flicked with her middle finger. The next year they had Derek, four years later they had me, and some-where along the way Mum lost her mind and stumbled into the fog to find it, and I sprang

down from the loft

padded into a simmering living-room, Derek swearing to Dad he was going, he was sick of this house, he'd go as far as London if he had to, Dad growing roots into that armchair of his, staring at his rebellious son. His frown hung heavy at each corner, laden with toast crumbs, and he groaned like a coffin closing. Derek made some last resort, stabbed the TV off with the same spite that had spat from Dad's own teenage face in the photo. He whirled his jacket onto his shoulders and stamped towards the front door, where a car filled with booze and boys waited to spring him out of there. Door slammed.

I sat down. Dad scratched his chin. Alvin, he said eventually, as if someone had had to wind a key on his back for him to do it.

Aye?

Put the telly back on, son, wid ye?

I trekked the icy wastes of the room, and just as I bent to touch the button of the television, Dad's slump was reflected in the blank face of the screen, then there was a quick crackle of electricity and

the cover for the new U2 album looms like the mothership at the end of Close Encounters of the Third Kind as me and Frannie rush to the window of Virgin, pressing our faces against it, toddler-amazed, and everyone in Falkirk High Street stares, concerned, like we're a couple of esaped Jack Nicholsons and someone should really call Nurse Ratched, but they don't understand. The world is about to be put right! All hatred, famine, war, sorrow, eradicated in one interstellar burst!

All That You Can't Leave Behind.

'Ye ken whit this means?' Frannie grins.

'Whit?'

'There's a new U2 album oot.'

'So there is!'

An Asian man in the High Street strolls despondently with a sandwich-board that says LOOKING FOR ANSWERS? but we're too excited to pay him attention. We nod at each other, satisfied, workers just completed construction of the Forth Bridge, the sweat and the grime soaking out from our blue collars, God smiling down at our Protestant work ethic and delivering this boon, this glinting jewel on a velvet cushion. The amount of living we have compressed into these days before the new U2 album, the way time has been stretched by desire. Last night, Saving Private Ryan seemed to last for about ten hours, and all the way through, instead of feeling thoroughly ashamed of myself for not dying in a horrible war, I could only picture me and Fran with big headphones clamped to our ears, chilling to the new U2 album like superstar DJs and

'Fucksakes,' Brian sighed, shaking his head at the telly. His own dad was in the army, Brian barely saw him, and now they don't talk. This is why he has the house to himself usually, with all its lonely family-less space. Onscreen, a soldier hunted for his missing arm on the grey beach, a wall of rain on the horizon sweeping closer. The soft fall of pain. Someone shot through the skull and

Me and Frannie pogoing with 40,000 nutters to Pride (In the Name of Love), Frannie ignoring the Irish tricolour flags, Dolby's there! He's pretending that he doesn't think Bono's a knob and has even learned the words to everything on Achtung Baby and

'Aw them lives lost.' Brian's eyes became misty. He wiped at them manfully, dignified, and I wondered when the last time he spoke to his dad was. Bodies littering the beach, the surf a light crimson colour, lapping like a stray dog at a scrap of bare meat and

Soon Bono calls me up onstage during With or Without You for a slow dance and I'm cuddled into him and even though he's been performing for two hours he's not sweaty and

'If I was a religious man I'd say a prayer for them boys,' said Brian, sort of talking to himself, distant, humble and

We slide towards the derelict car-park like sharks.

Across the horizon, lights in a row mean parents with children, watching telly, maybe Who Wants to be a Millionaire. The industrial estate in

Middlefield has concrete walls spidery with lichen, vacant windows. Idlewild are singing Actually It's Darkness on Radio 1, but Dolby cuts them off as we turn the corner, making Belinda a vacuum, making the noise from the car-park bubble and spit to life. Laughter, young and male, honed on garage forecourts. Motors revving like dogs on leashes. Music, dance mostly, but bursts here and there of Shania Twayne from a pink Fiat Punto, Coldplay, Limp Bizkit. My blood drums along. Brian going, 'So my Uncle Tam oot in California says I can join him any time I like. Just needtay get ma visa. California boys, eh?'

'California girls!' Frannie nyuk-nyuks.

Light sluicing from the cars up one side. Silver metalwork with a rainbow flip. A girl answering her phone, her silhouette knife-thin against the headlights. A tower of Reebok checks his texts. Phones ringing everywhere, a seizure of bleeping, drug deals spiralling into the air above us.

As we cruise up the line, Brian points at the boys, 'Fiat Uno . . . Ford Fiesta . . . Golf . . .'

As we cruise up the line, Frannie points at the girls, 'Rancor Monster . . . Snaggletooth . . . Hammerhead . . .'

Two guys place loose change on the roof of a Vauxhall Corsa. The bass throbs and the coins dance, a miniature rave. 'The guy's name wis Shiny,' Dolby's muttering, as we smooth past a gang of girls. They are lionesses spotting a wildlife photographer. 'Met him on a chatroom last night.'

'Shiny?' Frannie says. 'Sortay fuckin name's that?'

'Sortay fuckin name's Frannie?'

Chatroom, I'm thinking. Internet, I'm thinking. First killings by internet cult, I'm thinking.

Tyra Mackenzie was wearing a salmon-pink blouse today with a silver chain, her skin lightly freckled like eggshell.

63

There's a tap at the window. Some dude gestures for us to roll it down. He casts an eye over our dashboard – for woofer speakers? strobe lights? – and snorts to see it bare. 'You Shiny?' Dolby asks him, guarded.

When he smiles his front teeth jut out like a rodent's. 'Why?' he yips. 'Whit d'ye want?'

'Just telt tay ask for Shiny.'

His teeth nibble at his bottom lip. 'Aw, you the chatroom boy? Uriel?' Frannie glances at me, smirking. 'Nay bother, pal.' Our host breaks into a grin. 'I'm Shiny. Just makin sure ye're no the pigs, ken?'

'Of course,' Dolby manages nervously, 'em . . . whaur do we go then?'

Shiny's smile is bringing on nightmares. It seems to eat into the sides of his face. He's dressed head to toe in Adidas, his hair slicked back as though he's just climbed out from a toilet. He catches my eye, sees my discomfort, and his grin burrows further into his cheeks. Then he's rubbing his hands. 'Got yer readies there, gents?'

We fish in our pockets for a couple of quid, Brian grumbling like an old colonel, which we hand to Dolby, which he hands to Shiny, which Shiny pockets in one of those bags that hang at your belly, the kind used by those guys at the waltzers who shout, 'scream if you wanna go faster!'

'Just drive up there, mate. Watch the races if ye want. Wait yer turn for the burnout.'

Dolby nods.

'Burnout?' says Frannie, as we are corralled to the head of the car-park, past – I don't believe it – a van selling Mr Whippy ice-cream. 'Fuck's a burnout?'

'Just think it sounds gid,' Dolby mumbles, turning the wheel smoothly, treating Belinda like she's a girl he wants to keep sweet, as though their relationship hangs in the balance. We park behind a purple Mazda, two neds dropping bottles and chart hits from the window, elbows (Nike) leaning nonchalantly. There we wait, listening to Primal Scream, not talking, watching the cars purr in and out, creating a secret language with their engines, windows rolled down, banter and fags lit, a sudden laugh like a firework, someone boasting, not caring who hears, 'I've written aff three motors and a mountain bike,' as a girl with a clipboard – neat hair, like a secretary – asks if we want to put our names down for a race.

'Um,' I say, 'I've no brought ma trainers.'

'Shut up,' she tuts savagely.

'It's awright, hen,' Dolby says, 'we'll just watch.'

The Lads glare at me, mortified.

after a while, in which Frannie bores us with another Tesco's story, motors start gathering in the middle of the car-park and the air tightens. There are whistles and catcalls. Expectation. 'Shiny was tellin me the things they get uptay,' Dolby's saying, 'like recreatin the Grand Prix course every year round Falkirk.'

The secretary girl is holding her hand up.

'Maistly, they meet up in places like this and–'

The crowd clears. She picks up a flag, holds it aloft, stretching her arm so high her back becomes a drawn bow.

'– race.'

Two cars appear in a burst, tyres screeching. They jostle, neck and neck, fumes billowing, everyone cheering. They accelerate towards a wall at the far end of the car-park, but the crowd converging behind them block our view. Squealing breaks. We crane our necks.

Light confusion settles to the ground. Girlfriends' anxious hands flutter at their throats.

Two figures step out from the cars. Applause. Arms wave in the headlights like a strobe show. Friends grab the victor, shaking his hand, patting his back, telling him he's mad, mad, he's a mad bastard, but he doesn't seem quite there for a second. He smiles vaguely, then takes a long unbroken gulp from a can of Miller, throwing back his head, beer pissing from his lips, and something animal is roared at the black sky.

the burnout goes like this: a gang of people stand in front of a car with their hands on the bonnet. The driver pulls the handbrake and starts revving up the engine, gradually increasing pressure on the accelerator. When it hits the floor he drops the clutch, and the wheels spin madly on the spot. Then he releases the handbrake and the crowd scatters like a shoal of fish and everyone laughs. Up to you to get out of the way in time.

Three of these break up the races. One car sacrifices its clutch. The second roars forwards like a tiger, neds slapping the bonnet as it is freed. The third car revs too long and the engine fails, a genie of smoke hissing from it. All the other cars honk horns and flash lights and we watch. The dangerous allure of it. The way girls drift towards the drivers and hang at their sides like ornaments. Low-grade electricity buzzes between us. 'This is the shout,' Brian says, charged, ready, and then we're leaping out of the car to join the crowd, wringing each other's shoulders, yelping like children and it's

Witnessed: Frannie copping off with a skank in the backseat of Belinda. We stand outside in the night air, freezing and full of wonder. The dazed shouts. The way drivers stopped expertly before the wall. Surely, they all know that someday one of them won't stop in time.

morning and I'm standing with the hash-heads at the back of the History huts. Not that I partake, mind, just that Barry and Gordo – the Cheech and Chong of Falkirk High – have between them the Floyd's entire back catalogue on CD. Today it's my copy of The Wall for Barry's Delicate Sound of Thunder for Gordo's Piper at the Gates of Dawn, as hands appear from the wreath of smoke then withdraw covertly.

'Sure ye dinnay want a draw?' Gordo offers, squinting through the grey fronds. 'Just one for Syd Barrett?'

He and Barry laugh explosively (at?) before descending into a whispered exchange and brief paroxysms of giggles. It's guys like these who were responsible for Hallglen becoming Hash Glen, sniggering, slack-eyed Syd acolytes that have a thousand potholes scattered around Falkirk High. Harmless. Sometimes even good for patter. They definitely know their Floyd. But when I'm with them I feel funky and unfunny, on the edge of things. This is what I do, float from group to group, liked by all, accepted by none. Like Icarus, I soar against the underbelly of the Livingstone set, then descend, wings fluttering, to the level of the grasshoppers. Each thinks I surely belong with the other lot.

'This is cheap shite,' Gordo splutters. 'You been buyin aff Big Mark again?'

There is a famous story of Barry, when he was twelve, buying off Big Mark Baxter. Barry boasting to everyone at Gordo's house that night that he knew his shit, that he was 'well in wi the Fear crew likes,' not knowing that Mark had sold him two Oxo cubes. 'Ha fuckin ha,' Barry tuts.

Gordo is the rumour conduit of Falkirk High, an oracle in Nikes. He hears things vibrating across the floor, or spoken to him in a dream. You can see him lounged in some doorway at break, a pale wraith in a shroud of ganja, murmuring, 'New Chemistry teacher's a dyke, gen up.' He knows where every boyracer in Falkirk has been in the last month, who they saw there, what they were listening to, probably knows where they're going next. We could consult him, cross-legged before a poster of Bob Marley, for Cottsy reports, leave rizlas at his door by way of thanks. Gordo knows all about Brian's head-to-head with Cottsy at the bowling-alley and he knows where all the races are happening and he knows about a Snobs Party coming up, Jennifer Haslom's birthday. 'Should be a classy do,' he muses, then takes a long toke. 'Nay skanks like us there.'

'Fuck that, man,' says Barry, shaking his head, 'be fullay knobs. David Easton, James French, Louisa Wanwright, Tyra Mackenzie, Connor Livingstone . . .'

'I hate that cunt,' Gordo tuts sourly. He offers me his roach, which I refuse, then they start a raunchy conversation about Tyra in various states of undress and position, Jimi Hendrix playing in the background, which makes me quite uncomfortable, so I distract them: do they reckon we'll get an invite?

Loud cackling.

'Us?

'Ye jokin?'

'Sure ye're no wantin some ay this?'

'Naw.'

'Anywey, Alvin,' says Gordo, 'you'll be awright. Tyra's keen on you.'

'Is she?' I say, too quickly, and they collapse again into an ecstasy of giggles. I sigh, turn, see First Years hurrying back before the bell past these Fifth Years with their funny cigarettes. They peek at us and scurry on. Their shoes are gleaming black. Their hair is cut straight. Their eyes are alive with zest for life. They are wondering how it all becomes a sad toke behind the History huts.

'Naw, seriously,' Barry remarks, sticking the next spliff behind his ear, 'you're brainy. You'll end up invited.'

'I will not,' I tut, secretly thrilled at the prospect. 'I'm no like them.'

Gordo shrugs, staring into the distance, 'Might no have their money, mate, but I dinnay see ye fillin yer brain fullay this shite either.'

Smoke hangs around their heads like gaseous lead. Their eyes are downcast, dismal with hash. The bell rings and they look up slowly, as if god has just spoken to them. So I leave them there, standing dumb as drugged rabbits, revelation floating between their fingers. Copy of Delicate Sound of Thunder in hand, I head for class . . . a party invite? one foot in the camp of Cleopatra? I picture myself surrounded by Jennifer Haslom, Louisa Wainwright and Tyra Mackenzie in silken garments, all dancing seductively to Delicate Sound of Thunder (Dave Gilmour's guitar solo at the end of Comfortably Numb) and I am not coping. Today, someone stopped me in the hall and said, 'heard Cottsy kicked your mate's heid in,' and I stood there, listening, restraining a need to run away, far away from him. But I did nothing. Except stared. Nodded. Snarled convincingly, 'the cunt whit said that better watch oot,' and later, in the toilets, I wrote feverishly on the back of the door THIS WORLD IS KILLING ME.

so we're in Brian's living room, right, and Batman is on the telly (a good one, before Jim Carrey and Arnold Schwarzenegger came along and ruined it for everyone) and we're swapping a single can of Irn-Bru since none of the Lads has been paid from work yet. Brian makes a pile of toast a la margarine while we watch Batman at work, munch, snigger at the décor of Brian's house while he goes and makes more toast. 'Who lives in a house like this?' goes Frannie, sweeping a finger along a shelf.

'Shaft!' goes Dolby.

'Can you dig it?'

soon we're slouched like collapsed deck-chairs, Homer-bellies on show, only vaguely registering the film. Frannie and Brian moan about the length of their shifts, and when they ask about Tyra I say that, like Juliet, she is the sun. No, I definitely don't. They lapse into a brief self-pity, until Frannie, quite unexpectedly, leaps from his seat and shouts, 'It's him!'

'Who?'

Frannie stabs at the rewind button. The screen whizzes back to a scene with a reporter walking into his office. All of his colleagues are mocking his interest in the story of a caped vigilante stalking Gotham City. One of them says

Hey, I got something for ya.

and hands him a cartoon of a guy dressed as a bat. Frannie continually replays

Hey, I got something for ya.
Hey, I got somethi
Hey, I got

this scene, mesmerised, freezing on the frame of the sarcastic colleague. 'It is him,' he gestures. 'Look.'

'Who!' goes Brian.

'Ye ken Rodney fay Only Fools and Horses?'

'That's no him.'

'Obviously. Ye ken his girlfriend Cassandra?'

'That's no her either.'

'Ye ken Cassandra's Dad? That's the guy that plays him.'

'Fuck off.'

'It is, look.'

'Frannie, aye,' goes Brian, 'Tim Burton's puttin the gither the cast

70

ay Batman and he's like, "Hey, any of you guys seen Only Fools and Horses? Y'know the guy who plays Cassandra's Dad?"'

'Ya bastards, I'll prove it.'

Frannie skips to the end credits, his face scrunched with determination. He traces his finger down the cast list until, right at the bottom, he finds

Bob the Cartoonist   Denis Lill

'How much?' he demands, palm open.

'Frannie, come ontay–'

'How much?'

Brian responds firmly. His eyes narrow on an irresistible bet. 'I'll bet ye the bottle ay Macallan in that cabinet, there is nay way Cassadra's Dad ootay Only Fools and Horses is in Batman.'

'Bottle ay Macallan?' Frannie's eyebrows raise as he is challenged to a duel. 'Nice whisky that.' Straight away he's cracking open an Only Fools and Horses video, forwarding Rodney and Del Boy and Uncle Albert and Cassandra and Cassandra's Dad, who jerk about like androids, until the credits roll up and he stands poised at the telly

Cassandra's Dad   Denis Lill

then he's whooping and leaping about the room, punching his fist in the air. I have never seen him so happy, which is some feat, since he's not exactly known for his sullen approach to life, and me, Brian and Dolby just look at each other, shaking our heads. 'That has made ma year,' Frannie goes, plucking the Macallan from Brian's fist. 'Denis Lill. That has made ma year.'

71

He pours the whisky. I decline a glass, content to watch rolling hills and heather and ancient claymores strike victory round their mouths. Frannie closes his eyes, blissful.

he's got a new phone for Christmas which seems to keep wanting to play us Never Had a Dream Come True by S Club 7 and the first time he gets a text on it we're in the middle of the Howgate centre on Boxing Day, just outside Argos (which has two frankly gorgeous lawnmowers in the window) and Dolby's jacket beeps. We pause our argument over which one is the sexiest – 'surely the Flymo' – Dolby taking the phone from his pocket, eyes wide, as though about to discover the location of secret spy plans. Heavenly white tiles surround us, reflecting light which shafts like knives from the glass ceiling, and Boxing Day shoppers are roaming, dazed as lab rats, the four of us crowded round this miniscule machine to read the words

hows ur new phone son. hope u get this!

'Wow.'
    'Looks cool.'
    We watch this message glow, each impish pixel another small step for technology, one giant leap in the lives of four piss-poor Playstation players, and grannies, who probably marvelled at the invention of the tin-opener, stare incomprehendingly and

later, with Frannie, on the way to watch the Rangers game in Smith's

U stink

later, with Brian, selecting a late Christmas present for his gran

U r a jobby

later, with Dolby, browsing for comics in Forbidden Planet in Glasgow

Spiderman is a POOF

until it gets to the stage that, as we're taking Belinda back out to greet the new year, they're actually sending texts from the front seat to the back. I see Brian smirk like a kid with a whoopee cushion, punching secretively at his phone

Frannie more like fanny

to which Frannie replies, chuckling, and before long Belinda is a roving arena of techno warriors, sponsored by Siemens, O2, Nokia, and Brian is moaning, 'put a fuckin smile on yer face, Alvin.' He fingers the new tattoo on his bicep, the Stars and Stripes, which beams his Californian dream. If any of us should've been born yank it's Brian, Cruiser-loving barman bastard that he is. He'll fit right in over there. 'Just havin a wee laugh eh.'

'Hilarious,' I brood. Frannie, beside himself with glee, shows me the text he's typing, which rhymes Brian Mann with frying pan.

'Get yersel a mobile and join in then, ya miserable—'

'Take that fuckin baseball cap aff!' Dolby interrupts him, furious. 'Ye'll gie us some bad name, you.'

'Aye, whatever.'

'I'll whatever ye. I'm in the hairdressers hearin them gon on about these "boyracers wi their baseball caps" that are menacin Falkirk. I dinnay want lumped in wi losers like that, aw cosay your fuckin heid-gear.'

73

'Nothin tay dae wi the speed ye're daein?'

'Shut it, runt.'

Frannie presses send, giggling mischievously. Brian feels the message invade his phone, grins, and I don't want to spoil their fun or nothing but, 'c'mon, is this no just a case ay wee boys and their wee toys?'

The question goes unanswered. Grim heads shake, despairing of this sole refuser of their redwhiteandblue utopia.

Dodging down into Princes Street, the cinema showing Another Massive Film (the poster has an explosion on it), Rosie's devouring an endless line of teens, Pinocchios waiting to be made real, the Lads quietly resenting the fact that, cos of me, they're not in the queue, wishing they could scoot me to the pier in Big, that Tom Hanks film, to make me older and be back in time for last entry.

in the window of a bridal shop for a brief second think I see

'Mum,' Frannie yabbers into his phone, 'tape Big Train for me. Whit? Naw, it's a sketch show, Mum, it's no about trains.'

The sky is the colour of lemonade and middle-aged women, the kind we like best, are about. 'A flash ay bra strap on aulder woman is the sexiest thing in the world,' Brian muses wistfully, as though he's a Yorkshireman petting his whippet and praising fond mornings on the moors. The soundtrack to Bram Stoker's Dracula is on the stereo, a track called Vampire Hunters Prelude, which builds with a slow menace totally ruined by Frannie yelping Big Train quotes at his mum. I wish Brian will one day invite us to his ranch in California, cold beers in the fridge and cowboy boots hardening in the noonday sun. I wish it wasn't so long until the next Clive Barker novel comes out. Dolby ejects Dracula and replaces it with Radiohead, starts plaintively crooning to Exit Music (For a Film). Thom Yorke's sorrow crackles and fizzes with technology as we slide from the town centre down, down, up, across, like video game characters, towards Carronshore suburbia,

74

while Frannie's phone chatter twists and rises into the desolate space above Falkirk.

there's too much. there's too much

'Mobile phones are essential purchases, Alvin.' Brian turns to me, still simmering at my 'boys with toys' comment, the bare-faced cheek of it.

'Naw, Mum,' Frannie's yabbering, 'just cos Black Books is about a bookshop still doesnay mean Big Train's about a train.'

'For emergencies and that,' says Brian.

I take a deep breath and uncage Mrs Costa's Modern Studies lesson from that morning, which takes even me by surprise and goes something like

> Mobile phones are the product of a consumerist culture which propagates the myth that luxury items are 'essential' purchases in order to keep the economy buoyant, thus ensuring the survival of the capitalist organism and

'Fuckin Radiohead,' Brian tuts, ejecting OK Computer. 'Just about fuckin greetin here.' He replaces it with the Best Eighties Album in the World . . . Ever, starts humming/droning along with Kim Wilde. Songs from before I was born and phones chirping like bio-mechanical birds and texts sprinting towards screens everywhere and Dolby veering us onto a long cool album-cover stretch of Scotland as

> We're the kids in America
> (whoa-oh)
> We're the kids in America

the past, present and future slide, merge, exist simultaneously in the furry dice ambience of this car. The sound of the year commencing, measured in the increments of phone technology, while in the time between U2 releases we grow older

just too much

A mother with two kids walks past. 'Fwoar,' goes Brian, 'the experience on that yin.'

'Ken,' Dolby says, the only one who was paying attention to my (I personally thought) brave anti-texting stance, 'Alvin's got a point.'

'On tappay his heid.'

'By next summer,' he muses holding up his phone with an opera-critic frown, 'when we're drivin about, this thing's gonnay be totally auld-fashioned.'

'Fucksakes,' Brian moans, 'ye're takin the runt's side? Ye'll be listenin tay fuckin Suede next.'

accelerating so fast it's like erasing Scotland from the

smoothing Belinda in, out, streams of traffic, never dropping below seventy, the winter sun a web of light on the windscreen. We overtake a fellow shitty-in-the-city Belinda, which flashes its lights and we flash ours back and the driver, a young guy like us, grins. A connection.

'Just,' Dolby explains, 'I wis readin an article in the Guardia– I mean, the Sun, and it was sayin that in a few years we'll have phones, like, embedded in oor skulls–'

'Cooooool.'

'– and microchips in oor eyes that can make us see in the dark–'

'That no whit light bulbs are for?'

'– and tellys that ken the things ye watch and record them for ye.'

'Ma Mum does that.'

'Your Mum does everythin,' Brian quips filthily.

'Shut it, skank.'

'I mean,' Dolby continues, 'the world's goin by so fast we can hardly see it.' He keeps checking the speedometer, Keanu-refusing to drop below seventy. 'It's only a few years ago that fax machines and the CGI special-effects in Jurassic Park were a big deal. Think about this: oor grandchildren will look at us like we're a fuckin joke.'

The laughter stops.

It's as though the Vatican have released to him the date the world will end, and he cannot tell anyone, and he has to encode it for us like this. The road becomes a conveyor belt, rolling a million souls towards the void, and Dolby is dumb with the fear of being obselete by next summer. His hands on the wheel: curved, tight, hard. A sort of look in his eyes that reminds me of the sky as night and day merge and things are cold and sluggish.

The four of us here, now, present, correct, as real and vital as the first flash of a phone screen as it's switched on. But one day we'll be De Niro at the end of Raging Bull: fat, fucked, perched on the end of the bar in Smith's, mumbling Brando's 'I coulda been a contender' speech, and as the implications of this start to roll like a boulder through our minds, none of us catch each other's eyes, in case we see ourselves old and cough-ridden.

We avert our gazes to the window, where magic is thinned into a straight line by the endless course of tyres on tarmac, rushing monotonously. Another U2 album is already an illusion on the horizon. Billowing air falls behind us then becomes still again.

I think about Dad's face when Mum disappeared, how small he looked, in his chair in the corner of the living room, everything he'd done with his life converging in that instant, lost in that instant, but then

Brian farts

'Aw, you are stinkin.'

and we piss ourselves laughing.

We're the kids
We're the kids
We're the kids in America

white Fiat Punto, the word GIRLZ printed on the windscreen, draws up alongside us. Dolby beeps the horn once, twice. Frannie is up at the window like a dog when the door goes. A parallel female universe of our own car, four girls giggling behind glass. At the next set of traffic lights, he rolls down his window, gestures for them to do the same. Their Brian complies. Frannie hands her a card with his mobile number on it, and as Dolby pulls away and their car drops back, we see the girls laughing, passing the card round. 'Now you, runt,' Brian points out, 'should be able tay pull at least wannay them babes.'

'Or?'

'Or cut yer dick aff and stick it behind yer ear.'

'Fuck you.'

'Fuck *you*.'

'Fuck her in the front seat,' Frannie murmurs, then mouths at them: You talkin to me? You talkin to me?

His phone rings. He answers quickly, 'Chris Tarrant here from Who Wants to be a Millionaire.' The Punto behind us fills with mirth. Frannie's nodding, 'Aye? Aye? Aye?' then splutters, 'They wantay talk tay Alvin.'

'Heddy haw,' goes Brian.

'Whit should I um . . .' I stutter, Frannie's phone landing in my lap like a grenade and I stare at it, terrified, until Dolby explodes.

'Fuckin talk tay her then, ya dick!'

'Whit dae I say?'

'I dunno, anythin. Tell her ye play for Rangers.'

I pick up the phone cautiously, place it to my ear as though it's

78

about to bite me (which, since I've seen Nightmare on Elm Street, I know it could). 'Hello?' I try to control the rise and fall of my chest.

'Turn around,' the voice purrs.

Bobbing behind us, girls exist. They are all older than me – about the same age as the Lads – and stunning. The girl in the front seat opens her kisser and we talk for a wee bit, as Frannie and Brian watch me take this Champions League penalty kick. This is what happens when one of us gets a click: he is himself, at that moment, the essence of Lad. I'm so swept away by this thought that when she asks where I work I say, 'I play for Rangers.'

When next the Punto skids back into view, all four of them are staring at me, wide-eyed. 'Rangers?' she says. 'Are ye no a wee bit young?'

My eyes glint at her. 'If ye're good enough, ye're auld enough.'

She scrunches her mouth gamely, drawing nearer to planet Impressed but still not sure she wants to land. 'Put yer mate back on.'

Franman haggling, loving the fact that a car full of girls is following us, as though we're the Beatles. Brian telling Dolby about neds he's had to turf out of Smith's. He suspects Cottsy has been sending boys in to noise him up, and one night we're going to get the call for back-up. This is Dolby's worry. He and Brian go back the longest of the four of us. They met in Primary 4, after Dolby let Brian have his Optimus Prime at the weekends. These days, half the fights Brian gets into are because Gentleman Dolby, the people's friend, will offer to hold the door open for the girlfriend of the wrong guy, or cheerily ask some Barlinnie turk what his favourite Queen song is. It's like that bit in Casino, when Joe Pesci wades in to defend De Niro

While I was wondering why the guy was saying what he was saying, Nicky just hit him. No matter how big the other guy is, Nicky'll take him on.

and I know Dolby could never have fucked off to university and left Brian, even though, if Brian goes to California, it'll be the end of the four of us, so if I win the lottery I'll buy Dolby a big widescreen telly and he can watch Gladiator and the X-Men and Star Trek all day and I'll get Frannie a seat in the director's box at Ibrox and and I'll phone them up from the States, where I'm chilling with Brian and young blonde California girls.

Frannie snaps closed the phone. The Punto veers away. 'Fucksake,' I say, 'whit's happenin?'

He rubs his chin, inspecting me the way a scientist inspects rainwater. 'I hope ye've brought yer shaggin shoes, wee man.'

'Why?'

'Cos they wantay meet ye at Callendar Park. Ten minutes.'

door swings out like a pod cracking open in a sci-fi movie. Dolby steps intrepidly out first, looks at Callander Park as though it's undiscovered country, holsters his phone. The sky lowering itself onto the ground awkwardly like a fat man going to bed. My heart is making the sound of a rabbit calling for help theywantmetheywantmetheywantme but not the me with hair that looks like a squirrel's slept in it and a dick that could be used for fishbait. No. They want the me that plays for Rangers. I don't have hair that plays for Rangers. I certainly don't have a dick that plays for Rangers.

Dolby sits on the grass and plucks a flower and lies back and places it over his face. The sun flicks red and yellow paint at the skyline. The winter air. Dolby blows and the flower spins into the air gracefully and he says, 'I have given a name to my pain–'

'– it is Batman,' I finish for him and we both cackle, as if this is the funniest joke in the world ever, 'Good auld Denis Lill.'

Brian the Mann's gazing round Cally Park, restless. What's on that craggy mind of his? The trimmed, tourist-brochure grass? The high flats, where his dad used to stay before he joined the Forces, before he left him on his own in Falkirk, alone except for us? The laughing, colourful mouths of the flowers? Cally is Falkirk's very own, itty-bitty Central Park, and Brian strides across it as though he's in the wild west. If he smoked, I'm sure, Martin Scorsese would use him in films. If Martin Scorsese was in Baxter's Wynd and fancied a pint or the racing results, that is. Brian hurls a five-pence piece at a nearby tree. It hits without leaving a mark.

Frannie does his his hair in Belinda's wing mirror, saying, 'I ask you to kill Superman and you can't even do that one simple thing?' before lulling into silence again. There is an unspoken sense of girls about to be on the scene. Dolby picking flowers, Brian gazing into the Sergio Leone distance, Frannie flexing his repertoire until Brian growls, 'Fuck off wi the impressions, dick.'

I do my hair in the other mirror, mimicking Frannie's movements. They seem to work for him. My bovine face peers at me, awkward, as if I'm somehow not who my reflection expected. Sometimes, way across the horizon of a decade or so, I imagine myself as a phoenix, risen: a film star working the room, slipping tenners into the hands of waiters, my movements smooth, immaculate hands reaching out to touch me but

No mistake, right now I'm the ashes.

'Sure they said Callendar Park?' I ask Frannie across the roof of the car.

'Sure.' He wets his fingers and flattens a bit of hair, squinting.

'No Dollar Park?'

'Naw.'

'Or Callendar Square?'

'Stop shitein yersel,' Brian humphs, reaching into the pocket of his jeans and tossing me a small packet. Drugs? Brian? Drugs! The man

81

who threw two Boag widos out of Dolby's sister's seventeenth for taking ekkies and trying to sneak rave onto the stereo? But the word Durex speckles the packet.

'Fuck's this for?'

They all look at me sharply. 'Fuck ye think it's for?' Brian laughs. 'Skimmin across the loch?'

'I'm no gonnay need this.'

'Ridin bare-back?'

'I'm no shaggin any ay them.'

Brian strides over, puts his hand on my shoulder. 'Wee man. I ken ye're no shaggin any ay them. But there is that tiny, million tay one chance that wannay them might fancy yer miniscule tadger.'

I repeat something they've all heard before, tapping the condom into his shirt pocket. 'Sorry, Brian, I am savin masel.'

'For who?'

In my mind she's a belly-dancer, shimmying up to me in her Falkirk High blazer, a veil and nothing else. One of her breasts peeks out from behind a prefect stripe. 'Tyra,' I reply defiantly, 'I am savin masel for Tyra Mackenzie.'

Brian covers his face with his hands. 'Alvin,' he implores, 'if a girl asks ye tay shag her it's considered extremely impolite tay say no.'

'Peer pressure.'

'Alvin, son, you are the only virgin we ken.'

'Nay mingers for me,' I emote, waving a Shakespearean finger, 'when this shagger starts it will be with the finest creation on god's earth.'

'Tyra's probably gettin a ride at the backay the Martell right now,' Frannie adds. 'Brian's probably shagged her already.'

'I probably have,' goes Brian.

'Aye,' laughs Frannie, 'Although he canny get it up unless he's surrounded by binbags.'

'Ha,' goes Brian, 'listen tay mister While U Wait. Just up against the Corn Flakes boxes, Elaine, ma shift starts in five minutes.'

I sit down on the grass next to Dolby. He is tinkering with a daisy chain. Someone has turned the thermostat on the day right down without telling the sun, and birds everwhere frantically clipe. We can see our breath. We look out at the swing park, where wanes climb things and throw balls and there is laughter, light as party balloons. All of this is ahead of them. Their mothers scattered across the park, the useless flapping of their coats, the opaque tragedy of their eyes. I want to tell Dolby everything, right now. I want to take my pain in a lump sum and dump it here on the grass, so we can poke it with a stick and humiliate it. Instead I say, 'Whit about that new Clive Barker book?'

'Aye,' he replies, 'shite.' He shrugs and starts to chew the end of the daisy chain, making it ragged.

'Brian, ye shagged Snaggletooth oot the backay Laurie's, ye shagged Chewbacca oot the backay Storm.'

'Ya liar, I never went near Chewbacca. You shagged Chewbacca.'

'Right enough,' muses Dolby, 'didnay see oor books in WH Smith when I was buyin his.' We put our hands behind our heads. In the sky, a cloud shaped like an angel glides past in slow-motion. Parts of its wings detach and drift away.

'Chewbacca? Fay Shieldhill?'

The angel fragments. A mouth forms in its head as it screams at being pulled to pieces. There is vast, vague terror in the sky. I can't get out of my mind that night I sat in front of the police – one bar of the fire on – and they asked if Mum had anywhere to go, anywhere she might want to run to. The policeman leaning in close, the smell of grown up: 'Now tell me honestly, son. Yer Dad disnay needtay know. Did yer Dad ever hit yer Mum? Did he? Cos him hittin yer Mum's whit might've made her run away.'

The sound of Brian and Frannie arguing is almost as calming, reassuring, as the singing of the birds, and I can't imagine not being with them. They are as intrinsic to life as fresh air, pollen, chlorophyll. My sullen, slow rot. My mind running to stand still. My casual slide into freakishness.

'Should you no be studyin for yer Higher prelims?' Dolby asks.

'Aye,' I shrug, 'but fuck it eh.'

Dolby does not respond, at least not with the, 'aye, fuck it, live it up while ye're young,' that I'm expecting. He grunts despondently, the angel is blown to bits, its mouth expanding, corrupted by sky, until its face is filled with a single, silent wail.

'Dae ye think Brian'll really gotay America?' I ask him, but he doesn't answer. He's glancing up, listening, getting to his feet like Richard Dreyfuss spotting the shark coming at them in Jaws.

'Oh boys,' he interrupts Brian and Frannie, who're disputing which of them has slept with the most Catholics. 'Oh *boys*. Looks like they've come for their feeding.'

The girls in the front seat of the Punto do not resemble anything from Jaws. Or Star Wars. At all. We watch them like castaways struck dumb by an approaching ship. Frannie starts singing under his breath

fun
girls
wanna have
fun
girls

Slam. Slam. Slam. Brunette. Blonde. Brunette. One of them lands a pack of Smirnoff Ice on the bonnet. Another adjusts her hair. The third draws on her fag, sizing us up like a pretty inmate. The Lads stand.

'Awright,' says the smoker.

'Awright.'

'Hiya.'

'Hello.'

I don't say anything.

'Youse the boyracers then?'

'No,' Dolby growls, whipping the baseball cap from my head, 'we are not.'

Her eyes flick between us, as if selecting a victim, the whole thing like a re-enactment of that cellar scene from Pulp Fiction. I keep waiting for one of the Lads to say something, anything. Brian to ask where their brothers drink. Frannie to do his Ali G impression. Dolby to say, 'We're called Trekkers, not Trekkies.' But they just stare, arms stiff by their sides, like three Gregorys on a planet of girls. 'Whit wannay yese plays for Rangers?'

'Him,' they all say, their gazes swinging round to me, and I am thrust forwards, looked up and down, summed up and chewed over with bubblegum.

'He disnay play for Rangers!' one of them hoots, breaking into the Smirnoff Ice. 'Ho, son, whit's yer name?'

I scramble my mind for the most hunlike name I can think of. 'Ally,' I stutter, 'Ferguson.'

'Ally Ferguson? Wendy, you ever hearday an Ally Ferguson?'

Wendy steps out from the car. Rangers shirt. 'Ally Ferguson?' she muses. 'Whit position dae ye play?'

'Centre right. Back. Forward.'

'He's in the reserves,' Brian adds hurriedly, and doesn't need to groan for me to know that he's groaning.

'Aw,' Wendy smiles, 'Ally Ferguson? I mind. Did you no come on as a sub against Motherwell last season?'

85

'Aye, that's me.'

'Scored two goals?'

'Probably.'

Wendy nods. 'Pleased tay meet ye, Super Sub.'

we are spreading out into the park, the girls clinking Smirnoff Ice and blowing smoke genies, as the water from the loch laps against the bank, as the bare trees spread branches, as the world revolves through space in slow motion and I think

Girls!

Halfway round the loch, I drop back. Wendy drops back with me. She offers me a Smirnoff Ice, but I shake my head. 'I dinnay drink.' She offers me a fag. 'I certainly dinnay smoke.'

'Ye don't drink, ye don't smoke,' she tuts. 'Whit *do* ye do?'

She winks.

Eventually she says, 'Look at your mates.' The alcohol has relaxed them from their C3-PO stiffness. Slaggings are batting back and forth. Anecdotes. Nothing seems forced about it. The girls look on, amused, injecting the banter with stories of their own. Sometimes we think we're the only group of mates in existence, sealed in the world of Belinda, breathing an atmosphere of our own in-jokes, then we meet these girls

fun

wanna have fun

girls

with their over versions of Dolby, Brian, Frannie, Belinda, their own running arguments, their own favourite films, albums, books, parking places, seats in McDonalds, phone brands, a history we've crashed against by accident, and this is how it works, meeting lassies, and it's easier than I thought it'd be.

'Lassies are just like guys really eh,' I say to Wendy.

'Except they're lassies.'

'Aye.'

'I've got bigger tits than you.'

'Aye.' I cough, trying not to look at them. 'So how did youse four meet?'

Wendy crosses her arms over her chest. Really suits that Rangers top. I like the way she keeps folding a wee twist of her hair past her ear. 'Well, me and Lindsey used tay hang about at Graeme High the gether. Caroline knew Lindsey through the karate. Sarah met Lindsey eftir shaggin her boyfriend. They had a fight about it likes, until baith realised it was the boyfriend that was the dick, ken?'

'Em, aye. Whit a dick.'

'Wan night, for some reason, we aw ended up at the same hen party the gither. So here we are now.'

'Heddy haw.'

'Heddy whit?'

Frannie laughing up ahead, the sound like bucks fizz over a barbecue at a mate's house. One of the girls is creasing herself, Dolby is covering his face, pretending to be embarrassed, and Brian has heard it all before. We've all heard it all before. But Frannie has this infectious laugh. None of the four of us, I realise, are bad guys. A wave of affection rolls across me and I fade, viewing the scene from a distance, as though I've sent someone else out to speak on my behalf, a cooler person than me

now tell me honestly, son, yer dad doesnay needtay ken

'So when did you join Rangers?'

'Last season.'

87

'Do ye think Tore Andre Flo is worth £12million?'

'Oh, without question.'

'Gies a drinkay yer Cherry Coke.' She takes the can and slurps greedily, a single bead trickling from the side of her mouth. She finishes the can. 'Cheers,' she gasps, forearm raking across her mouth. 'Did I catch you lookin at ma tits there?'

'Naw.'

'Just as well.'

She holds my gaze.

We've reached the other side of the loch, where it's still, and you could believe for a second that Callendar Park has been plucked out of a holiday brochure. At the other side are the swings, rowing boats, climbing frames, all the places you make for when you're a bairn. Over here feels like a different realm entirely. Like Eden after the apple was bitten.

'I am Brian Mann and I don't care,' Frannie sings, 'I love the Rangers and I've got chest hair.'

'Frannie, you are one Tesco's-lovin scumbag knob.'

'Hiy. I do not love Tesco's.'

'Your pals must get loadsay lassies,' Wendy smiles.

'Ooft,' I say, 'tons.'

'Youse are obviously oot chasin a shag the night then.'

I turn to see Wendy on guard with an arched eyebrow, carefully gauging my reaction. 'We certainly are not,' I protest, 'you've got us aw wrong.'

'Naw I've no,' she grins. 'Cmon, why did youse wantay meet us here? Whit are yese eftir?'

She has the accuracy of an assassin.

'I'll tell ye why. Deep doon, right, aw I want. Aw I have ever wanted. Is just tay wake up in the mornin wi some really nice lassie, and hear her say those three special words.'

88

'Which are?'

'You're so cool.'

'Right.' She presses the blade of her gaze further in. 'I've got yese aw wrong, have I then?'

'Listen,' I say, sweating now, 'this is whit lassies dinnay understand about guys, right. Other *guys* are mair important tay a guy than lassies. It's no aw about the shaggin. We're cultured. Me and Dolby have read Lord of the Rings. Aw three books.'

'So?' she says, 'Whit makes you so special?'

Good question. Horribly good question. I'm on the verge of answering like Morrissey

I am huuuuuuuuuman and I need to be luh-ah-uved
just like everybody else does

but I don't, cos that would make me a dick, so instead I say, 'See for my Higher English personal study, I'm looking at Stephen King and Clive Barker, explorin these two masters ay Horror. I'm totally gonnay get an A.'

'That's whit makes you special?' she says uncertainly, 'Stephen King and . . . ?'

'Clive Barker. They're easily the best authors in the world today, and no just Horror. Stephen King wrote Stand By Me and the Shawshank Redemption–'

'Stephen King wrote the Shawshank Redemption?'

'– but he's scary tay. I mean, jesus, that scene in The Shining. Heeeeeere's Johnny! Clive Barker has a better imagination, and he tackles more philosophical issues than King.'

'Ye're cute, Super Sub,' Wendy smiles. 'God knows ye cannay relate tay lassies, but ye're cute.'

'Weaveworld is probably Barker's best book. Followed by Imajica, and then the Great and Secret Show.'

'Take ma arm.'

'I'd also recommend Stephen King's novellas, especially the Different Seasons collection, which has both Stand By Me *and* the Shawshank Redemption in it.'

'Take ma fuckin arm!'

'Um, okay.'

The wind lifts leaves into the air and back down again. The winter sun brushes the trees with gold and at last I feel a calm, an optimism settling on me. The Lads and Lassies are still making woopee up ahead and I'm walking arm in arm with a girl, *an actual girl*, and U2 are touring this year, and everything feels vibrant and alive and young and exciting, and Wendy leans close in so the others can't hear and says, 'I bet you've got a tiny dick.'

Cherry Coke catches in my throat. '*Cough!* Whit did you just say?'

She's allowing the group to drift further away, her hand snaking round my waist. 'Gon, let me see it.'

'I will not!'

'Why no?' she smirks, 'Must be tiny then.'

'No it's no.'

'Well.' Her hand reaches down, her breath on my cheek, and something stirs. 'Let's have a look then.'

'In the middle ay Callendar Park?'

'Nobody can see.'

I glance round. The Lads are oblivious. The space around us is filled with leaves, branches, empty cans of spray paint, and a squirrel which is surely not much bothered about seeing my willy. It's suddenly a great idea.

'Gon,' she says, 'I'll show you if you show me.'

My gaze falls to her chest. I fumble with my zip, feel the cold air on my exposed knob and go, 'There!'

She peers down. Nods approvingly. Then she gives a sharp whistle, and everyone turns to see me standing in the middle of Callendar Park, my willy hanging out like a tiddler. One of the girls puts her hand to her mouth and goes, 'Oh my god,' before Wendy triumphantly says, 'As if *that* plays for Rangers.'

free periods this morning, rolled up in bed, the world the colour of slumber. Don't have to be at school until assembly, just before lunch, don't want to move from here ever, it's so warm and lovely and Dark Side of the Moony and nothing can harm me, there's nothing to fear. I smile against the warm covers.

Downstairs, Dad looks in good form. 'Ye missed it,' he says, 'Richard and Judy. This wee lassie agein prematurely. By the time she's 16 she'll have the body ay an 82 year auld.'

'That's a shame.'

'It's a wee bit funny though.'

'Naw, it's no a wee bit funny.' He has a habit of laughing at things like dying puppies on Animal Hospital. 'It's a tragedy. That could've easily been me or Derek, so don't come it.'

He mutters under his breath, folding toast into his mouth.

'Whit's that?'

'Nothin.'

Stroppily, I roam the kitchen for mail. Doctor's appointment card for Dad, probably to blame for his mood this morning. No fucking bread left. When Mum was here there was always bread in the bread bin. Usually a few other things too, right enough. Vodka. Pills.

Coco Pops, king of cereals. I set them down on the table.

'Dad?'

'Hm?' he munches, non-committal, Doesn't like it when I argue back, retreats like a dog with its nose skelped.

'I minded somethin the other day.'

'Hm?'

'See when Mum disappeared? The polisman who came up asked me if you'd ever hit her.'

Dad's eyes, calm, still tuned to the telly. He picks up the remote control and changes the channel, muttering, 'Canny stand that Richard Madeley.'

'He said that might be why Mum left.'

'Him and his wife. Obnoxious pair.'

'Was it, Dad? Was that why she left?'

'How should I ken why she left?' he shrugs, then says, 'Pass me up that Daily Record, will ye.'

I pass it to him and wait while his eyes travel the first couple of pages.

'So did you ever hit her?'

'Look,' he sighs, crumpling the paper, 'did ye ever havetay share a hoose wi somebody who hadnay been sober for a week? Who nearly burnt the place doon twice?'

'Aye.'

'Or find three bottles ay whisky under yer bed?'

'Ye ken I did.'

'Or come hame and suddenly find objects ay value missin?'

'I did that tay.'

'Well then.' Dad opens the paper again. 'Just think aboot that.'

latest postcard from Derek in London, has a picture of a sunbathing woman carefully combing her pubic hair. On it, he's written, 'From one fanny to another,' and it makes me head out to school in a better

92

mood than I should be. I miss him. He used to do this monkey face at me when I was wee, rubbery bottom lip and ears sticking out. When Mum and Dad took us on walks by the canal, me and Derek would always be mad-charging around the next bend, desperate to see what lay ahead, Mum warning us not to run too far off, the anticipation so great it was painful. Anything could've been waiting for us. A fire-breathing dragon? A lagoon? Or, if were on a drive at night time, and we saw the lights of a town in the distance, we'd always think it was the shows. 'Dad, Dad, it's the shows. Can we go over there tay the shows?' Then we'd get there and realise it was just another scheme like Hallglen.

I wind my way through the labyrinth of the place, past the primary school where my childhood was spent in a warm haze of Barrs lemonade and football. Some of the school weans follow me, shouting, 'Awright, big man, like yer PVC jaiket, ya mad jester ye,' and I slip my earphones in and the Velvet Underground drones them away.

Onto the Glen Brae, across the ash park at Lochgreen, underneath the pylons. The Falkirkscape is wide and still below, god's dust-jacket for his crappiest book. Grangemouth refinery unfurling pollution into the sky

I am tired
I am weary
I could sleep for a thousand years

barely make it into assembly before they close the door, and big Ronnie Melville strides up to the podium. His red hair seems to burn with an Old Testament authority. Some prefects follow him, Connor Livingstone among them, hair flicked into place, and I'm sure he sees me standing dishevelled at the back of the assembly hall, and then

Tyra!

Her name is like two notes of chamber music. Murmurs of approval from the boys as she takes the stage, her face cool and smooth. She sits, hands on her knees, her tantalising legs pressed together. Connor smiles at her and she smiles at him. Melville gives one last sweep around the hall for latecomers, before booming, 'We have a special guest for today's assembly.'

Two Tamfourhill neds in front of me fizz with sarcasm: 'Kelly Brook in the scud, heh heh.'

'Now, most of you are at, or coming to, an age when those privileges which you have been hitherto denied will be made available.'

'He means shaggin, heh heh.'

'The consumption of alcohol and tobacco.'

'Shaggin. Gon, say it. Shaggin. Heh heh.'

'The right to vote.'

'I bet he doesnay say it.'

'I bet he does.'

'And, of course, intercourse with members of the opposite sex. Or the same sex, if you prefer.'

'!'

'!'

'These are not privileges which are accorded lightly.' His eyes bulge for a bit. 'As you pass into adulthood, you will be accorded even great responsibility. An occupation. A family. A home.'

Brian watching Saving Private Ryan with moist eyes. The young hurled, flailing, into the fray.

'These responsibilities must be exercised with proper consideration for the society which has conferred them upon you.'

Gunshots. Bullets. Blood.

'We have here Mr Giles Johnson of the Automobile Association, who is going to speak to you about the issue of safe driving.'

Brian muttering, 'If I was a religious man, I'd say a fuckin prayer for them boys.'

Giles Johnston starts and I am instantly bored, even though he does his best to scare the shite out of us. Slides of car wrecks and burning motorbikes flash past. He sighs, 'and the driver of *this* car was only 21,' at the appropriate points. But his presence here has the opposite effect. Fifth year is the year when we all turn 17 and can legally sit our driving tests, hence the timing of the talk. Cars. Driving. Freedom. I gaze round at these hopeful faces, their bright young arrogant eyes, glinting at the highways of the future through an imagined windscreen, feet pressing invisible accelerators, dying to be let loose on the world.

Then the assembly mutates. Every one of us old and bent in the year 2060, staring vacantly at a giant TV screen in an old folks' home, while the 17 year-old kitchen boy mocks us over bowls of gelatinous soup, dying to get out from work and into his hover-car with his mates, to attack the motorways that float eerily above Falkirk. 'Auld bastarts,' he smirks, turning the key in the ignition, taking off with the rest of the boyracers towards the ozone layer, or what's left of it.

Tyra shines amid this apocalyptic ruin, perpetually young. I catch her eye and she smiles as if to say 'boring or what?' or maybe 'kiss me out in the milky twilight,' but it's all I need. Something has possessed me. The spirit of all those dying cars? The prospect of being trapped in an old biddy's home of the future with a silver-haired Connor Livingstone and his golf buddies? I have a few thousand days in which to live and I will not be mute, because when I am jammed in that armchair near the end of my life, the decades spilt like coins beneath the cushions, I want to know that I did what I could to have the woman I loved. Carpe Diem, and all that shite from films that Dolby likes. I'm going to ask her. Right now. Straight after this assembly.

she is

the

most

beautiful

On the screen above her, a twisted Ford and a wrecked Cortina embrace in a metal union, their fenders locked, their smashed windows touching lips, the love leaking from he radiator, down, down, towards the drains.

'Tyra!'

I try to push through the throng, but she's being led away towards the Rector's office with Melville and the prefects and Mr Giles Johnson, Connor at her back, musing falsely, 'Well, yes, I thought there was quite an *impact* to the presentation, if you'll pardon the pun.'

'Tyra!'

My heart going at it like a Motorhead album. The fear, and the defeat of fear. Three bints reading a prelim exam timetable in my way and Tyra almost disappearing from sight into the admin corridor. I slam against the double doors, shout

'Tyra!'

like a shot prisoner, but Livingstone is holding them closed, appealing sweetly. 'Sorry, Alvin, Tyra's busy with prefect duties at the moment. We have to lunch with Mr Johnson to thank him for his informative talk.'

The veneer slides from him, slick, making me feel like I need to wash.

'It's just for a second, Connor. I wantay – '

'Not now, Alvin,' he commands, like I'm a collie dog. Half expecting him to shout 'Stay' and throw me a rubber bone. 'It's really very important that you don't interrupt. You might get her in the prefects' hut at the end of lunch break.'

'Connor,' I mutter, exasperated, 'as you well ken, I'm no a prefect. I'm no allowed intay the prefects' hut.'

The Brian Mann creeping out from under my clothes. This must be how the Incredible Hulk feels (or would feel, if he had to contend with the likes of Livingstone instead of the Abomination). Connor closes the double doors on me officiously.

'Sorry. No non-prefects allowed in the admin corridor. You might see her in English class after lunch . . .'

'Connor.'

I start knocking on the glass. But Livingstone is retreating further up his own privilege, his last look towards me a handsome shrug.

She isn't in English class after lunch.

Mrs Gibson is reading a solemn passage from The Great Gatsby, shuttering the blinds, making the classroom dark, and I am trying to conceive strategies for getting into Rosie's and

> The music had died down as the ceremony began and now a long cheer floated in at the window, followed by intermittent cries of 'Yea-ea-ea!', and finally by a burst of jazz as the dancing began

as I gaze longingly at Tyra's vacant seat, I will the emptiness to take on her shape. She appears, in a special-effect, morphing out of thin air. Her whole body is the colour of iced water, voice the sound of classical music. When the bell goes for the end of the period, she explodes like a shot aquarium, and I push my fingers to my temples and rub at a whining pain.

> 'We're getting old,' said Daisy.
> 'If we were young we'd rise and dance.'

Despite the randomness of events in my life, despite the speed at which it all crashes past, despite the Lads, Belinda, the colour, the laughter, a new and grown-up world opening around me, the big bursting choruses followed by inventive guitar solos, despite friendship, family, education, the welfare state, the abolishment of nuclear threat, I still sense horror lurking. At the end of the road. Something dark, unformed, mysterious, waiting for me to hit it like in the prologue to a werewolf story, the Lads all hanging around for something to happen, for the alarm bell of their thirties to go off maybe.

If being a teenager was a job, you wouldn't apply for it. 'Enterprising youths wanted for angst-filled soul-searching. Seven year contract. Will affect your sex life.'

Dolby's mad keen on going back onto the crusing circuit, been bugging us about it for weeks, since he's found Shiny on the chatroom again, going on about 'the buzz yi get bettr than drugz' (sic) so we give Belinda the old spit and polish and head to another secret location in Grangemouth and it's all covert and mad, like being in that Al Pacino/ Johnny Depp number, Donnie Brasco.

On the way there, Frannie tells us about a group of ducks he saw on his way to work this morning, 'obviously lost like, cos fuck knows whit they were daein ootside Tesco.'

'They'll be fay Cally Park,' Brian suggests, scratching his stubble, reading an article in Maxim about a bottomless bar in Texas, which I glance at over his shoulder.

'But Tesco is, like, a mile fay Cally Park.'

'Aye,' Brian tuts. 'Hence bein fuckin lost.'

'Anyway,' Frannie continues, 'dick. It's a mammy duck and her wee chicks, and one of the chicks is laggin behind in the car park—'

'They were in the car park?'

'Aye,' Frannie seethes, impatient. 'As ye just pointed out, they were fuckin lost, weren't they?'

'Go on.'

'So, this wee chick's laggin–'

'Duckling.'

'Whit?'

'Duckling, no chick. Chicks are baby hens.'

'Aw, right, so this wee *duckling's* laggin behind, and I'm watchin it squeakin away, tryin tay keep up like. Wee shame for it. I wis gonnay go ower and give it a hand, but then somebody shouts on me – ken big Maxie? – and when I look ower again it's disappeared.'

'Disappeared? The duckling? Are you sure it didnay just catch up?'

'Will ye listen tay the fuckin story?'

'I'm listenin. It's just takin too long.'

'It's takin too long because ye keep fuckin interruptin.'

'It's just dull, Frannie. It's just a dull story. Chicks in a car park. So whit?'

'Oh, I thought you said they were ducklings?'

I pick up the copy of Maxim that Brian has disregarded in favour of refining Frannie's storytelling, to read an interview with some girls on a night out in Glasgow

MAXIM: Are Scots lassies up for it, then?

Heather: We're quite forward, if that's whit ye mean.

Lisa: Aye, I mean, if we see somethin we want, we just go and get it. Life's too short to be a wallflower eh.

MAXIM: How far would you go in bed?

Karen: Threesomes. Foursomes. I've even dressed up in ma school uniform once.

MAXIM: Who was that for?

Karen: Ma science teacher.

Lisa: Truth is, I'd love tay get off with another woman while a man watched.

Heather: Aye! That's like givin him his fantasy on a plate but. Ye havetay make him work for it.

MAXIM: What do you look for in a man?

Lisa: I love it when a rough man just takes me, and he's aw sweaty fay a day at work and we have really filthy sex all ower the hoose.

Frannie and Brian have resolved the issue of whether or not a duckling can be called a chick. 'So the *chickling's* disappeared, right, and I'm a wee bit concerned for it eh. Cos it's a wee shame bein lost like that, an the mammy duck's noticed, an she's gettin aw frantic, lookin for it, so I starts lookin for it. Then I realise whaur it's went.'

p.12 VIRTUAL MAXIM Score with Courtney online. Can you get to first base with out cyber-babe? www.maxim.co.uk

p.22 YASMIN BLEETH 'In Baywatch, I didn't just play a model or a bimbo; I played a responsible role model. It just so happens lifeguards wear bikinis.'

p.28 LADS NIGHT We take you to Sheffield, for the ultimate night out with the boys.

'It'd fell doon the drain.'

'Aye?' goes Brian, trying not to piss himself at the image of a wee duck floundering in the fag-ends, quacking helplessly.

'So I lifted up the grill, an I'm just about greetin by now, like, cos the thing's so panicked, an its fur's aw dirty an it's wee heart's beatin like a drum and I haud it in my hands and carry it ower tay the mammy duck, really feelin like I'd achieved somethin, ken?'

page after page of Porsche Turbos, Gent USA gear, Nokia ('Fun Outside, Serious Inside'), Ralph Lauren shaving products, Jimmy Bee shoes ('Jimmy's Gonna Sort You Out'), Pierre Cardin t-shirts ('Label Envy'), the twenty most wanted stereo systems in the world ('I prefer large knobs')

'But the mother had been killed,' Frannie concludes, 'run ower by a car. Aw the ducklings were hoppin and flappin round her body, splashin about in the blood.'

There is a space in which no-one says anything. Frannie gazes towards the window.

We drive on.

races are busier than last time. There's about eighty motors, and puffa jackets dash across the car park, leaning into windows, making preparations, revving engines, comparing sound systems, wheel trims, while Grangemouth oil refinery looms above us spewing smoke. A sticker saying MAD MALC. Neon tubes and dry ice and a Blade Runner effect glowing on the sprayed shells of cars. Alloy wheels gleam futuristically. The words BORN TO CRUISE. A repetitive whump of bass.

Shiny is here, even recognises us. 'Just watchin again, gents?' he calls, making us feel like perverts. As we cruise past, Brian mentions a rumour that Cottsy, the ned from the Hollywood Bowl who gave us a pasting, might be sending a squad to Smith's to turn the place over. We watch the action: the pod race from The Phantom Menace with Falkirk scenery. A Renault Megane and a Clio neck and neck and I notice one of them has an Irn-Bru can on the dash and I ask Dolby again why this can wouldn't land in the back seat if dropped in the front but he shushes me.

Three neds are heading our way, glowering like plumbers faced with a perpetual leak. Dolby rolls down the window. 'Can we help youse chaps?' one of them (sort of) growls.

'Just here tay watch the races,' Dolby answers. 'Cleared it wi Shiny likes.'

The neds frown. 'But yese are no, eh, racin yersels?'

'Be a funny thing tay race yersel,' Frannie laughs, and they look at him, and he shuts up.

'Naw,' Dolby says, clutching Belinda's wheel. 'We're no up for that.'

'And yese arenay doin the burnout?'

One of them has walked to the rear of the car and is checking the licence plate, and it occurs to me that if we just come along here and watch every time – spare pricks that we are – they might actually think we're

'Polis,' one of them says.

'Fuck off,' Brian splutters. 'Look at the age ay this wan. He look like polis?'

The three neds turn their attention on me, sitting there hunched on the back seat as if on a potty.

'Runt's no even auld enough tay vote,' Brian laughs.

'No even auld enough tay vote,' I repeat.

They nod, still checking for a hidden blue light or the letters POLIS scratched away from Belinda's bonnet. 'Well, if yese arnay polis,' one says calmly, 'ye'll no mind if we use yer car for the burnout?'

'Course no,' Dolby replies, powerless.

We wheel Belinda over to a corner, where lassies surround an XR3i. The car is being redecorated with dance music against its will, its features tested by cackling youths (electric sunroof, voice that intones 'rear door not shut' as though in a Radiohead track), and as they notice our arrival I feel like a castaway walking into the native tribe unarmed.

'Ye sure Belinda can take this?' Brian whispers to Dolby. His large hands cover his knees, flexing.

'Ye sure *I* can fuckin take it?' Dolby replies, breathing deeply, as we get out of the car, leaving him in the front seat like a Lego test-pilot. 'Just make sure ye get oot the fuckin way in time.'

Me, Brian and Frannie are in central position. Our hands splay, our shoulders tense. Three neds (Adidas, Nike, Fila) jostle and grin and I swallow what feels like a ball of paper in my throat and just before Dolby, staring blankly through the windscreen, turns the key, one of them turns, shouts

'This is what it's fuckin aw *aboot.*'

and Belinda roars, a waking dragon. We take the strain, our heels digging against the tarmac. The car makes a noise like a rottweiler on its leash, the tyre screaming as the six of us push against it. Frannie looks like a rock singer midway through a ballad, and just as I start to laugh

our ground slips

Belinda inches forward. Someone shouts, 'Clear,' and we leap away as she accelerates, Dolby hard at the wheel, the adrenaline shooting into a five-point star inside me. I whoop, delirious, then hear a

crack

Someone screams.

A tyre bumping back to the ground.

A long, uncontrollable wailing.

'Chas? Chas? Ye awright? Ye awright, man?'

Me and Brian glance at each other. My lungs suddenly feel like lead. Dolby, pale, behind the wheel. The noddies all surround Chas, who is howling like the war wounded. The surface of the world ripped open.

103

'We should mibbe get ootay here . . .' Frannie whispers, but Dolby is a salt-pillar, mouth hanging open as if he's killed someone, so we just stand there, useless as grandparents at a rave, watching

ShiningTheGoodTheBadandtheUglyRagingBullDirty
HarryPredatorCarrieJawsForaFewDollarsMoreJerryMaguire
ArmageddonTradingPlacesCasinoTheBreakfastClub
BornOnTheFourthofJulyEntertheDragonBoogieNightsLA
ConfidentialDieHardTheThingFullMetalJacketLockStoc
kandTwoSmokingBarrelsTheGodfatherPartsIandIIbutnot
IIISavingPrivateRyanScreamAliensTrainspottingTheX
MenTheTerminatorTheUsualSuspectsCocktailTopGun
TheEmpireStrikesBackStarshipTroopersRobocopScream2

the same argument erupting as we retire to Blockbuster, Brian a bull-dog, objecting to every suggestion. Dolby usually mediates, but nobody has seen him all day (probably out with Prontaprint Lisa, latest Lassie Pal, for whom neither Brian nor Frannie has given approval). Frannie has demanded Eddie Murphy's 1983 classic Trading Places ('And listen tay you *quote* it aw night?') while I've opted for a film starring Katie Holmes from Dawson's Creek, but Saving Private Brian gets his own smug way as usual, and we're forced to suffer another three maudlin hours in the trenches with men. With men. Without Katie Holmes. When he sneaks to the toilet, Frannie grumbles it's as well we never fought in the war beside Brian Mann. 'Cover ye, ya cunt?' Frannie mimics, 'Who's been coverin ye the hale war? Cover yersel ya lazy bastard. I've a pub tay run.'

Back at Brian's. Outside the window, the day and night have appeared at once like a tragi-comic mask, and the three of us are yakking about Brian's new barmaid (not only a visible bra strap, but pantyline) when Dolby comes in. His face is heavy. He looks round the room, his tongue running over his top lip.

'Where've you been?' Brian grunts, pausing on Tom Hanks'grime-covered face.

'Something tay tell yese,' Dolby mutters, ashen.

'Whit? If it's about that guy's broken leg–'

'It's no about naebody's broken leg,' he says, 'things just have tay change, awright?'

'Aye, okay,' Frannie placates him, 'whit's the problem?'

'I'm . . .'

He breaks off, wipes his hand across his face. There's a hole in his Ghost Rider t-shirt, just above the eye socket of the Spirit of Vengeance, and I'm sure it's nothing to do with his news but it terrifies me all the same, like a hole in the universe. Dolby adores that t-shirt.

'Hurry up,' demands Brian. 'Whit is it?'

'I'm no afraid tay admit it anymair.'

'Admit whit?' A shard of panic in Frannie's voice. Each of us suddenly reassessing all the times we've been alone with Dolby – did he say anything? make any untoward gestures? – our mental picture of him shifting. Brian's face avalanches with terror.

'Tell us.'

'Yer no-?' Frannie can't even bring himself to say it.

'I'm,' Dolby holds up his head, 'Uriel.'

The room resounds with the clang of a piano falling from a van. For one brilliant second I imagine Dolby is going to open his jacket and unfold a pair of wings.

'Whit d'ye mean, ye're Uriel?' Brian sneers. 'Is that some sortay gay code?'

'I've changed ma name,' Dolby nods defiantly. 'Deed poll. It's done. Nay mair Martin Dolby.'

105

My head is roving from Brian to Frannie to Dolby and back and I laugh out loud. The three of them stare at me.

'Uriel,' Brian groans, hiding his head with his hands, thinking, no doubt, about the first punter in Smith's he has to introduce to Dolby.

Frannie looks almost betrayed, as if Dolby has kept a lottery win quiet or something.

'Let me get this straight,' he snaps. 'You want us, yer best mates, tay call ye Uriel?'

'Or Uri,' Dolby nods. 'For short.'

'Uri?'

His hand shaking, Dolby whips the TV Times out from under Brian's coffee table, where it lies with the Rangers News and all the books on British undercover agents in the IRA. 'Oh,' he goes, totally without conviction, 'Buffy the Vampire Slayer's on.'

'Uri?'

Dolby's flicking through, rapid, searching for exciting television preferably on now, right now.

'And Live and Let Die. Dunno bout youse, but I always preferred Roger Moore, like. The actin eyebrow.'

'Uri?'

'Fuckin Uriel?'

'Uriel? Man, ye canny be serious.'

'Look, lads,' Dolby collapses back into the settee and his eyes roll up, corpse-like. 'I'm 19. I've been fittin bloody whirlpools the last three years ay ma life–'

'So?' Frannie says. 'I stack shelves for a livin. Dinnay see me changin ma name tay Frodo.'

'Alvin. You've read 1984. At the school eh? I tell ye, I'm sick ay bein a fuckin *prole*.'

He leans back, hands behind his head, weary gaze unravelling the patterns on Brian's artex as though they are an escape map to a battlefield of orcs and elves, gladiators and wizards, dragons rearing up from the mist of his imagination and flashing the undersides of their gilded bodies.

'I'm sick ay being Mar-tin-fuck-in-Dol-by,' he seethes. 'Whirlpool fitter.'

Frannie mouths at me: 'the fuck is a prole?'

'But Uriel, man?' says Brian, fraught, as if by changing his name Dolby is telling Brian to quietly go fuck himself. 'Ye canny seriously expect–'

'Listen,' Dolby snaps, scissoring upright. 'If you're aw ma mates.' He glances at me: help me out, Alvin. Please. 'Then ye'll be happy for me.'

The only thing I can think to do – what else *can* I do? – is, uselessly, stand up and cross to the drinks cabinet, pick up a bottle of peach schnapps, watch the clear liquid slosh and sway seductively and

you ever have tay restrain a drunk woman wavin a knife in yer face

unscrew the top before my conscience can stop me and

the awful sound of it gurgling, my knees pressed together at the top of the stair, listening to the sound of the cap unscrewed in the kitchen, the hurried gulp and gasp, and though I couldn't sleep I would not go to her and

'Since, fellas, we're aw forgettin that I turn 17 the morra.' I hand one of the glasses to Dolby. 'And tay celebrate oor mate's news.' I swallow the schnapps. They watch me swallow the schnapps. They can't believe they're watching me swallow the schnapps. 'Let's get pished.'

so Brian cracks open the Glenfiddich he's been saving for Judgement Day – 'heddy haw' – The Best Rock Album In The World . . . Ever turned up, up, way up, Frannie hollering

Follow follow
We will follow Rangers

107

and though a I try a sip of the whisky it makes me feel sick so I stick to
the peach schnapps, my stomach fluttering and the Lads raising holy
hell and I smile weakly, drain the dregs which are turning, slid

ing snidily, like poi

'Ur-*i!*'

'Ur-*i!*'

'Ur-*i!*'

son, Dolby slugging the Glenfiddich, shaking his head, dazed, while
outside the clouds unburden themselves, washing the scum from the
streets and Led Zeppelin is allowing No Quarter inside and the next
door neighbours start to bang and Brian bangs back, laughing, 'Fuck
youse! Ma mate's an angel!' Dolby and Fran flick through Brian's classic rock collection, arranged chronologically – Black Sabbath, Iron
Maiden, Motorhead, Guns n Roses, Metallica, Nirvana – sudden up

surge of schnapps in my gut and I burp, and as Brian absorbs the
sight of me skating towards drunkenness he beams, arm trapping my
neck, whispering something buddy I don't quite catch for Dolby and
Fran raking through drawers for the photos from our first fishing trip
(the one where I fell in) and he's going, 'Am I right? Am I right? Aye,
ye're a good wee cunt, Alvin. Number 1 Runt,' and round about here
without me even noticing the decision is made to go to the

'Toon centre, mate.'

Brian slams us into the taxi, falsetto Blondie-singing, the driver,
unamused, another squad of lads at large, an average night, until Dolby
leans forward, puts his hand on the cabbie's shoulder, and goes

'I'm so happy, mate. This is the maist important day ay ma life.'

'Wettin the baby's heid?'

'Naw. I've changed ma name tay Uriel.'

'. . .'

108

We pass Belinda, waiting cold and patient outside Dolby's house, but tonight the Brae is a magic carpet-ride into a town of riches, excess. Daylight disappearing rapid-style, covering its own ass, because the town is alive and we slam into Smith's first, Brian commanding his lassie staff, 'Get ma guests here a round ay Aftershocks,' while me, Frannie and Dolby gridlock round the jukebox. Smith's is a proper pub off the High Street, cobbled lane, everything made from wood, real horse-racing on the telly, real old geezer to hassle you like fuck at the jukebox. Scrooge, they call this annoying bugger.

'Pit Sinatra oan,' he croaks, like a wean pleading for a Christmas present. 'Sinatra. Everyboady likes Sinatra.'

Dolby cares not. 'Sorry mate. We're payin for it eh.'

101/4 Wamdue Project – King Of My Castle
120/6 Oasis – Rock 'n' Roll Star

'Fuckin Sinatra, boys, eh? Nane ay that modern stuff.'

'Look, pal, it's oor money, we'll pit oan whit we want.'

'Shelley! Ho! Shelley! Round ay Aftershocks? The laddie's seventeenth . . .'

098/13 Radiohead – Paranoid Android

'Naybody likes that garbage. Got tay play stuff everybody likes.'

'Naw ye dinnay. It's ma pound coin, ma choice.'

'Sinatra! 0 . . . 6 . . . 7 . . .'

067/01 Frank Sinatra – My Way

'Hoi! Did you just type that in there?'

109

'Boys. Haw, Uriel's Angels? Leave that fuckin jukebox, here's yer Aftershocks. Sawright, Shelley hen, I'll ring it through the till later.'

151/12 Bruce Springsteen – Born To

'Runt,' Brian toasts, raising his wee beaker of Aftershock, gentlemanly, 'here's tay yer seventeenth, and yer first night pished.'

'The runt.'

'Runt.'

'Runt,' I manage, staring at the tiny red abyss at the bottom of the glass (blood? medicine?) before I throw it (mouthwash?) into my throat and screw shut my

'AAaaaaGGGHH . . .'

'Eeeeeeechhhhh . . .'

'UH. UH. UH.'

Brian swallows calmly, then places the empty beaker onto the bar.

'Right Shelley. Same again.'

The taste of washing-up liquid and nitrogen and aniseed in an illicit rave on my tongue, Frannie, Dolby, hunched, deformed with the awfulness of it. Frannie moans and I shake my head. Buffalo charge from one side of it to the other. Shoogle my arms like

plasticky

glasses lined back up on the bar, filled with, filled with

Scrooge wandering up to the jukebox, fumbling through the discs and wincing as

> toniiiiiiight
> I'm a rak n rowww staaaar

Oasis churn up the pub.

'Hey, wee man,' Scrooge calls to me. 'Borrow a pound for the juke-box, pit some Neil Diamond oan?'

'Borrow?' I blink at him. 'Ye'll gie me it back?'

'Aye.' His lip raises, showing a rusty car grill of teeth. 'How cheap d'ye hink am are? Jist tay pit Love Oan The Rocks oan.'

I flick a pound coin at him, and Brian's new barmaid Shelley is totally un-ugly! As she leans to pour the Aftershock, her cleavage looms, but she catches my gaze, pushes it away from her breasts.

'Right.' Brian lifts his beaker. 'To ma boy Uriel. The artist formerly kent as Dolby.'

'Uriel.'

'Uriel'

'Hmp.'

I gulp, knocking it back, and when my head revolves back to planet Earth I see Shelley sort of frowning, her brittle whisper to Brian, 'you watch that laddie, the night,' while I just grin at her, foxily, glowing.

'She is so cool,' Dolby mutters, wistful. 'A cool girl with cleavage – who kens howtay mix cocktails.'

'Oot ay oor league, boys.'

'Never!' I proclaim, slamming my beaker onto the bar with manly conviction, startling even myself.

Brian laughs. 'You, runt? Every punter in here's tried tay pull her.'

I glint drunkenly, watching the expert way she whips a packet of Ready Salted from the box, her arse rolling in her skirt, and I almost tell her I am human and I need to be loved, just like everybody else does, but I'm just one of many bodies crushed in a cluster round the bar, waving empty glasses at her. Yet it's me she responds to, promptly, maternally, and soon I'm trying to get my pound coin back from Scrooge and his ugly puppet features are outraged. 'Ye want it back, wee man? There it's back then. I'll gie ye yer measly one pound back. Ken how? Cos I'm no a cheap cunt like you.'

He totters to his warren in the corner, muttering, and in the mirror that hangs solemnly above the bar I see myself, hands curled round a drink as though trying to keep warm, and I'm suddenly a young version of my own Dad. The hair swept back from a worried forehead. The frown. Life minus four decades

sledgehammer break from the pooltable shatters

Frannie groans as Shelley passes, her 22 womanly years moving, sensuous. 'Shelley, psst.' I gesture her over like a bairn who wants the teacher to see his best work. 'Shelley, tell us. I'm dyin tay know. Whit's yer favourite Narnia book?'

Shelley frowns at me, washing a glass.

'Ih?'

'Yer favourite Narnia book,' Frannie translates wearily. 'It's his chat-up line.'

'Oh. I'd say, um. Probably The Lion, the Witch and the Wardrobe.'

'Wrong!' I make a noise like a buzzer on a quiz show. 'Everybody says that.'

She nods, and I can tell she's impressed by the subtlety of this sociological experiment, and Frannie is hunkered right up to me on the bar stool and Brian and Dolby are taunting each other across the pool table like Apollo Creed from the Rocky films

When I first met you, Stallion, you had the eye of the tiger, man, the eye of the tiger

fog outside the house schoolbag on the kitchen floor mum? what's for dinner? mum? mum, are you

112

'Long have I kent you?' I ask Frannie, minding fine games at the Hallglen ash park when I was 12 and Frannie was about 15. Matches that would last till the sun dripped away behind the roofs of the scheme and we couldn't see anything and we were a horde of bairns playing spot-the-ball in the dark, kicking clods of ash and falling in, falling out, falling about. Everything simple. Dolly dimple.

'Dunno,' shrugs Frannie. 'Four years?'

'Man,' I marvel. 'I've always admired your attitude to life. Ken? Always a smile on yer face. Always tellin jokes, nay matter whit. You're the man.'

'Naw,' Frannie mutters, his face darkening, 'I'm no the man, Alvin.' His voice is ironed out. Insistent. 'I work in Tesco. That disnay make me the man.'

'It does!' I protest. It is suddenly the most important thing in the world, that I make him see this. 'You, Dolby, Brian. Youse are aw ma heroes. I owe youse everythin –'

'Alvin, yer no listenin tay me–'

'Naw, you're no listenin, Fran. You're the man. Fran the man. You're, like, Bill Murray in Ghostbusters. You're Ally McCoist.'

The shutters are coming down on Frannie's eyes, revealing someone quietly loading a shotgun. He talks firmly, as if aware that there are lawyers present.

'Noo, listen–'

> finally you're paranoid
> but not an
> android

'– I'm no Coisty. Coisty lives in a big hoose in Bearsden. Coisty's scored mair goals than anybody in the Scottish League, ever. Ye listenin? I'm the guy that cleans Coisty's windays.'

113

'. . . the Man, ken . . . ?' A dribble of schnapps runs down the inside of my glass.

'I dinnay lord it about at university. I dinnay even run a bar like that big-nippled prick ower there.'

Brian cannons a ball into a pocket and smugly sips his pint, preten-eding it wasn't that great a shot

mum? ye upstairs? mum what's for

'. . . aw ma heroes, ken . . .'

'I work,' Frannie raises his eyebrows, as if to make me see the simplicity of this, 'in Tesco.'

'But you fuckin love it there, man.'

He sighs and shakes his head. 'I love it cos I'm 19 and I've nothin tay spend ma money on but petrol and U2 CDs–'

'. . . always gawin on aboot how much ye love it in Tesco . . .'

'No sure I'll love it when I'm fuckin 30 though, get me?'

Brian's barmaid patrols the counter like an Amazon, pausing to wipe a spillage just in front of us, catching my eye again. She has a smile like the actress Kirsten Dunst. Man, I'd love to

'Get me?' Frannie is not angry, but he's that way someone goes once they suspect an argument about music is actually a thinly-veiled attack on their belief system.

'Aye, man, I get ye.' I mumble, knowing my compliment has shot past him and into waste, into the cold of outer space, into

the queue for Rosie's, here, suddenly, before I've hardly even noticed. The wind whipping bits of paper across a neon sky. Cosmetic faces creased against the cold and I feel lost, orphaned, fighting to be awake to the evening's possibilities, then I am, I'm into it/up for it! Wahey! A

114

storm rumbles out from the doors of the nightclub and I will get in this time, even though I haven't thought of a fake date of birth or nothing. Dolby and Frannie arguing about petrol money owed from last week and the Aftershock is at the piano in the front cortex of my brain, taking requests, and the cinema is showing Shrek and a girl from Graeme High School pretends to be with me and the bouncer doesn't even

'Heddy haw!' Frannie roars. They slap my back, making me cough, laugh, splutter all at once. 'The runt's made it in. How does it feel?' Brian says, before gesturing to a barman he knows who serves him before a wall of pissed-off clubbers. Dolby waves to a girl on the stairs.

'Wee man,' Frannie beams, proud. 'Ye made it. Whit d'ye think?' Well, I think

dad where's mum I've just got in from school and she's no

it's rising around me like a temple of hedonism and I drink it in, the Aftershock and schnapps swilling a miniature wave-machine between my ears. Young boys/girls darting behind the bar, shaking drinks, lifting glasses, pouring smiles. The dancefloor filled with prettiness. A staircase rising in the centre of everything, girls lounging on its celestial steps, as if in a colour remake of some classic black and white film. They release smoke into the strobe-lit air, turn, slowly, posingly, as muscled shirts appear by magic and hover at their sides. Gyr

if you buy this record your life will be better
your life will be better
your life will be

ating hips, kiss-tinged schoolgirl lips, locked in an ecstatic jam, waves of pink, violet, red smashing and rippling against a shore of heads.

!This is it!

Dolby shouts something as we're contracted into the crush of bodies. Two women, breast to breast, blocking my path. 'Whoa, hen –' I laugh, unsteady on my feet and they chuck me a dirty look, as I am forced to the stairs, sole oasis in this coruscating beauty reach the

front step

gasping. Sitting down. Laughing. Sweat beginning to rise and coat my skin and I scan round. Brian caught in the snare of the two girls. He raises a sly eyebrow at their jiggling bodies. Frannie frantically tapping his mobile.

'Is

it

ringing?' he says, his facial movements seeming to down-gear as if on slow film stock. 'Hoi,' the bouncer commands, looming above, and I don't believe it. It's the Outlaw. 'Need tay move. Canny sit here, mate.' Further up the stairs, three gorgeous girls are sharing a Smirnoff Ice and office stories, arranged like empty dresses.

'Whit about them?' I nod over towards them. 'Are they movin?'

The bouncer's lips lift, like the thing in Alien, to show a row of rock-hard teeth. 'Are you givin me hassle?'

'I'm . . . just . . . ken . . .' stuttering my way back to the dancefloor, terrified, retreating from the xenomorph in the bomber jacket. He stares after me, mad, death-filled.

'Alvin!' Dolby/Uriel grabbing my shirt, pointing towards a Britney Spears lookalike and her mate. 'Two stunners up ahead. I dare ye.'

'Watch this,' I nod to Dolby, then grin and saunter towards them, a superb chat-up line forming. I am confident of this. I am King Alvin of the Allison clan. I am young and I am alive. There's a flicker of life from the girls as I approach, but their posture is locked. Wary. I am not

116

wearing Ben Sherman and my hair is not cut in any sort of fashionable style. I am a threat. I must be opposed.

'Evening,' I smile, Fonzily.

'Hello.'

'Hiya.' One of them scratches the bridge of her nose. It is slim and faultless.

'My mate over there –' I gesture to Brian, formally slugging his Becks. This is a cracking chat-up line. 'Do you reckon he's gay?'

'What?' One of them blinks. The other one, who is nothing like Britney close up, stares away, distracted.

'I said my mate over there –'

'I heard you.'

'Well.' I try to connect with her large, blue eyes, though this is like trying to shake hands with smoke. 'I was watching Rikki Lake, and she said that you can't tell if someone's gay or straight just by appearances, so . . .'

The girl stares at me over the rim of her Bacardi Breezer, looks across at the queue for the toilets, perhaps needing to go? No, I refuse to believe that this princess has a bladder or bowels. But she's not getting the subtlety of this chat-up line at all.

'Sorry, what did you say?'

'Well, I was just wondering if . . . it's possible . . . if you can tell . . .'

'Tell what?'

'Um . . .' I say, 'if he's, um, gay or, um not . . .' My god, what am I talking about? What the fuck am I doing here?

Non-Britney picks lint from the front of her dress. 'What does it matter if he's gay or not?'

'Uh, that's not what I'm getting at,' I point out. 'Do you think you can *tell* if–'

'It's what's inside that counts,' she shrugs, devoid of empathy with

117

me. 'You shouldn't judge people by whether they're gay or straight. That's phomo-hobic.'

'Homophobic.'

'No I'm no,' she says, 'but you are.' Both girls are looking away now, one up at the stairs, the other smiling flirtatiously at someone in the bar queue. Both of these girls are achingly beautiful, as though they've just stepped through a curtain of rain from another dimension, not seeming to know, or care, that I've read, like, a whole Thomas Hardy novel, seen Citizen Kane twice, maybe three times.

so I buy myself a double peach schnapps, having lost the Lads somewhere in the dry ice, and down the drink, and thin figures are rising from the mist as I punt myself away from the bar into the dancefloor, into dazzling eyes, slim cheekbones, soft cleavages. I am in the final reel of Apocalypse Now with all its strange sounds and imagery and Brando mumbling

> but you must make a friend of
> horror
> or it is truly an enemy to be feared

as the DJ, one of those wannabe Fatboy Slims, does theatrical turns on the deck and shouts, 'Lemme hear ya say yeeeaah!' (yeeeaah!) 'Falkirk, the weekend has landed!'

Tanned legs and the smooth smalls of backs and fingers circling glass rims become unf

ixed the more I stare, dissolving into a chaos of loveliness, the floor tipping like a disaster movie. Tyra isn't anywhere here. Disappeared into the mist like the Blair Witch. I search out her milk-white form, try to find her outline through the spectrum of lights that blink and swan-dive and rise, then I see

long has your mum been gone? son, this is important

the Lads like a cluster of barnacles in the far corner. I stagger into their communal space, shared with a couple of chicks Frannie went to school with. Their mascaraed eyes bear down on me like sharks and I feel a dull, lifeless pain at my heart and pick up a drink someone else has left and down it greedily. 'Where d'ye go tay, ya wee rodent, ye?' Brian asks, patting my ba

ck! 'Ye find any babeular action on the floor there?'

'Naw,' I bray, my voice like Pinocchio's turned into a donkey. A churning pressure in my gut. I slug another double and Dolby and Fran are telling the lassies about how

she'll come back don't you boys worry okay if your mum was drunk she won't have an

arm locked round my neck, his fist gnashing my hair. I am released to breathe smoky air. Ceiling the colour of fireworks. The world explodes with lustful glances, glinting earrings, remixed house tracks. Tongues darting from lipsticked lips. Happiness spreading like a disease across the dancefloor. My mouth tastes sickly. I feel ill, unravelled, depressed. No-one can help me. I realise this. Things only end badly, otherwise they don't end. The Cruiser said that in Cocktail, y'know.

Frannie and Brian fight for first slaggings of Dolby's new name. 'Thing is, right,' Brian says to him, 'we were sure ye were gonnay tell us ye were a poof.'

'A poof!'

The school-girls have faded like lions into the black, afraid of our Lad-light. The four of us embrace, sloppy, pished. True love amidst all this

record your life will be better
your life will be better
your life will be life will be

decadence, and Brian going, 'Dolby, man, nane ay us would mind if ye were a poof.'

'I wid,' says Frannie.

'Dinnay listen tay him. Nane ay us wid mind. No me. No wee Alvin there. No that Orange cunt either –'

'Aye I wid.'

Brian and Dolby lean boozily, pressing their foreheads together. 'Disnay matter if ye decide ye were bent, straight, black, white, chinky, reptilian, or had yer arms and legs cut aff.' He pauses. The music seems to fade. Their eyes locked, a meaning almost biblical transmitted between them. 'You. Will always be. Ma best –'

whoooa

Dolby holds me up, leading me to a free table, my hand stretching for the unattended drinks, Dolby (Uriel!) slapping it away, 'Alvin, ya skank, they're no yours.' Fran and Bri start dancing with a girl who resembles Uma Thurman in Pulp Fiction but I'm sure she comes from Reddingmuirhead, Brian stiff and robotic as if on old, flickering footage. He dances like someone is threatening him with a knife. The music shuddering and a billion girls silhouetted against the party, against the world, but Tyra's absence walks the room like a spectre. My stomach weeps, the booze staggering through capillaries to my head and Dolby (Uriel!) is saying, 'Listen,' his eyes bright, his tone demanding. I am dying, convinced of it, cos when I open my mouth this happens:

'Yrr ma fckin best pal. Aw yese. Fckin lve yse gyys –'

'Alvin,' he's barking, though the bass blasts most of his words away, '. . . talent, wee man, ken whit I'm sayin . . .'

120

'Ken whit yer sayin,' I reply, a (Becks? Miller?) stain seeping into my shirt, which I know won't come out. 'Loads fckin talent in here.'

'Naw, that's no whit I'm sayin.' He slides his chair closer. '. . . listen tay me. You've got brains, man . . . get tay fuck away fay Falkirk . . . it's deid! Ken whit I'm sayin?'

'Naw, man,' I protest, hugging him, 'us frr will eywis be thegither. MeenyounBriannFran. We'll fckin eywis be thegither . . .' The love swelling beneath my shirt like a big cartoon heart.

'. . . no listenin tay me,' Dolby's carrying on, 'get studyin for yer exams, man . . . go tay university and marry some wee psychology student . . . want tay be a dick aw yer life? Ih? That whit ye want?'

'Dolby, if you'd been a poof, I widnay've minded. No wan bit. I'm so happy, man. Yss are ma best mayss. Ow mfuckin life t . . .'

I tail off.

There is a moment of clarity.

The dancefloor is spread beneath like a menagerie. The beaks of vultures, dipping into Bacardi. Squawking lies at the bar. Everything is evil. One of the most gorgeous girls I've ever seen turns to me and hisses, 'Fuck ye lookin at, wido?' Bodies, germinating, mummified in a wrap of brand names and

the horror
the horror

this is what I've been inducted into. Adulthood. The parallel universe behind the glass. I tap a girl on the back and ask if she's read Clive Barker's Books of Blood and she pushes me away. 'Ye havenay seen the film Carrie either naw, jst checkin, jst checkin.'

remember reading somewhere about how sleepwalking starts in children as they become aware of their mortality and all the clubbers here are shrunken and dressed in pyjamas dangling teddy bears and looking for mothers, padding single file into a vast, consuming darkness and

If we were young, we'd rise and dance

everything dead. And lovely. And dead. Pre-programmed dance moves. Youth risen for one last final oh-fuck-it-then rave before the whole charade collapses and when I turn I see a

ned at the summit of the stairs, being told the News by his big weapon mate. His face turns bad, like fruit in speeded-up film, his mouth hurling sounds into the thick air. Hair seeming to grow on his arms. Oh jesus, it's Cottsy and he's looking at us. The words 'kill that cunt' stab from his mouth and Cottsy has Dolby down on the ground and is trying to kick the shit out of him but Brian and Frannie are racing from the dancefloor and everyone is staring, appalled, and I charge into the fray like a super-hero, like Spider-Man, grabbing Cottsy's arm, booting at his ankle, biting his elbow, and then someone's hand closes on my shoulder and I'm

in the back of the taxi

headlights passing. Sullen shop windows, street names. Me slumped in the corner of the cab singing Animal Nitrate to myself, which is on
the first Suede album?
Dog Man Star?
anyway, the boy in the song, he's just an animal and
My black eye pulses and my back hurts, my Mum on the corner of Montgomery Street, waving fondly, so I wave half-heartedly back (just *totally* can't be arsed with her right now) but Shelley from Smith's is in

122

the back seat next to me, stroking my hair, saying to someone on the phone, 'Brian, how did you let this boy get in such a state?' and

Shelley from Brian's pub?

likes stuff from the Gadget Shop, her flat crammed with toking aliens, bottle openers in the shape of scarab beetles, inflatable chairs, lava lamps. She crosses the room, puts David Bowie's Hunky Dory on, laughs at me trying to remove my shoes, as a chess set, with shot glasses for pieces, is brought out from a side cupboard, more Gadget Shop shite, Shelley filling one side with whisky, the other with vodka, and before I can protest I've lost a bishop and three of my pawns and Shelley's lost her blouse, her socks, her earrings, the lobes burning a sexy red, her upper chest flushed with whisky, the CD jumping at Oh You

Pret

Pret

Pretty Things, and her bookshelf filled with fat Marion Keyes paperbacks (Rachel's Holiday, Watermelon). 'You're next,' I try to warn her, like that guy at the end of Invasion of the Body Snatchers. 'The whole world's fucked,' I say, but she doesn't hear, drawing my zip down, down, without any fuss, and Shelley's mouth touching the bruises on my neck, and she's whispering 'sssshh –' and all I can think about is that line from Robocop which goes dead or alive you're coming with

I wake.

The morning light twists in smooth, slow curves.

A dream about the River Ganges fresh in my head. Me and Robert DeNiro in a canoe, the soft sound of paddles in water, lulling. Nice dream.

The first thing that seems out of place is the duvet. It's not mine.

My bed doesn't usually have a woman in it either.

123

Shelley from Brian's pub is zonked out next to me. Her hair plasters her face, Medusa-like curls. I lift the duvet cautiously. Look down the length of her body.

Yep, she's naked.

making my way home is like scaling the north face of the Eiger with a head full of Nirvana b-sides. The Lads are ship shape in Brian's kitchen, folding toast into their mouths and flicking through the Sunday papers, various cuts and bruises on their faces, and I can just about read one of the headlines through the slats of my eyes (a Rangers win) as they clock me and roar, as though I've knocked one in during the last minute of an Old Firm final. I crumple, wincing. Posh and Becks loom apocalyptically on the front of the News of the World.

'Well then?' Brian beams.

'Ye shag her?' Frannie beams.

'Long did ye last?' Dolby beams.

I can barely swing my head round to look at them. TLC singing No Scrubs on the radio and I feel yuk. 'Just think,' Brian seats himself next to me. 'Everyone in that pub has been dyin tay dae what you did last night.'

'Look, I'm sure she's a very nice girl,' I protest, 'but –'

'Nice-girl shmice-girl. Ye shagged Shelley. Be prouday it.'

and I can only groan at the stark sound of it. While they celebrate my virginity drying on the bedroom sheets, I press my face to the formica, where it's nice and cool and nothing is demanded of me and Life's Little Instruction Booklet lies innocuously open, saying

76. Remember, overnight success usually takes about five years.

77. Never indulge in lawsuits.

78. Always keep warm blankets in the boot of your car.

79. Avoid sleeping with barmaids you hardly know.
80. Forget about Tyra Mackenzie now, knobhead.

and I catch sight of the date at the top of the paper, just above Beckham's fringe.

Happy birthday to me.

week later, Richard and Judy are featuring a slot called 'Back From the Brink', about suicide. Linda from Sussex, Eloise from Maidstone-on-Kent, Susan from Peebles all call up with heart-wrenching tales of shaking in the doctor's surgery/being driven to drink/failed infertility treatment. I watch, transfixed, the tea in my hand cooling until I look down and find it's grown a limpid skin.

'An hour at a time, a day at a time,' Richard says sincerely, 'and reach out to the ones who love you.'

Dolby is beeping the horn outside, but I am slack-jawed, struck dumb by the level of grief in the voice of Susan from Peebles. I cannot move. Dolby continues to beep, the noise of a cartoon character opening and closing its mouth on the edge of a galaxy. I cannot face him. The possibility of movement. Richard and Judy are conducting a phone in quiz

What planet is named after the goddess of love?
What nationality are Abba?
Who is married to Brad Pitt?

creep to the window, kink the blinds and see Dolby looking at his watch, hear Belinda's engine chug. The caller has won a cash prize. A rebellion seems to be occuring deep within me, then fading, then resurging again. I nearly run out into the street in my socks to tell Dolby to step on the gas, collect Brian and Frannie from work (like in An Officer and a Gentleman) and drive, drive to Florence or Reykjavik or the Côte d'Azur, where we four can live in illicit comfort, sinking pink drinks and summoning ladies to show us their tan lines and

the lack of love from Tyra Mackenzie, like cold light from a distant star. In its beam I am hunched, riddled with evil (Dolby is still beeping) and if you're going to force the issue – though please, for my sake, don't – I remember this:

It is the beginning of the nineties. Everything is black and white, the furniture is angular. That is what is in. I am eight years old, and Mum is about to burst with fury, and Derek, tearful, is trying to subdue her. I am watching Children's BBC. Mum has chain-smoked her way through a packet of Silk Cut, twitching, bird-like, with the effort of each sentence.

That day, she'd taken me and Derek down to Falkirk to buy new clothes for school, when she'd bumped into a couple of old schoolfriends, now doing well – why they were planning to buy their house, where you should really go for your holidays – and Mum'd been hesitant and clipped, her nerves sucked down to the filter. Me and Derek made faces at each other, monkeys and donkeys. Falkirk had newly opened the Howgate shopping centre, heralding a bright new dawn for the local retail economy. Mum dragged us in and out of Poundstretcher and What Everys. She moved us with the agitation of a cat. Derek didn't like the the shoes he was fitted with, couldn't he have Nike or Adidas like everyone else at school? I'd whined at the scratchiness of the shirt, imagining who might have worn it before me, gripping the guard of an electric fire when Mum tried to pull me over to the trousers. Grey and flannel. Me and Derek stopping at the paradisal window-fronts of John Menzies, Woolworths, Toys R Us, awe-struck by towering blocks of Gameboys and Nintendos. Can I get that, Mum Mum, see when Dad gets his wages, can I get that Can I get! Can I get! Mum repeated, trying to haul us onto the Hallglen bus, Aw I ever hear fay you pair is *can I get*. Into the house and the TV switched on and Derek in a sulk and Mum's voice peppering the cartoon soundtrack, ordering me to get that turned down and stop diggin intay they fuckin Coco Pops, ye'll spoil yer tea. Whit is it for tea, Mum? Ye'll get whit I fuckin make ye. Aye, but whit is it? Is it stovies, Mum? Mum, is it stovies? Is it Mum? I hate stovies! Mum, I hate stovies! Tough. Ye've ate them afore, ye'll eat them again. Weans these days have got awfy fancy stomachs. Mum, I've jist goat a normal stomach, but I still hate stovies. I'm no wantin stovies. Mum clattering with the pots and Derek with a petted lip in the corner and the Teenage Mutant Hero Turtles blaring and I'm wailing about the unfairness of stovies, following Mum round the kitchen to tell her this. My bare feet cold on the black and white tiles, chipped from things being dropped, thrown. Derek, tell her, eh we're no wantin stovies? Mum, dinnay pit stovies oan. I'll just pit some oven chips oan fir Alvin. Yese arnay gettin oven chips, yese are gettin fuckin stovies. Yer Dad wants stovies, so I'm makin fuckin stovies. I've no goat the time tay make four separate dinners, Derek, noo get oot the road tay I get the ironin board doon. The starved horse of the ironing board clanks to the floor. Mum sweating, the dinner erupting in plumes from the hob behind her. She kneels to my level. I wish I could remember her eyes, even their colour. Alvin, son, d'ye ken whaur I keep ma crabbit pills, upstairs at the side ay the bed? Can ye go up and bring me wan doon? Will ye dae that for me? I wid, Mum, but that wan I got for ye earlier was the last yin. There's nane left. Mum stands, sighs, runs a hand through her hair, covers her eyes. Derek is peering over the top of the ironing board at me, making more monkey faces. I laugh; Mum swats him away, lifting the iron,

127

muttering. The water hisses a steamy tantrum. Me and Derek play furniture Olympics, an assault course of coffee table, sofa and drinks cabinet. Empty drinks cabinet. Will you pair fuckin shut up through there? I'm tryin tay make the dinner and iron yer Dad's shirts and ma period's due and I've nay crabbit pills till I can get tay the doctor's the morn. Mum, he kicked me! Shut up, ya wee clipe. Mum, I did not kick him. Mum, Derek kicked me! Will yese fuckin shut up the pair ay yese. Mum stomps towards the drinks cabinet, finds it is empty, clutches at her own ears and squeezes closed her eyes. Bastard never even left me a drink. Mum, Dad says ye've no tay have ony mair drink. He telt us it's bad for ye. Aye, well, yer faither disnay need tay pit up wi you pair aw day, wi yer fuckin can I get and yer I dinnay want that an will you fuckin stop jumpin on that couch, there no enough holes in it awready? Mum? Mum? Ye dinnay make holes in a couch by jumpin ower it. Aye well, jist quit it. Aah! He's kickin me again! Mum! He's twistin ma arm! Mum! Aah! Muuum! Will yese fuckin shut up I swear tay Christ yese are drivin me roon the bend, ye'll have me in fuckin Bell's Dyke before the year's oot. I'm tellin ye, if it wisnay fir you pair an yer faither oot at work aw day an I've nay fags whaur's ma drink go an get ma crabbit pills the fuckin doctor's is shut I'll no be able tay get them tay Tuesday ma fuckin heid that's ma migraine startit an I've the claes tay finish an the dinner tay iron an the dishes tay buy an the messages tay be washed afore he gets in will yese fuckin just gies peace Bell's Dyke ya wee bastards that's whaur I'll end up will yese just sit soon an I canny cope I canny cope I canny fuckin–

Derek puts her to bed before Dad gets in. He takes the stovies off the ring and makes me oven chips. And when I go up to see her, she is staring slackly into the middle of the room. There is a beaded chain of saliva, like a dewy web, connecting her mouth to the pillow. She doesn't seem to hear me when I try to say sorry. And everything is black and white and angular, because that's what is in that year, but I wish I could remember the colour of her eyes.

Dolby slams his hand onto the horn one last time, making me pull on my trainers, grab my bag, breathing hard, and run down to

the surf, and two men in waders trying to haul a small boat. It bobs and pulls against them, an unruly child that wants to stay out longer. Forcibly manacled to a tractor, it is dragged home, shamefaced, across the length of the beach.

Two girls carry surfboards towards the water, blonde hair waving in a sea breeze. They skim the boards nose-first onto the spume, then charge into the cold like foals. In the foam and dip of the grey waves, they darken, wetten, shine. Their eyes press into the saline creases, as they ride, and fall, and rise to ride again.

Small boys digging plots on the tideline. The muscles of their faces are determined. They dig, flicking the sand behind them into the sea, which creeps silently and fills the hole again. The boys dig and flick, strenuous, the centre of the earth beckoning, the sea inching and swallowing up their world, but they must keep at it, keep it at bay.

Further up the beach: the ritual of the upturned bucket. Other children burying their mothers in a dress rehearsal of death. The old folks, nosing mournfully towards the real thing.

This isn't a holiday, I think. It's Saving Private Ryan.

'Braw drive. Lovely wee beach. Plenty young yins! Nice pubs. Away doon. Enjoy yersels fir god's sake, ya miserable–'

We'd been lurching towards boredom in Falkirk. The same roads. The same conversations. There's only so many times you can smirk about the size of Brian's nipples. I've been unable to think about anything but the recent, tragic loss of my virginity to Shelley the Barmaid, the fact

129

that when Tyra Mackenzie gets around to doing it with me, I'll already be spoiled goods. So me and Dolby chucked a couple of sleeping bags into the back of Belinda (as well as a pile of practice exam papers, York Notes, Torrance's Higher Biology, just in case I get the inclination/fear) and after we drove past Tyra's house (so I could look, yearningly, at the light from her bedroom window), we took off to one of my Dad's old pit stops in his days before Mum. Saltburn-by-the-sea, North East England.

It was like running away from home. Putting the foot on the accelerator and following Belinda's nose and the spirit of adventure. The surging landscape, the pulse of road signs past the window. The second we pulled away from Hallglen, the patter and the laughter jet-planed, the sun crashing against the windscreen, Dolby starting to insist that I call him Uriel (still can't believe he went through with it) and Scotland mutating into strange regions – every time we say the name Hawick, we pretend we're dragging phlegm – over the border to Angleterre and the window rolled down and Bat Out Of Hell roaring fantastically, triumphantly uncool and

> I'm gonna hit the highway like a batterin ram
> on a silver-black phantom bike
> when the metal is hot
> and the engine is hungry and

we arrive to find this. Grim England.

The window-wipers sweedge wearily before a beach.

'Whit d'ye want tay dae?' says Dolby.

'Dunno. Whatever.'

'Could go for a swally?'

'Heddy haw.'

We exit the car and head along the promenade. The sand skitters across the shop-fronts like insects. We're both thinking the same thing:

we could have been this bored just staying in Falkirk. We could've sat one more night in Brian's living room, Frannie listing the minutiae of his daily routine in Tesco, Brian tour-guiding us through his favourite Bruce Lee scenes. We could've drank the money we've forked out on petrol, or gambled it, Kenny Rogers warning

> know when to fold
> know when to hold em
> know when to walk away
> know when to run

the two surfers have tired of wrestling the elements, jogging to their car across the beach. They begin to strip, chilly, behind the cover of a car door, and we both try to transmute the metal into glass. Then, so suddenly it's funny, one of them hoists the leg of a shop dummy onto her shoulder and carries it to the boot.

'Hey,' Dolby shouts, friendly, 'sorry tay hear about the accident!'

'Up yours,' she replies, as her friend wheels her chair out from behind the car.

'Aw, eh, I didnay mean . . .'

In the Ship Inn later, I'm still giggling.

Dolby moodily sucks his pint and frowns, that I'm-no-happy-wi-you frown he could have copyrighted after Frannie snogged his sister once at the Maniqui.

'I dinnay want the Lads hearin aboot that,' he warns, pointing. 'I mean it. It wisnay funny.'

'It wisnay funny wan bit,' I agree, trying to gag my splutters, knowing Brian and Frannie will think it's Christmas Day when I tell them.

Dolby, you see, until he changed his name to Uriel (which the Lads have embraced with the same enthusiasm as they did Celtic's 3–1 defeat by Caley Thistle), was notoriously difficult to slag. I have crap hair. Frannie has a love of Tesco bordering on the obsessive. Brian has nipples like satellite dishes. Dolby? Has the same name as a sound system. Hilarious.

But that 'up yours' is going to stick to him like shit and he knows it.

'Mocking the afflicted's nay laughing matter, man.'

'Aye, awright,' he mutters, ripping up a beermat, 'wido.'

Our accents have attracted attention. England neds. Funny differences between the neds here and the ones in Scotland, they're all blond, for a start (probably a remnant of a Nordic invasion they're desperate to take out on somebody) and they don't have that crewcut so beloved of the Scottish ned. They don't growl, either, or ask if you've 'got a fuckin problem'. They just stare. Like menacing fish.

I ignore them, listen to some crap old Sixties song on the jukebox, my gaze roaming the decor of the inn for distraction, learning that Saltburn used to be a smuggling haven. Mocked-up Wanted posters and sepia newspaper cuttings warn us to be on the lookout for strangers. Well, we won't be smuggling anything in, me old mateys, but we might just leave with the hearts of some of your local wenches. I'm even more ecstatic to learn that the King of Smugglers, their very own local hero, was a Scot. A poster recounts a pitched battle on this very beach front between Scots bandits and King George's tax men. For once, we won.

Heddy, and indeed, haw.

Dolby is blethering away about Prontaprint Lisa, as he did the whole way down. We couldn't leave Falkirk until he'd cruised past her shop twice (once catching her – gasp – photocopying). Plain looking lassie if you ask me, but she's lit Dolby's fire. No doubt Brian the Mann's right in his prophecy that she'll join Dolby's bulging club of Lassie Pals, these being the ones he invites out to listen patiently to their problems, before dropping them off at their door resolutely unkissed, untouched.

'Gettin a peck on the cheek an bein called a nice guy at the end ay the night?' Brian usually sneers, thumping his Rangers badge and slurping a Stella. 'Whaur's the fun in that?'

I have to interrupt Dolby's rhapsody to point out the impending ned trouble we have, urging him not to look round, which he does, then snorts with such Brian Mann contempt that I have to check I've come on holiday with the correct Lad.

'Them? Weapons? They're wee fuckin laddies, Alvin.'

He laughs, but indulges me, draining his pint. I finish my peach schnapps and lemonade, and we head out to judge the local talent contest. Mother Hubbard's cupboard is bare, however, and no heddy haws are uttered the entire way to the chip shop, where, unbeknownst to us, a third En-ger-land encounters awaits.

'Whatsit called, mate?'

The guy sticking his hand behind his ear theatrically, leaning across the hiss and fizz of the batter.

'Irn-Bru,' Dolby repeats, keeping his annoyance in check, drumming his fingers on the sauce-stained counter and contemplating, I can see, the wisdom of the whole trip.

The guy shakes his head, his assistant giggling behind her hand. 'Sorry mate, don't know him. Live round here, does he?'

'Gies a can ay fuckin Tango, then.'

Outside, two girls sit hunched on a wall like frogs, straws jutting out at odd angles from their mouths. Thick jackets, thick stares. They look us over, snigger, and in such a situation Brian would be asking them what the fuck they're laughing at, Frannie would be dashing over to offer them a chip. Either way, problem nullified. But me and Dolby trundle on, moodily, picking at our soggy haddock as our enthusiasm for Saltburn, for life, for the space-time continuum itself, unspools. Their taunts follow us, like extras from one of Brian's Clint Eastwood movies, eyeing the new gunslingers in town and croaking, 'ay, Greengo.'

'Wankers!'

Dolby's fists clench the newsprint. He turns, sees what I see: the animals that were lurking behind the facade of this seaside town have reared out into the dusk. The genus that hunt in packs and use Childline as a defence policy. I count one, two, four, seven beady eyes blinking like Midwich Cuckoos.

'Whaur's Brian Mann when you need him?' Dolby mutters, retreating quietly as more of them emerge from the shadows, following, yelping.

'Hey, jocks.'

'Och aye the noo, MacTavish.'

'Where's your haggis?'

We thrust our hands into our pockets, upping the tempo, no idea where we're going, ducking from street to side-street, each empty, dust-blown. A chill blustering off the sea, howling, dropping, and the beach-blond weapons laugh and close the distance.

'Belinda?' Dolby mutters, glancing back.

'Heddy,' I agree. 'Haw.'

We make for the beach-front, speeding up, vaulting walls, cursing my Dad, but when I look back to see how close the raised knives are they've Gone.

The street hangs, patient. A shopkeeper pulls the grate down over his store, stares warily. His quaint Saltburn-by-the-sea shop taunts us with granny ornaments, when truncheons and black masks are more the sort of thing I'm thinking tourists are likely to need. Seagulls wheel above us. Slivers of adrenaline thread through my veins.

'Hey,' I whisper. 'is this no like that scene in Jaws?'

'Whit?'

'Ken – when the shark disappears under the water, an everybody's holdin their breath, waitin for it tay smash oot fay the sea . . .'

Dolby stares at me. 'Fuck are ye talking about?'

'I dinnay ken. I feel a bit light-heided.' I swallow. 'Are we gonnay get battered *again*?'

'Shut up.'

The beach-front is deserted. The Somme veterans trying to sunbathe in the drizzle have died, or given up, along with the one-legged source of Dolby's shame. Only sea ghosts are out now, writhing in the moonbeams.

'Beaches are terrifyin places at night, eh?'

Dolby doesn't reply, picking up the pace of his strides.

I'm glancing at the brood of waves, which bring to mind another scene from Jaws, the one I remember being glued to, wide-eyed, in front of my Auntie Marlene's TV. The girl's nude, phosphorescent form enveloped by waves. She rubs the sea into her hair, smiles, calls, 'Come on into the water!'

'Hey. D'ye ken Bram Stoker wrote Dracula twenty miles from here? Place called Whitby.'

'Aye.'

Dolby grunts again, picking the cold fish from the newspaper then dumping it back in its puddle of vinegar.

'And Queen once played in that pub we were in earlier?'

The sand hops across the salt-encrusted concrete, in and out of the thin gaps. The sea hisses like one of the relaxation tapes my Mum was given by the AA.

'Aye.'

Dolby scrunches the newspaper, chucks it grimly across the car park, then peers through the darkness, eyes pinched, troubled.

'And did ye ken Saltburn was where the vibrator was invented?'

'Aye.'

'Ya liar. I'm making aw this up.'

'Shush the now, Alvin.'

I squint, trying to make sense of the grey shapes, blurry without my contact lenses. Belinda's still waiting at the far end of the beach, coldly wondering when we're coming back

except

Perched on the bonnet, his fag-tip glowing lke a firefly on a stalk, sits a local ned. Arms folded. He sees us coming and smiles, almost charming. I don't believe it, the stereo's playing, which means the little bastard has managed to get into the

'Owya doing, lads?' the cheeky fucker's beaming, off on some James Dean fantasy I'm looking forward to seeing Uriel, avenging angel, end for him.

'Awright,' Dolby replies, and gestures. 'Want to get off the car, mate?'

The ned frowns, peers down at Belinda's scratch-work, then shrugs, careless and free as a wean in a playpen. 'Nah, not rilly.'

Dolby nods, checking automatically for the boy's backup. We can see up the length of the beach, and like I say, just ghosts.

'Fuckin move it,' Dolby growls, my heart starting to pound with fight-nerves. 'We're wantin away fay this shit hick toon.'

The wee boy – about 14 we're talking here – raises his eyebrows and places his palms on his cheeks. 'Ooooh,' he says, like a camp game-show host.

'Whit's your name, pal?'

He explodes. 'Andy-fookin-Pandy's my name. You keep yer mouth shoot, yer fookin jock bastid.'

Dolby retreats a step, wondering, as I am, what's making this under-age knob so cocky. He soon supplies the answer, calmly taking his

136

phone from his puffa jacket. Punches numbers. The song playing inside the car says

the English motorway system is beautiful and strange

'Jez? Gaz? Yeah, they're back at the car. Givin me plenty hassle too. Fink they're summat out of Trainspotting, this pair, Scots gits. D'yer wanna send a squad round, sort em aht?'

Dolby's calm, listening to this, but I know he's sweating. A small lump expands in his throat. Brian, Frannie, two hundred miles away, and a platoon of Englishmen about to get us back for Braveheart.

Then Dolby surprises even me. He takes out his own phone and starts dialling.

'Brian? Aye? Listen, how far away are ye? Well, we're just doon at the beach and there's a wee noddy sittin oan the bonnet, willnay move.' He glances up at me, then away. 'Doon in a couple ay seconds? An ye'll bring the whole team? Cool.' He snaps closed the phone, turns round and gazes out to sea as if studying it for a photograph.

The ned looks at the back of Dolby's head, then at me.

'You erda the S-Burn Posse?' he asks. 'Craziest fookin gang in North England.'

'That right?' I nod, as if he was telling me about some mark he'd managed in a science test at school.

'Be ere any second. Any second nah.'

Dolby leans over to me, speaking just loud enough for the boy to hear, 'Brian bring that stanley blade doon wi him?'

'Um. I think so.'

Dolby nods. The ned's hand strays to the phone inside his jacket. Dolby reaches for his, and the boy draws his hand back, slow. They stare at each other like gunslingers.

Headlights.

At the far end of the car park a motor swings into view. 'Yer dead naah,' the weapon says, 'S-Burn Posse.'

Dolby walks towards the car, raising his hand. It stops. Too dark to see in, but me and the nedboy try anyway. The far window is rolled down and Dolby leans in to speak to the driver. I can't hear what he's saying, but he points in our direction. Two silhouetted heads in the back seat turn to the ned.

But he's gone. A vacant space on Belinda's bonnet where his mardy arse was.

The car pulls away, slipping out of the other side of the car park and onto the main road. Dolby trots back to Belinda and glances at me across the roof.

'Directions,' he says, and we
exhale

On the pier, we breathe in the salt air and try to calm down. Dolby grins/sighs/laughs. The adrenaline has washed away, leaving my insides a desolate shore. The sky meeting the sea before us in a seamless black accident and there are gunshot stars and lights from the boats and cold rolling off the sea in waves and the sound of slopping water and my virginity floats on the surface like a discarded polythene bag. Everything mesmerisingly bleak.

'How ye gettin on studying for yer exams?'

'Shite.'

'Who's yer teachers again?'

'Harry Kari for Geography—'

'I had him. Mad bastard.'

'Deansy for French, Picairn for Biology, Gibson for English.'

'Gibson? There's a wifey who wants tay change the world.'

'Ye reckon?'

'Aye. Shame she'll wake up in twenty years and realise she made fuck-all difference.'

Dolby stops. Spits. Watches it fall spit-kilometres.

We stare down into the water, vast, black as dreams. His words ripple in the empty air

fuck
all
difference

When I was wee, I was terrifed of swimming, could always imagine this massive prehistoric shark, Megaladon, roaming the pool, waiting to swallow me whole, Poundstretchers trunks and all. That beast grins beneath the surface now, tail beating the deep. Its mouth stretches as wide as a cavern, my arms spread as I leap and fall, the wind wrapping my face, the brittle sea collapsing under my weight, the waters rolling over my head. Endless. Comforting as death . . .

'Alvin?'

'Whit?'

'Ye gettin a feelin like ye want tay jump in?'

'Aye.'

A beat.

'Want tay head ho–'

'Aye.'

and so we smuggle ourselves back to Scotland under cover of darkenss. The lights of England shrink into the night. I think about the shark, swimming in huge circles, leaning its smooth head out of the water with its mouth yawning. Dolby steps on the gas.

if you travel at lightspeed, or fast enough, then things become illusory, ghosts are produced

when I get back, I find my brother in the living room talking to Dad. I linger, dumb, by the door for a second, almost believing the jazzy eyes and pearl-white grin aren't really there. Then Derek jumps from the chair and we shake hands in the middle of the room, beaming.

'Looking good, Billy Ray.'

'Feeling good, Valentine,' I reply, a quote from Trading Places, one of our favourite films. He curls an arm round my neck and we box a bit and nearly hug, but don't. 'When did you get back fay London?' I say, stunned by how pleased I am to see him.

'About an hour ago.'

His accent is odd and anglicised. He steps back, gives me the once-over, folds his hands back into his worn denim jacket. Grins again. 'Well,' he says, rubbing his hands together.

'Well,' I say.

'Well,' Dad says. His fly is undone.

We all smile.

Derek looks more like a Highland chieftan than a banker. The paltry stump at the back of his head is the beginning of a ponytail. His denim jacket is frayed at the cuffs, the elbows turning the colout of old men. He hasn't shaved and his bum-fluff is growing in ginger, like mine, like Dad's, and the overall impression is of Damon Albarn during the recording of Blur's 13 album, as though he's just split with Justine from Elastica.

'How was the journey?' I say, a fill-the-space type question I'm disappointed with myself for asking.

'No bad,' Derek shrugs, grabs a rake of bourbons from the biscuit barrel, shovelling them one at a time into his mouth while he speaks. 'Sitting next to this guy on the train – mind Handlebarus Moustachius?'

140

'Naw. Him that used tay sit ootside the shops? Eywis –'

'Pissin himself.'

We both laugh.

'It wisnay him, wis it?' Dad interrupts, from the edge of things.

'Looked pretty damn like him.'

'Nay way. Whit did he dae?'

'He pissed himself.'

'On the train?'

'Never.'

'Always. I think it was him.'

We slot into routine, each absorbing the contrast between old footage and new: caravan holidays; Derek bringing me home caked in mud; Sunday dinner and our grubby hands reaching out to grab the bread, Mum slapping them away and

mum slapping them away and

Dad folds his hands over his stomach, burbles softly with middle age. Something not quite fled from his face suggests he and Derek met at a strange, unwieldy angle. I realise they have been sitting in diametrically opposed chairs, like facing statues in an old, sealed tomb. Guardians of the dead.

'Ye see the Old Firm game last week?'

'I ken. 6–2. Poor Rangers.'

So much not being said, the absence hovering between us. We fill it desperately. The last time we saw each other, what were we wearing/ listening to/on about? Who's number one in the charts just now? What did ye make of that new Radiohead record? I think it's shite, too experimental. All of this sends emergency air into our punctured tyre, keeps the family unit trundling on, and the three of us are gathered here after all this time, all that's happened. Polite. Nodding. Like all the remaining Beatles meeting up on John Lennon's birthday.

141

take Derek to Comma Bar. 'Did this no used to be a bookshop?' he asks, as we wait for the waitress (not unlike Winona Ryder in Heathers, except prettier, not so pale). It did used to be a bookshop, called Inglis, and I can still picture the shelves, their ghostly spines emerging from the glamour. The Children's section, where a machine is now selling damaged lungs. Horror/Sci-Fi now a framed print of Manhattan at night, its lights unblinking, the clouds eerily frozen, and I remember Dolby buying his first Tolkien in that corner, rapt by its paperback immensity, and as an oblivious waitress disperses him, it occurs to me just how many worlds are going on at once that you don't notice. An untrendy town staggers through trendy blinds and Derek orders something called *mocha*, gazing up almost hopefully at the waitress, who smiles, which is of course an excellent quality. Brian thinks a good arse is important for bar staff, but I've always liked people who smile at their work. It makes a difference, it really does. I order a peach schnapps and lemonade. Winona seems impressed, doesn't even ask for ID.

Ordering drinks. Paying my own way. Handing over money. Not being a virgin.

'Ye remember when ye were ten in here and you bought that book about the boy who turns into a dog?'

'Woof?'

'An for two months after, you were tryin to change into a dog. Crouched down on all fours, yer face screwed up like ye needed a shite.'

'Chrissake, man.' I redden, as the waitress is in earshot. 'I wis only ten.'

'An me an Davy Pearson bet ye couldn't, and down you went . . .'

The memory hisses back, singeing my skin. Me with my eyes clamped shut, straining the word *dog* into my sinew, then standing up, utterly the same, utterly embarrassed. Hallglen seemed greyer, more drained of mystery, after that day.

The waitress places our drinks down.

'Woof,' she says.

'I wis only ten!'

I remind Derek of the time he jumped from a tree in Callendar Woods, snagged his trouser leg on a branch and swung, screaming, upside down for five minutes. Our laughter ripples.

It's good to see him. It is. I've decided.

Derek peers at the shoppers outside, their different shapes, fads, hairstyles, somehow worried, and he so much does not look like a banker. Do they allow him to go to work unshaven like this, I ask him, but he just shrugs and looks away, doing a double-take on a passing girl. 'So, whit are ye daein back?'

'The streets of London are not paved with gold,' he grunts, and seems edgy, almost paranoid, resisting my attempts to find out about his job or London with a firm, 'Let's no talk about work.' His face, which was always either a glinting humour or a sullen brood, has now settled permanently between the two. His boyishness is gone.

Dolby said once, when I asked him how he could be bothered getting up and fitting whirlpools every day, 'ye just dae it. Ye get up, put on the work heid and just day it.' After he said that, I realised that just doing it had pulled all of us – me, my family, the Lads – this far. Broken. But doing it.

and there is a quiet heroism which goes on every day

Me and Derek chat about what I'm up to (revision for my Highers mainly, these days), and thank god he doesn't ask if I'm still a virgin, and although I try to tell him that Dolby has changed his name to Uriel, that Brian is still planning to emigrating to California, that Frannie's Mum and Dad are on the verge of splitting, Derek's some-where else. Vague. Haunted. He's blinking, nodding, saying 'aye', and laughing in the right places, but he's not there.

143

'When I got in,' he whispers, interrupting my story about Cottsy and Brian, 'I found Dad in the garden, holding Mum's wedding dress.'

This is a sight I've seen more often than he has, so it doesn't faze me.

Derek recounts times when he found bottles of vodka hidden all over the house; when he had to go out on his bike to look for her, see if she'd collapsed anywhere, only to come back and find her snuggled up in the loft with Smirnoff. I stare at the mahogany knots in the table while he tells me this, wondering at the strangeness of the past, how if you drop it in the front seat of the present it does not land in the back.

'I'm amazed she survived as long as she did,' I say.

Derek looks at me. 'That's what I wanted to talk to you about.'

The waitress comes over, but Derek hisses her away and she withdraws, sullen, unsmiling, and just before he starts talking I notice a photo of Marilyn Monroe reading Ulysses, sitting in a swimsuit with her legs drawn up and her face slack with incomprehension, like a little girl trying to keep up with the teacher. The book is huge and heavy and has JAMES JOYCE on the front in big, bold letters, and I'm surprised she can hold the thing up, let alone read it. She is almost on the last page, and though I don't believe that she's managed all that, I feel bad about not believing her, believing *in* her. Maybe she has read it, and I'm being a dick. The photograph disturbs me for the length of time it takes Derek to say, 'I think Mum's still alive.'

The three of us talk that night for the first time in years, dotted in separate corners of the room. Things are fraught with restraint. When we speak, cages are opened a crack. The beasts inside sniff, consider, then retreat. There's too much.

there's

too

much

blame almost attached and just lifted before the sting, and Dad plays an Elvis Costello song, Alison, flickering in and out of my awareness, making it feel as though Elvis is strolling the room, crooning, knowing this world is killing me and I can't concentrate on what Derek's saying. I feel far away from things, behind glass, mouths moving but no sound coming out, a vague terror mounting, a feeling I get in Belinda sometimes as we cruise in and out of Scottish new towns like panthers in the night – when the Lads are talking about wages and shagging and beer and Rangers – as if I've gradually slipped down a crack beneath the seat and none of them can hear my plea.

Derek thinks Mum's been following him.

He's turned, several times, and glimpsed her standing on street corners, staring coldly at him, then disappearing – blink! – and he reminds us (why? don't we know this?) that the police never found her, that there was no body, while on TV a male goat stands waiting to be castrated, which I watch on the edge of my seat. The goat blinks at the camera, chewing stupidly, making me wonder if it's, like, the goat version of Brian Mann, and has to return to its mates in the pasture dickless.

I feel like telling the two of them that hope is born, but lives in a short, frantic burst, like an insect, and then dies. But instead I find myself screaming hysterically, 'That's a lie. She *never* said that. You're a fucking liar, Derek Allison, you cunt.'

Sunday night.

The three of us not talking now, lurking in different rooms. Like the good old days. The walls feed off our resentment. The shower slow-dripping. The garden slabs broken. I head down to Dolby's with an idea for a new Clive Barker novel that I'm thinking of sending to his publishers. Dolby's Dad says he's at Brian's (Dolby, that is, not Clive

Barker!) with DVDs and popcorn, but when I chap on Brian's door nobody answers, though I want, *ache*, to head out in Belinda tonight, break onto uncharted roads at the speed of sound, shouting, 'Heddy haw,' from the sunroof, Led Zep playing loud enough to obliterate all this shit. I knock again, peering in the window. The lights are on. I knock a third time – still no answer – then, warily, like in a murder mystery, squeeze the handle.

Brian and Dolby are eating popcorn on the couch.

'Aw. Alvin. It's you,' Brian says, flatly. 'How did I ken it wis gonnay be you?'

'Never mind that,' I say, 'why did yese no answer the door?'

'We, eh, thought it wis the guy for the TV licence,' Dolby says, and Brian nods. 'He's no paid the bill, ken?'

'No paid the bill,' Brian mumbles.

'Ye forget I said I'd be doon the night?'

'I did,' Brian sighs, unpausing the film, then pausing it again as I tell them, excitedly, about Tyra's nipples straining at the fabric of her blouse today, and my idea for the Clive Barker book which has a really cool baddie and should be made into a film and

Brian yawns.

next morning, the school assembly hall is filled with universities plying their trade. Suits, stalls, clans of prefects all honing their careers over milky cups of tea. Mrs Gibson has forced me to go. I was hoping to use that morning's free periods usefully, to watch Scarface or something. As I wander round the stalls, several scenes from the film keep
stuttering in my head

You kno what capitaleesm ees?
I tell you.

Get fucked! Dat what capitaleesm ees.

Get fucked!

All the other local schools are visiting ours today. The hall is a tide of bobbing blazers. Photos of campuses, scientists and smiling students of every ethnicity are arranged on the walls in a collage. Tyra Mackenzie, who I've been following all morning, meets-and-greets boys from Graeme High, St Mungo's High, Denny High, who she knows through the Debating Society, her face lit up for them. She is handing out invitations to her forthcoming 17th birthday party, gushing, 'Oh, I'd *love* it if you could come, guys,' but I can't get close enough for her to accidentally find herself beside me and realise she hasn't given me one, so I manoeuvre myself in and out of the crowd so that the next stall she visits, St Andrews, I will be there, casually perusing a prospectus, ready to exclaim, 'Oh, hi, Tyra. St Andrews? Yeah, I dunno, I suppose you just feel a calling to some places. What? A party? Oh, I'd love to.' But just as she says goodbye to some Denny High prefect with awful acne, her hand lingering (too long) on his sleeve, just as I start discussing with the rep the fact that no decent bands ever came out of St Andrews – ever – there's a tug at my arm.

'Alvin,' Mrs Gibson says, her smile glowing. 'There's someone here I'd like you to meet.' I'm pulled away from Tyra's light like in a near death experience, as she finds herself alone at the stall, glancing round (for me?) before her image is obscured by a drifting cloud of blazers.

!Fuck!

Mrs Gibson drags me to the Stirling Uni display, giving it mucho peptalk. Photos of greenery, rabbits, freshfaced boys with folders grinning ouside lecture halls.

'This is Alvin Allison,' she says, introducing me to the stiff behind the stall, 'a very talented student of mine. He sort of needs a bit of convincing to go on to further education, though, so if you could . . .'

I am only half-listening, scanning the crowd for Tyra, who is blowing through the far end of the hall shedding invites like sweetie papers.

'Well, I think you'd really warm to the Stirling Uni environment, Alvin,' the rep's blethering. 'It has excellent facilities, a beautiful campus, and–'

'Hmm. Yah. Supah,' I say, rubbing my chin.

The suit coughs, perturbed, looking at Gibson, who frowns and explains to him my keen interest in, uh, Gothic literature.

'Alvin's Higher English review is on Stephen King, and it's quite an insight into, the, um, mindset of, um, pathological violence . . .'

'Pathological violence,' I repeat, smiling.

'Excuse us a minute.'

Gibson draws me aside, glowering. 'What do you think you're playing at?' she snaps, hands on hips. 'Is your future some sort of a joke?'

'Oh, come on Miss,' I protest. 'I ken whit yer daein, an it's cool. You *shall* go to the ball an aw that. But mibbe I dinnay want tay go. University's full ay tossers like this–'

and I sweep my arm around the pack of well-bred crocodiles snapping for tidbits at the Edinburgh stall, but Gibson's having none of it.

'Will. You. Just. Stop,' she says, the magic wand replaced in her act by a whip. 'Think about your potential for once. This isn't a class issue, Alvin.'

'Everything's a class issue,' I mutter, switching to Smirk Automatic as I wonder why Bernard Butler really left Suede (cos he would have sounded great on the Coming Up album) and shrug, walk away, strangely furious with myself, and I don't mention that my future seems like one yawning great chasm in which nobody loves anybody else and Scotland breaks away from the British Isles and crumbles pointlessly into the sea – plop – since each of my thoughts is precious, hidden, hoarded and pored over, and Mrs Gibson shouts something

148

like, 'promise me you'll think about it,' but I can't promise anybody anything of the sort.

'Well, if we're talking forte,' one of the prefects is braying at the Dundee stall, 'we'd be talking chemistry.'

'Do you have active theatre groups?' asks another.

I start drifting round the tables, only half interested in the patter, humming

> still haven't found what I'm looking for
> no I still haven't found

and realising that Tyra has left. Her invitations are given out. Her purpose is spent. Her perfume is only a lingering scent, which fades into mindless excitement for Business Law at Glasgow, Media Studies at Napier, Accountancy at Strathclyde, and so I drip back to the Stirling stall, which Gibson, exasperated, has quit.

> and I still haven't found what I'm looking for
> no I still haven't

Connor Livingstone is beside me all of a sudden. He's had a haircut, and looks like one of the actors from the Scream movies. He says, 'Stirling?' Shrugs. 'I suppose it's the right place for someone like yourself.' And the weird thing is that I can see on his face that he *probably means well*. After my set-to with Gibson, my uninvited status to Tyra's (the world's?) party, and a mother who has every right to be dead after all this time surfacing just when I need my sanity most, I'm spoiling for a fight.

'Could you, um, clarify that, Connor?' I ask, gritting my teeth. 'That, ah, "someone like yourself"?'

Livingstone has total recall to the Times Educational Supplement.

'Well,' he begins, smiling like a toothpaste advert, 'it didn't make the list of the top ten best universities in Britain in the recent survey. It clings a bit to its left-wing reputation from the seventies. And if you compare it to somewhere like, I don't know, Edinburgh, it just can't compete in terms of resources and finances . . .'

I'm nodding, encouraged by his insights.

'I didn't mean to sound patronising, Alvin. All I was trying to say is that, for someone like yourself, who's obviously talented but not, er, academically *gifted*, as such–'

'Academically gifted.'

'– it would meet most of your needs. You wouldn't find it as stretching as, say, Cambridge or Oxford, and some of the people there will be from your own background.'

'What kind of background is that?'

Connor smiles reassuringly, his prognosis delivered. Then he adjusts his hair, which, it has to be said, looks bloody marvellous.

I am totally sold on Stirling.

'Anyway, Alvin,' he says, patting my shoulder, 'I really have to go and see the Edinburgh rep, he's my dad's–'

'Hang on,' I stop him, 'can I ask one more question?'

'Of course,' he smiles, surprised but delighted by my willingness to learn.

'Who the fuck do ye think you are?'

He stares back at me, startled, as though I have jumped him on his way home from a fund-raising bash.

'Excuse me?' he says politely.

'Dae you ken me?' I snarl. 'Dae you have any idea who I am or what I feel? How dare you dismiss me like that, you cunt.'

I say the word 'cunt' formally, enjoying the experience of it on my tongue. It feels like introducing a madman to a dinner party. Connor frowns. My challenge has riled him, and he lets slip that facade which I knew, *I fucking knew*, wasn't the real Connor Livingstone.

'At least I don't spend my nights boyracing with a pack of neander-thals. I'm—'

'You're nothing,' I sneer, smelling a kill, seeing visions of myself as a shop-steward inciding the workers to arms, to rebellion, to crush the Suits. 'You're an empty blazer. A prefect badge. A fucking haircut. *That's* Connor Livingstone.'

He takes a step back, and I like that feeling of power, that reversal of power, my hatred for him actually hurting, as I stare, willing him to test me, force me to reveal the true, seething, nature of this outcast thing that dares litter the corridors of Connor Livingstone's school.

'You won't be going to Tyra's party,' is all he can say. 'You won't be going. I'll make sure of that.'

He stumbles, glancing back as if expecting me to come after him like a rottweiler, and I form a confident picture of the moment he reaches the prefect hut, trembling, some girl handing him a glass of water while he shakes and tells them about this rabid thing that would

take

no

more

and then I think Fuck! I'm never getting into her party now!

I rush to find Tyra before he can, checking the places she spends interval duty, the Maths corridor, the refectory, the tuckshop, then spot her at the top of the stairs. She is with Louisa Wainwright and Jennifer Haslom, all chatting excitedly on their phones, her words floating like pink paper on a breeze, so I bound up the first two, three flights, energised, knowing that I have to ask her now, right now, but I can't.

151

Livingstone's right. I am a broom-pusher. A car park attendant. My children are destined to work in McDonalds. Tyra and her friends live in houses that have actual names, not just numbers. Money swirls and eddies about them like confetti. I gaze at her from the lower step and she is a promise that I will not reach. She exists at the end of a long corridor in some perfect, white, silicon future world. The deft movement of her wrist as she talks, brands coasting her body like pilot fish, her phone is blue and

I still haven't found what I'm looking for

emits love songs and right now I am the feeling you get when you switch on the TV and see that the Simpsons has just finished.

'. . . and then he said to me, "I can see that you are a woman, not a girl", so . . .'

'. . . get your tongue out of my ear! But it's, like, this silver Merc, cos he is loaded . . .'

'. . . what? Oh? Like, whatever . . .'

Some people exist for the past. My Dad, for example. Some people exist for the present: ravers and extreme sports fans and party girls and armed robbers and junkies and boyracers. The present to me feels like candyfloss dissolving on the tongue: I can't quite hold on to it's beauty for long enough. No, I think that I

still haven't found what I

exist for the future, the hope that it's as bright as they promise. But it's just that the faster I charge towards it, the further away from me it seems to stretch.

I traipse dejectedly away from school, unable to face Tyra and the rest of my classes, just desperate to return to bed, soft safety, not even in the mood for Scarface now, and all I can visualise, with stunning clarity, is the sticker I once spotted on a car Belinda couldn't overtake, which said GO ON THEN, TRY AND OVERTAKE ME.

These are the top ten things Alvin Allison has looked forward to in his life:

10. The Blair Witch Project
(my generation's The Exorcist)
9. Guns 'n' Roses album, Chinese Democracy
(should be out later this year)
8. X-Men movie
(ohhhh they got Wolverine right)
7. The Third Book of the Art by Clive Barker
(Book Two published 1994. Still waiting, Clive)
6. Blair Witch 2: Book of Shadows
(my generation's The Exorcist II, unfortunately)
5. Spider-Man movie
(Peter Parker is the role I was born to play)
4. Kid A by Radiohead
(even though I didn't understand it)
3. forthcoming Lord of the Rings movies
(possibly makind's single greatest-ever achievement ever?)
2. All That You Can't Leave Behind by U2
(classic me and Frannie bonding moment, oh yes)
1. American Psycho movie
(there is an idea of a Patrick Batemen, some kind of abstraction, but there is no real me, only an entity, something illusory. And

though I can hide my cold gaze and you can shake my hand and feel flesh gripping yours and maybe you can even sense our lifestyles are probably comparable,

I simply

am not

there

singing like they're winning – Frannie with the actual money from his wages splattered against the windscreen, lording it over all the passing skanks and weapons, and after we picked him up in Belinda with a poly bag of Becks, which Brian cracked open and handed round to the sound of whoops, cheers and classic Bon Jovi (yes, there is such a thing) and it's the end of the month and the Lads have just been paid and the four of us are rocking and we drive to:

Stirling Castle.

'Dolby, Dolby, give us yer answer do.'

Linlithgow Country Park.

'We're half-crazy aw for the love ay you.'

B&Q.

'Been years since we had some nookie, and that was wi a wookie.'

Langlees.

'But you're still sweet, in the driver's seat, so pull us a skank or two!'

as Dolby puts his palms on the ceiling of the car for a few seconds, laughs, 'Well, one ay youse fuckin drive then,' and Brian swaps Bon Jovi for Deacon Blue, frog-singing away to Dignity, and soon we're all unleashing our throats on the bit that goes 'Set it up again! Set it up again! Set it up again! Set it up again!' like the Tartan Army invading

154

the pitch at Wembley, until I think some more about the words, pause, then say:

'Sortay patronisin, that song, when ye think about it really.'

'How d'ye mean?' says Frannie, bobbing his head in time to the music.

'It's patronising tay the working classes, in't it?'

Brian turns down the volume and I shift nervously in my seat. 'Whit the fuck are you talking about now?'

'Well, it's aboot this cooncil-worker, an everybody laughs at him cos he's cleanin the streets. But he's gonnay save up his money, buy a ship, an call it Dignity.'

Brian is waiting for the punchline. 'Aye?'

'So, it's sayin that ye have tay have money tay have dignity. That it's somethin ye can buy.'

'But he's no buyin actual dignity,' Frannie says, baffled. 'He's buyin a dinghy. Just wants tay go oot in his boat.'

'Aye. Called Dignity. It's a . . . metaphor for . . . aw, never mind.'

'Oh. I wonder who's daein Higher English?' tuts Brian. 'Anyway, whaur is the fuckin dignity in cleanin the streets! Nay dignity in that. Let him buy his wee boat for fuck's sake, leave him alane.'

'How's there nay dignity in cleanin the streets?' I say.

'When did the song come oot?' asks Dolby.

'Dunno. 1987?'

'Thatcher.' I pounce on this. 'Only Thatcher could convince us that cleanin the streets has nay dignity.'

'Here we fuckin go.'

'Wages Day is the same. Like, ye can only enjoy life if ye've just been paid.'

'Ye *can* only enjoy life if ye've just been paid.'

'I havenay just been paid,' I say.

'You dinnay work,' Brian sneers, wrenching his frame round from the front seat to take me, firmly, to task. 'In case ye didnay realise, aw these crisps an cans ay juice ye've been shovin doon yer scrawny throat are on us. Cos it's wages day an we've aw been paid an we're enjoyin oursels. You, *runt*, huvnay even goat a fuckin job, so dinnay talk tay us about enjoyment. Who's bein patronisin now, eh? Ye think we get up oot oor beds an work for the life-fulfillin experience ay it?'

'I'm no sayin that, but–'

'Once you've got a job, wi nay seven-week summer holidays an nay study-leave, then ye can fuckin lecture us about dignity, wee man.'

Brian grips his Irn-Bru with result.

We stop at a red light. A council worker crosses with a lumpen rubbish cart, as dignity-free as anyone I've ever seen. Neither does he look like he's saving up for any. The lights change. Dolby speeds up. Brian plays Wages Day, deliberately.

> You can have it all
> you can take it all away
> on wages day

'They're closing doon the ABC and opening up a multiplex,' Frannie utters this, monotone, as we pass the cinema for what seems like the millionth time this week. Tonight it is showing Jurassic Park 3. Rain starts to form little bodies on the glass. 'Think aboot aw the films that have been shown there ower the years,' Frannies sighs. 'Gone Wi the Wind. Star Wars. Robin Hood: Prince ay Thieves. It's sortay, like, a cultural history.'

'No it isnay,' Brian snorts, unimpressed. 'I'm sick ay this pish. It's *progress*. Sa shite picture hoose anyway. The seats are uncomfy as fuck.'

'Progress-shmogress,' I say, still rankled by the Deacon Blue argument and sensitive to Frannie's vision of folks in old-style hats traipsing out from a showing of Calamity Jane. 'Progress is a capitalist myth.'

156

'Capitalist myth?' Brian shouts. 'You're a capitalist myth, ya cunt! Whaur wid we be withoot capitalism? A fuckin borin world that, eh Dolby?'

'Borin,' Dolby replies robotically.

'Nay Nike. Nay MTV. Nay McDonalds–'

'Nay Glasgow Rangers,' I goad.

Brian glares, at the same moment in which the veins at my temples (which feel like they've been laced with fireworks and have been threatening gently all night) are set off.

'Whit ye tryin tay say about the Rangers, like?'

It's bound to be more complex than this. Economics is, isn't it? But I can't grasp it, not really, but on a classic Star Trek repeat the other day Mr Spock said

slavery can evolve into an institution, develop benefits, health care

then an advert for Doritos came on which had loads of mates laughing over a bowl of crisps and ended with the word Friendchips and these years I'm living in now, should I forget, are the Best of My Life, hey, so fuck it, fuck them all, I am not going to take on Brian because I've just

stopped

caring

but before I know it I'm talking like this, 'Glasgow Rangers Football Club does not represent the workin man, Brian. They dinnay even represent Scotland.'

'Oh. An whit dae they "represent"?' Brian makes inverted commas with his fingers sarcastically.

'The Queen, the crown, greed, exploitation, the Empire, Thatcherism–'

'Thatcherism?' he laughs, looking to the others for back-up, but they seem tired, ironed-flat by the whole topic. 'Come ontay fuck, Alvin, they're a fitba team, no a political party!'

'Everythin's political,' I mutter, staring at him, my mean headache turning sideways,

sideways.

'Yer arse is fuckin political!'

'My arse *is* political,' I laugh, hysterical and useless. 'Who owns my arse!'

We pass the carcass of a dog strewn across the road. It has an eye missing and tyre-tracks across its back.

'So let me get this straight,' Brian is a fighter jet screaming from Fortress Ibrox. 'Not only are ye a poof an runt, but now yer a socialist and a pape?'

'A pape?' I blink (really wishing Dolby would change this fuckin Deacon Blue album now). 'How's that, likes? Because I dinnay agree wi your narrow-minded-Brian-Mann views I'm a Catholic? That makes sense!' Adrenaline surging and I'm making this a bigger deal than it is and pissing the three of them off simply because Frannie mentioned the ABC is closing down, but I'm past caring, beyond the thunderdome, clouds are gathering on the horizon, things passing from simple to complex with frightening speed and a heroine is screaming somewhere each time I issue words, as though I'm a lunatic brandishing a knife, my life passing for Chinese water-torture, incidents slow-dripping in my head: my unquenchable love for Tyra, Derek coming home a defeated man, Connor fucking Livingstone, the Spider-Man movie only in pre-production, Mum undead, losing my virginity (did I come too early?), Belinda needing a service, a broken leg in an accident that wasn't our fault – I know it wasn't – but which could result in some drive-by outside the Callendar Arms bar, Connor-cunting-Livingstone, exams, U2 tour dates still unannounced, the future, I owe it to myself repeated like a mantra in each of my dreams, and during all of this I am trying to turn my squeak into a roar, become Russell Crowe fighting tigers in Gladiator while simultaneously placating my horror at the crushing boredom of everything and everyone around me.

'See these part-time bigots like you?' I am raging. 'I've less respect for them than the full-time wans. At least Nazis and the KKK believed in it. You just switch it on and aff when it suits ye.'

'Naw I dinnay,' Brian roars. 'Fuckin Protestant through and through.'

'No yer no.'

'Aye I am. Twenty home games last season, ya bas.'

I ignore this, hammering on Thor-like. 'You live in a fantasy world called "The Fortunes of Glasgow Rangers Football Club". It disnay matter if they win or lose. You're just a consumer – a means tay an end fir the fat fuckers that own the club, who're gettin rich aff the stupit fuckin emotional attachement tay Rangers they've managed tay sell ye.'

'Listen tay it,' Brian laughs. 'Me in a fantasy world? You're the cunt that still reads The Hobbit an Lord ay the fuckin Flies.'

'Rings.'

'Whaur's the reality there? Ye canny fuckin *deal* wi reality, Alvin.' He lunges into the tone of some angry beast, and though I'm out of order calling him worse than a Nazi, especially when his Dad is a British soldier, and though he's throaty with resentment, jabbing his finger at me from the front seat, and even though this is one of my very best mates and I really fucking love the guy, what can I do?

Things are getting difficult.

'Now you listen tay me, runt,' he snarls. 'Ye canny just tag along wi us in this car and go' (affects poofy voice) '*I tink tis is wrong and I tink tat is wrong.*'

'Tag along?' I say, startled.

'Ye're too fuckin young tay be hinging oot wi us, anyway. We've been tryin tay avoid you for months.'

'Brian,' Dolby barks, as I melt into the back seat.

'Ye want tay ken somethin else?' he laughs, blundering through my defences. 'You didnay even shag Shelley fay the pub.'

'Enough!' Dolby demands.

'You *couldnay* shag her, ye were that fuckin pished.'

Ice slowly spreads on my skin.

'Ye put yer heid on her tits and asked her tay hold ye.'

We drive for the rest of the night in silence.

Frannie mentions once, 'I dunno whaur they're buildin the multiplex.'

slam four doors, go four separate ways, and that night I argue with Derek across the kitchen table about his silly paranoia – Mum still alive? following him? the stupid cunt – and he sucks up spaghetti and replies that if I'd been more paranoid when she disappeared, phoned the police quicker, they might have found her, so I punch him, and then he punches back, then there's a flurry of punches which Dad breaks up, horrified, and I run to my room saying that I hate them both, knowing I've missed Buffy the Vampire Slayer and that I also have no friends in the world, that Tyra doesn't – couldn't ever – love me, that my Higher exams represent my doom and that I am totally alone, so I just listen to Stairway to Heaven, watching the rain drip transparent patterns on the window, marvelling at how they wrote such a song, so *intricate*, then read some of Stephen King's Carrie and just sleep.

I dream about aliens. Aliens and the Blair Witch. Frannie and Dolby picking them up in Belinda and taking them out and treating them right. The Blair Witch tastes haggis and Irn-Bru for the first time. She likes it.

Monday night.

I head down to Dolby's. Belinda is parked outside like an obedient dog, her rust flaking. Dolby is halfway through his dinner and an episode of Babylon 5, so I natter to his Dad, who for some reason is keen to teach me House of the Rising Sun on guitar. I can't get my fingers round the frets, and have to pretend this is really funny, since Dolby's Dad looks like Lee Van Clef in The Good, the Bad and the Ugly and is notorious for dispensing dead-arms with accuracy, so I try again.

'Gon,' he urges, all satanic, 'play Layla.'

Later, in his bedroom, Dolby chucks me a package. I don't catch it instantly, having lost all feeling in my arm, but I do recognise the cover. It's the new release by Pink Floyd, Is There Anybody Out There? It's essentially The Wall album recorded live in 1980 when Roger Waters was still in the band!

'That's from Brian,' Dolby says. 'He's sorry about the other night. Didnay want tay give it tay ye himsel, cos he's embarrassed.'

'Right,' I say, knowing it's a lie and that Dolby has bought this. 'Tell him thanks.'

'Cool, eh?' Dolby nods at the CD.

'Cool,' I agree, slightly disappointed that forever The Wall will remind me of Brian's mouth twisted with resentment, the *un*shagging of Shelley, until I run my hand across the hardback book that accompanies the CD, the four faces of Pink Floyd on the cover, their eyes cut out like empty masks, while inside The Wall concert explodes in a burst of stage lights. David Gilmour's guitar glinting and his shadow, thrown by a spotlight, bleeding across the audience, and huge, marching hammers, and a nimbus of mist, and floating, malevolent teacher puppets, all of this plucked from the fog of the past and made real, apparent, whole.

'Dolby,' I begin, but can't express any of it.

'I know!' he grins.

'Naw,' I say. 'It's just too . . .'

'I know!' he almost squeaks, his eyes screwed shut. 'I know!'

We listen to it.

For an hour and a half we lie still on the bed, watching the graphic equaliser blipping up and down, his plasma ball flicking tongues of electricity, the shifting blues and greens of the fish tank and the spectral, gliding shapes of the fish. It is our own private Pink Floyd light show. The scent of Dolby's incense (jasmine) curls in the air, revealing itself the way a pretty, stoned girl might take off clothes.

Outside the sky turns from grey to dark grey, the white concrete of the Hallglen scheme becoming dull alabaster, and we cannot hear the drunks shouting, the children baiting them, car alarms going on, off, bottles being kicked, smashed, while we lie on our stomachs with our chins in our hands, just listening to the Floyd.

Sometimes, the world is too fine, just stuffed with good things.

The CD makes a small *shick* sound as it spins to a halt. Dolby turns over, scratching his belly. 'If you make it away, Alvin,' he says quietly, 'make it for the four of us eh.'

and we both gaze down at the bedspread, then talk about the album, how Roger Waters is a songwriting genius, he really is.

but none of this resolves what to do about Tyra's party. It is the focus of my existence, the light above my bed, only a day away and going on without me. How can I concentrate on exam revision? I am doomed to spend loose hours feeling my mind pinball from the new

162

singles chart to the wrongs of global capitalism to whether or not we should print DA BOYZ on Belinda to the question of Tyra's underwear (betcha it's white lace) and Stephen King's best book (surely *The Shining*). Frannie's just off the phone. His Mum and Dad are finally divorcing. Maybe it's cos his Dad lost his job at Motorola recently, the contract punted off to Jakarta or somewhere else that sounds like a dance act. I dunno. He phones me up, and when I ask him about it, he falls silent for a good long while, only space crackling and hissing between us.

'So, how's work?' I say, and the silence mutates into a sigh.

'Fuck work.' Frannie sounds nothing like himself, as if he's been body-snatched by some lurching misanthrope. 'See bein a guy these days? It's a joke. Women are too smart for us. This *lifestyle* dangled in front ay you wi one hand while yer work steals yer soul wi the other. I tell ye, we've been betrayed. Fuckin betrayed.' I hear what sounds like Frannie putting down the phone, walking around the room and saying 'fuck, fuck, fuck' to himself in an infuriated whisper.

'Fran? Ye there?'

Then he's back on the line, exhaling. 'See the Rangers game last night?' he says. 'Ally McCoist wis commentatin.'

'I did, man.' I say. 'His patter's magic.'

So we talk about Coisty for a while before he puts the phone down, in a better mood than he was. I suppose our story – mine, Brian's Frannie's, Dolby's, Belinda's – will end up just another Scottish folk tale, no more than a modern day Fairies O' Merlin Craig or The Brownie O' Ferne Den – sort of shite you find in flog-it-to-the-tourists books with tartan spines and I'm not sure if Scotland even exists anymore. Maybe Scotland was only ever a dream agreed upon by people who shared the same land and the same shit life and that's it, and I stand before the bathroom mirror, seething with confusion, imagining myself as Mr Blonde from Reservoir Dogs, his open razor raised, smirking

Did you ever listen to K Billy's Super Sounds of the Seventies?

as I press the blade against my cheek and red oozes from its edge and

'Post been delivered, Dad?'

I'm padding downstairs after a (for once) dreamless sleep, my stomach roaring for Coco-Pops (king of cereals). The morning sun makes jungle-dapple on the floorboards. The neighbours exiting stage left for work. Birds tweeting. The Sex Pistols drowning out Derek's complaints at the Sex Pistols drowning out Derek's complaints. I pass the front door, vaguely registering that the postman has–

Joy catches in my throat.

I pounce on the pink envelope, buzzing with hope.

YOU ARE INVITED TO THE
17th BIRTHDAY PARTY OF
TYRA MARY-LOUISE MACKENZIE
at
11 ALBERT ROAD, FALKIRK
1st April, 8pm

And though my head is spinning like it's in a washing machine filled with petals, I notice

ps. Sorry I didn't catch you at school, Alvin.
Would love it if you came!

the rest of the day shoots by like a torpedo! The drugged, soulless teach-ervoices – droning on and on about transferred epithets, verb tables, isotopes – skirt the ground like dust in a breeze, while texts buzz back and forth between the desks and my mind soars upwards, whirls, becomes orchestral and limitless. I feel heightened, alive, muscle-bound, like Brad Pitt after being bitten by the Cruiser in Interview with the Vampire. The whole school is alive with talk of Tyra's party, and I, Alvin Allison, am centre of the whirlwind, a god amongst incon-sequentials. Everything is beautiful. First-years collared by Melville for running in the corridor have genius in their trespass. The word 'chil-dren' in Connor's Dad's notice on the PTA board

> request volunteers to organise more study groups for the senior
> children

strikes me as lawlessly funny, the way a swear word leaps out in the context of a poem (would these be the same 'children', Mr Livingstone, who recreate the Grand Prix in Falkirk town centre, masturbate like Duracell bunnies and run up phone debt with each twitch of their hash-stained fingers?) Connor gives a letter from his mother to Mrs Pitcairn, complaining that the class tests are too easy, not stretching him enough, and I can't bring myself to care about this as I've just realised I have another eighty or so years left on Earth in which I can do whatever the fuck I want and I'm wondering what booze I should bring to Tyra's party and

we swagger from the shop at the bottom of the Glen Brae with two bottles of Famous Grouse and eight Strongbow (for the price of four). Brian and Frannie insist on singing Hello, Hello, We are the Billy Boys all the way up to Tyra's house while I try to tell Dolby the latest on the forthcoming Lord of the Rings movie. The evening is blue and clean and billowing. My stomach is full of circus performers.

The music pumping from Tyra's house (Abba), the antiquity of Albert Road – its stoic, middle class retirement air – filled with Europop and Rangers terrace anthems.

'So whit's the name ay the birthday bint?' Brian asks, thumping my shoulder with a Strongbow. 'Tie Her Up?'

'Tire Her Oot?' suggests Frannie.

'No,' I say. 'Tyra. So the thing about the film,' I carry on, my jaw tight as we approach her door, 'is that they're using the same technology as Gladiator, except they have to make you believe in a fantasy world, not a real one.'

'That's very interestin,' says Dolby.

I ring her doorbell. The Grouse bottles clink gently. I can see dark shapes through the frosted glass; woozy, ghostly heads. I ring the doorbell again and the music is turned down briefly. Someone says, '. . . at the door? But everyone's here . . .' then a grey shape swells towards the glass.

'I could shag a whole room full ay schoolies,' Brian growls.

Frannie, in a 'Vietnamese' voice: 'You so honny! Two dollar! Sucky-fucky!'

'So, when's the movie due?' asks Dolby, but I shush them frantically and the door swings open.

'Alvin?' I actually intake breath at how beautiful she looks. Her hair has been set in golden curls for the evening. Her face is glowing with excitement. The temptation to touch her hand, resting on the door-jamb, is overwhelming.

The Lads say nothing, dumbfounded by her beauty.

'You. Uh – you're *here*.' Her voice goes up on the last word, flecked with surprise.

'Well, I'm a wee bit late, but–'

She's staring at the cut on my cheek, concerned. 'How did you get that scar?'

'Oh,' I fumble, 'shaving accident.'

I thrust the gift at her and she stares at it for a second, as if unsure of something vital to the cogency of life. Then she shrugs awkwardly. 'Well, I suppose you'd better come in.'

We stride past her into the lobby, the Lads mumbling 'Evenin'/'Happy birthday'/'Hiya' the same cowed way children speak to their dentists. Her hall is resplendent with balloons and streamers, littering the paintings and framed prints like clowns invading a serious arts debate and (I am in Tyra's house!) the mahogany thrums with drum n bass. The Lads spread sheepishly into the hall as Tyra unwraps her present.

'Oh,' she gasps, reading. 'Is this a box set of . . . the complete albums of Pink Floyd?'

'Digitally remastered,' I add.

'Thanks,' her small mouth utters. I was hoping she'd cry, but she's obviously too stunned and grateful.

'It's a real idea of how the band developed,' I point out to her, 'over fourteen albums.'

party is littered with star names from the senior school, the detritus of an exploded galaxy: Jennifer Haslom, earrings glinting, curls swinging gently on a slender neck; Louisa Wainwright brushing a fawning hand down David Easton's arm. All eyes turn as we enter, grinning like village idiots, hauling our Strongbow from the poly bag to offer them round. No takers. For most of the evening we remain in a tight, defensive phalanx, moving from room to room as a unit.

Brian's eyes goggle at Tyra's tanned, summery friends. 'Canny remember schoolies ever lookin like this.'

Frannie is horrified by evidence of Tyra's Dad being a Celtic fan. 'A Souvenir fay Dublin?'

Dolby scours the bookshelves for confirmation of his own good taste, his fingers resting on all seven of the Narnia books in hardback. The party shifts

up a gear. Someone plays Fatboy Slim's You've Come A Long Way Baby, Brian and Frannie rolling into an argument about lyrics. 'Does that song say *Carol Vordeman is druggy druggy druggy*?'

'Naw. It's *California*.'

Frannie cocks an ear, raises a finger

'It's Carol Vordeman. *Carol Vordeman is druggy druggy druggy.*'

'Shut up,' Brian rumbles.

Through the swelling crowd I catch a glimpse of my mother watching me the way she once looked into my cot, and for some reason Louisa Wainwright is giving Gordon French a massage, her hands easing and rising on his shoulder blades as a look of bliss breaks across his face, and a couple of guys – older guys who claim to know Tyra (they wink) *very* well – ask about Derek

'Is your brother back from London?'

'Naw, he's stickin it oot,' I say.

and I half-deflect, half-ignore their questions, Fatboy Slim's loops burrowing a dull worm of pain into my skull and Tyra is nowhere to be seen, and so, slurping at the syrupy warmth of the Famous Grouse, I go hunting, asking vague party girls if they fancy my mates, cos they're, like, all single, glimpsing Mum several times – sipping gin on the stairs, helping someone be sick in the garden, browsing the Mackenzie CD collection – and when next I return to the living room the hash heads from the back of the History huts are talking to the Lads, Barry holding court like Shaun Ryder, his lit joint making the Lads stiff, wary, subdued. He is telling Frannie and Dolby about his idea for a novel called Twelve Storeys High, which is, 'a bit like Trainspotting except set in this high-rise in Fawkurt, an there's like, twelve different stories for the twelve different storeys, an they're aw drug dealers so that's why it's cawed Twelve Storeys *High*. Robert Carlyle'll play me in the movie likes.'

Gordo, meanwhile, is imparting one of his prophecies to a rapt Brian Mann. I shuffle close, inconspicuous, to hear Gordo say, 'Just tay let ye know, man, I've heard it said that Cottsy fay Camelon's still gunnin fir ye.'

Brian grunts moodily, retorts something about Cottsy having to fucking catch him first.

'Whit happened at the races, by the way? I heard somethin like yer mate ran ower some nutter fay Langlees?'

A monosyllabic reply from Brian.

'Well, they're keepin an eye oot fir yese an aw. Cottsy's crew *and* the Lang Boys? Yese better stey aff they roads fir a while, man. They aw recognise that car ay yours. An mair important, they ken whaur ye work.'

'Fucksake!' Brian explodes, prodding Gordo's chest and producing a brief splutter of smoke. 'Gonnay tell us some good news?'

'If ye like,' Gordo shrugs. 'Celtic are winning 2–0.'

I head (am directed? divinely?) to the garden to write a birthday poem for Tyra, trying to ignore the Slipknot slam-dancers who've colonised the kitchen, one of them barging into me and dislodging a fantastic metaphor which I've just composed. On a low wall which borders the calm of the lawn, I listen to the gurgle of the fish pool over the screech of guitars, raising my face to the sky, burbling with poetry. The sky is an irresistible velvet blue, rippled with stars and an indolent moon. I try to picture Tyra's face – just at her moment of ecstasy when she opened my present – then write on the back of a napkin

you are the moon
celluloid-thin, white,
touched by the silhouette of
E.T.'s bike.

and get up to look for her, eager to impart these lines, my head swimming with whisky, romance and the complete albums of Pink Floyd,
but over the pogoing heads of the Slipknot parade, between the prefects
who smooch in drunken poses on the settee, beyond the champagne
pyramid which someone is attempting to build, I can't

see

her

but take the chance to steal carelessly left drinks (the tastes blending
in a gloop on my tongue) and no-one knows where she is, not even,
strangely, after I regale them with my joke about the Pope on a tour of
Ibrox, which suddenly seems important – vital – to my quest. The
party evolves into a vortex, me anchored to the centre by the logic of
my Pope joke as pretty, educated, drunken faces rotate around me then
away before the punchline and someone

!

I'm sprinting to the bathroom, hitting the porcelain and suddenly
making a weird sound like this, 'Blooooouuuurgh.'

'Bohemian Rhapsody will not be played on this piano, thank you
very much.'

'Blaaaaarrruuuugh. Uh. Help. Eough.'

'Me, Jonesy, Gordo and this bird wi huge–'

'Aah. Aaah. Heeelp! Boooooaaagh. (ohh)'

'invited that Alvin and those *awful* schemies . . .'

'(fugg) Gooooaaaagh. Goooaaaggh. (ohfug)'

'. . . you are my Falkirk, my only . . .'

170

then wipe my hand across my face, feel the slavers fall away in drips, and piss, making a Z in the foam with my urine. In the living room, people are gyrating hip against hip, kissing, and a copy of Empire magazine lies stuck to the coffee table in a glaze of dried beer, so I pounce on it, ignoring the lovers crushed against me on the couch, their sex-crazed elbows digging into my ribs. Winona Ryder is on the cover, her face clear and white like the moon above the trees on a fishing night with the Lads last summer, Dolby, pencil-thin in the dark, whispering so the fish wouldn't be startled, 'Isn't it beautiful?'

Winona has hazel-coloured eyes, with a sphere of reflected light glistening in the centre. Inside the sphere the photographer is visible, his sinister outline like a fleck of evil. There is a serial-killer in the chamber of Winona Ryder's eye. Empire are advertising a 2-for-1 DVD offer and I lose myself in the glossy sheen of the pages, the glinting promise of each crisp edge, and soon I notice that the sky outside the room is the colour of slate, remember there's one street in Bainsford that has three – count them – three chip shops and

All I want is to find a ruby in the trash.

Something that is true and good and right.

Every night we head out in Belinda like road warriors, avenging angels, and I search for it with Terminator-like determination, my eyes lingering on the actresses in the video shop windows and the drunks who appear randomly and who we ignore, laughing, nosing through a relentless shoal of streetlights but

I still haven't found what I'm looking for.

Dolby and Frannie are talking about some girl that Brian used to go out with. 'Mind ye telt her ye'd seen Noel Gallagher's willy in a toilet in Glasgow and when she asked whit it looked like ye said–'

'It's goat a big bushy eyebrow and sings Wonderwall!'

They both crack up and Brian tries to shush them, sorting out yet another pub crisis on his phone (which I hope isn't Cottsy wrecking the joint) and I obsess on that dark slice in the pure crystal of Winona Ryder's eye, then the fishing night, where beside a fitfully flickering campfire we talked about Jack Nicholson movies and listened to the midnight hymn of the water and Dolby, distantly, without emotion, mentioned that he would rather die than go back into Whirlpools Direct on Monday.

'Awright, Alvin?' Frannie frowns, lifting the drink from my hand. 'Bit green around the gills there, bud.'

> I wish they all could be California
> (I wish they all could be California)
> I wish they all could be California girls

best of the Sixties playing and what looks like a porno but is actually the new Britney Spears video flickering on MTV and an entire section of the living room turned into a hash-head zone which the Lads have quit in protest at the giggling, virginal dope-ridden faces of the prefects, and framed Scottish landscapes/glens/Tyra's modelling shots (so soft-focus as to be hallucinatory), and row upon row of Absolut Vodka/Omega cider/White & Mackay/Bacardi Breezers (such pretty colours) compete in my reeling vision and someone suggests heading out to Rosie's to which I snarl, 'No, I don't fuckin know what Derek does in London, okay? Where's Tyra?' and Frannie shakes Brian's hand, congratulating him on Celtic's 3–2 defeat by Aberdeen and I hear

telepathic messages?

saying?

Tyra's voice floats from the top of the stairs, so I stumble towards it, my poem about her and the moon memorised. Someone – Frannie? Mum? Stephen King? – tells me they saw her slip away upstairs, and I creep towards a door ajar and behind it Travis are singing Last Laugh of the Laughter and a voice, two voices are moaning, so I repeat the poem quietly in my head, pick up a photo of Tyra with her three sisters, who are all as gorgeous as she is, posing like the Virgin Suicides, kiss Tyra on the forehead, open the door and

My eyes acclimatise to the dark. Someone is kneeling on the floor. Tyra is on her knees before Connor Livingstone. He has a sordid grin on his face and his jeans at his ankles.

Tyra turns. Her eyes are steely as bullets.

'Alvin, get the fuck out.'

I stand frozen. I can only hear the door swinging on its hinges. I am trying not to look at Connor's dick dripping with saliva, or Tyra's vicious face. 'Well, fuck off then,' she spits. 'Shut the *door*.'

Dumbly, I retreat. Connor Livingstone's dirty laughter echoes. The door closes, the room becoming a thin strip of dark. Downstairs the party has become the universe at the dawn of time. Things fly, smash, die. Curtains balloon and fall. A window has been broken in the kitchen and people stand around like dead weights. The night roars in, black and relentless, while the room swirls in the breeze.

Brian comes over and fits a Becks into my hand. 'Aye,' I mutter to whatever he's saying, 'aye,' and the next time I look the Becks is drained although I can't remember having drunk it.

The smashed window has ended the party. People are fraught with concern, stomping to and fro, blaming each other, you drank this, you threw that. Someone has turned MTV over and a programme that nobody is watching is imploring us to look after our bodies, because

by the age of seventy we have lost a third of our muscle strength

the hairs in the cochlea die, leading to hearing loss

cartilage rubbing causes sharp pains at the joints

and computer graphics detail the cross-section of a knee grinding, twisting, gristling like torture.

Tyra and Connor. Oh god.

I stagger outside, my stomach so light it feels as though it has floated away. Dolby follows, worried I'm going to be sick again.

'Alvin,' he asks. 'Ye awright?'

My world pierced. The life escaping it in a thin, whining hiss. I feel functionless, fucked. I collapse on a sun-lounger by the fish pool, my hand dappling its cold shallows, a smooth silver body brushing against my fingers, then away. The sky is huge and timeless and black. The point is there is no point, etc. Oh god.

'It disnay really exist, does it?' I murmur to Dolby.

'Whit?'

'Youth.'

He doesn't answer. We stare at the shimmering skin of the water. Things dance, then disappear like phantoms.

'It's a con,' I say. 'A clear surface. It breaks when you touch it.'

There's a pause. Dolby blinks at me.

'It doesn't mean anything,' I say.

The cold wind on our faces. I lean back, realising how devoid that sky is of any secrets, how poor Oasis are now, all those Britpop bands, how fucking drunk I am, and after all that, all I can remember is Dolby stretching my jacket across me, the police arriving, maybe several times, and an anonymous kiss on my cheek, a brief waft of a girl's perfume, my name whispered once, only once, and then

Our living room.

Me, Derek, Mum and Dad watching Family Fortunes in the dark.

The light sharpening the corners of the ceiling. The TV makes everyone's face a flickering, aquamarine mask. I'm on my belly, jabbing at crinkle cut crisps, one sock dangling halfway off my foot.

Name something, says Les Dennis, you would use in the garden.

Derek passes me the George and Lynne cartoon from the Sun and we snigger sneakily at Lynne's melon-like breasts as she cooks breakfast, as ever, in the nude. Bet when she's in the shower, Derek's giggling, she wears a woolly jumper and a bodywarmer. Simmering resentment from the couch behind us. Mum and Dad's blank faces crackle with light.

Name something you can cut with.

A contestant buzzes, hesitantly. Paper?

Me and Derek trade punches to the arm.

Enough, Dad mutters.

He told us earlier tonight that he has been paid off from the oil refinery down Grangemouth. Being paid off always sounds exciting in gangster films, like here's some pay-off money for you to keep ya mouth shut, but Derek told me that it isn't good at all. There was a lot of screaming and banging from the kitchen after Dad told Mum (though Derek took me through to watch cartoons while this was going on). Mum always does the high-pitched stuff. Dad grunts, sighs, and asks whit exactly is it that ye want me tay dae? Sometimes we can hear her sobbing in the middle of the night, along with Dad trying to calm her down.

Derek turns to Page Three and shows me Lena, 19, from London's 'boob-ti-ful assets'.

Her jeans are faded at the knees, I point out.

Derek tuts and drags the paper away. That's the fashion, he says.

The TV fills the limp, blue darkness with chattering light, rising and falling across the cliff-face of my parents. Their eyes are lost to the loveless flow, the cue-track of laughter, the adverts flinging themselves into the hurtling path of programmes, or the other way around.

D'ye think Pepe jeans are better than Naf-Naf? Derek asks.

Pepe le Peu! I say.

Enough, Dad murmurs, automatically.

Derek glowers at him through the dimness.

Name a country, says Les Dennis, That you would

stairs rising to a glue-patch of darkness, and I can hear skulking, moaning sounds coming from it. Mum awake and roaming. Derek has a new haircut. He is being insistent about something.

Listen Alvin, I'm fed up. I'm gon oot. I'm sick ay tellin ma pals that I'm no well, just cause ay—

He glances upstairs; there is a crash and some muffled swearing.

Sick ay it full stop. Ma pals are aw oot havin a laugh, gettin birds. Whit am I daein? Babysittin ma Mam.

I gaze down at the carpet. A bleach stain.

Whit time does Dad get back in? I mumble.

Late. He's oan the back-shift.

The darkness at the top of the stairs is silent now.

If she tries tay get oot, lock all the doors and windays. Ye ken the drill. Then just put on a video or somethin. She'll soon faw back asleep. Ye've goat Dad's number if there's an emergency. He cocks his head. 'Okay, pal?'

I nod.

C'mon Alvin. Ye're 11 now. Auld enough tay help look after her. Canny sit wi yer face shoved intay a Spider-Man comic aw yer life.

I nod again.

He ruffles my hair. The hallway feels like a vacuum. The ear of the china dog on the phone table is chipped. So are most of the ornaments in this house.

One night oot we ma pals. That's aw I'm askin.

Derek opens the door and goes out into a hubbub of 15 year olds, hands thrust into his jacket, their fags making smoke graffiti in the air. I watch them cross the grass and wander off, whooping. The throat of the stairwell is cold and narrow. Shaking, I climb the stairs.

She lies in bed like pale driftwood. Her skin is 34 years old, but shineless, worn. Her hand clings to the edge of the duvet. Her eyes are her only motion, the only tiny, wet sounds. A breeze makes a belly in the curtain.

Son?

I ignore her, tidying. Everything in its right place. More chipped ornaments. A china donkey. A ballerina on tippy-toes.

Son. I need ye.

Dust wafts through the light in the room. There is a smell of talcum powder and stale nicotine. I raise the duvet so that it covers her bony shoulders. Outside, cars speed past on the main road, the sound a pulsing rush. Here, there is stillness. Son, I need ye to do somethin for me.

Whit is it, Mum?

Her lips make a small clicking sound as she moistens them. Her pills lie spilled on the carpet.

Yer fuckin Dad–

She coughs. The window is open too wide. I close it.

Yer fuckin Dad willnay let me hae a drink. No even wan, the bastard.

Mum, ye ken why that is.

She raises a hand, slim as a flower stem, and points to the ceiling.

But I've goat a wee bottle ay vodka in the loft. I just use it for . . . for a treat. Will ye get it fir me, son? Wid ye dae that fir yer mammy?

I walk to the edge of the bed. Run my finger along the stitching of the duvet. She looks up at me, hopeful. Her tired lips are fighting with a smile.

177

You were eywis ma favourite, wee Alvy. Ye mind me takin ye oot in yer tartan shawl tay watch the stars? Ye mind the songs I used tay sing tay ye . . . ?

Her eyes start to close. The spilled pills.

I pull back the duvet and get into bed beside her.

. . . yer tartan shawl . . .

I kiss her head. Her hair is papery on my lips. Her face closes.

. . . just a wee treat . . . dinnay hate me son . . . dinnay . . .

Outside the cars hurtle past. The sound of air whooshes and falls. Her mumbling finally ceases. I lie down next to her and sink into the pillow and

wake in Tyra's garden?

An orchestra of birds is practising somewhere, so I know it's either early morning or dusk.

Fuck, man.

Weak and shaky. My neck's complaining loudly. I lift and sniff a rose which has been soaked in beer. The windows of Tyra's house hang tall and desolate and her garden is a mess: broken window, cans floating in the pond. I imagine groans shuffling out from sleeping bags all over the house. Maybe I'm the first one awake. Maybe everyone's died in the night and I'm the last man on Earth. The idea appeals to me.

I watch a butterfly for a few minutes, listen to the birds, feel the day warm up, the useless beauty of things. I think about nothing in particular, just look about, peaceful, swallowing, until eventually I stand up and head for home. Always home. There is no other place to go but home.

I bet if I could look at the street plans of Falkirk town centre, I'd see that it's shaped like a loop. I suspect that's why it's called the boyracer circuit: they just go round and round, like little Scalectrix cars. Round and round. Which reminds me, shit, today me and the Lads had agreed we would be

178

singing in unity – Brian's voice basso-rumbling, Frannie's high, squeaky, Belinda a clanking, disharmonious backing-track, while we eat, drink, be merry, tearing down the motorway and stopping for a ripe pish every 15 minutes. A competition soon starts over who can think up the most ridiculous insult – 'Unlicensed Bug Lover', 'Dirty Big Purse Snatcher', 'Promiscuous Potato Peeler', but I win with 'Chrome Plated Wife Swapper' (my reward, Frannie's unfinished packet of peanuts) – as we drive and drive and unfurl our collective petroleum self and Dolby interrogates Brian about the chick he pulled at the party – a distant cousin of Tyra's called Morvern who had dragonflies painted on her shoes and a spiderweb on her skirt – and Brian is describing every part of her anatomy except the ones we want to hear about. I ask Frannie if he pulled.

'Only ma pole,' he grumbles, then relates to us his horror at Dolby introducing himself to someone as Uriel.

'Well, it's ma name,' Dolby complains, adjusting the plastic Han Solo on the dash, which is in difficulty, hanging by one foot and a blob of Blu-tac.

'No,' Frannie says, 'it's no. Yer name is Martin Dolby. Ye were born Martin Dolby. You will always be Martin Dolby.'

Dolby's face closes and he shakes his head.

'Thing is,' I pipe up, 'there's probably some boyracer in Brazil with the name Uriel who's desperate tay change it tay Martin Dolby.'

The three of them laugh, hearty, genuine, and a warm glow suffuses my chest until Brian growls, 'We're no fuckin boyracers,' and everyone goes harumph.

accelerating across the surface of the land leaving a wake of crisp packets/Springsteen lyrics/tyre tracks to mark our passing while the Ibrox Twins discuss which Rangers Wives they (don't) want to shag – 'Seen his girlfriend? *She* could play for Rangers.'

179

Monday at school is abysmal. In my practice English essay I completely mix up George Orwell, Orson Welles and H.G. Wells (how easy is that?). I have to endure a common room on the boil with the news that Connor and Tyra are, officially, an item. On the desk at the back of my Modern Studies class I write

Is there anybody out there?

before initialling and dating it. Later in the day I get summoned back to Mrs Costa's room and handed a scrubbing brush.

When I get home I find Derek sititng in the garden, a joint in one hand and his pinkie extended. His ginger beard and chest fuzz have grown out of control recently. 'Whaur's Dad?' I ask, waving the smoke from my face. Derek just shrugs, rustling through the Daily Record

'Upstairs,' he says eventually.

'Have ye had a fight?'

He doesn't answer.

Our garden was slabbed with concrete in 1989. This was Dad's idea, meant he didn't have to cut the grass and pull the weeds every summer. Now the paving is cracked and cock-eyed, lying at slants as if an earthquake's hit. Weeds creep through the gaps like bits of broccoli between teeth.

I pull up a seat next to Derek, noticing Dad's slippers parked at the side.

'Does yer boss no want ye back at work soon?' I ask, pretending not to be concerned at all. 'Ye've been back here three weeks.'

'Long holiday,' he says tonelessly.

'Whit about yer rent?' I continue. My family aren't the greatest communicators, but I can guess their moods from only half-glances, since their faces pretty much, unfortunately, match mine.

'Taken care of,' he mumbles, clawing at his beard the way Dad does, the fingers hooked and inquisitive and quietly scratching out: Get. Tay. Fuck.

I snap, snatching his paper. 'Gonnay talk tay me, fir chrissakes?'

Derek calmly removes his shades. His eyes are blazing. He leans over to me. 'Our Dad,' he whispers, 'is going insane.'

Upstairs, Dad is face-down on the bed, spread like a starfish, surrounded by photographs. Dozens of them.

'Dad?' I say, and he makes a surprised noise, turning around. His eyes are mild, red and ringed. He wipes at them manfully.

'Sorry son,' he whispers. An effort to smile. 'Just me an yer brother havin words, that's aw. He sometimes disnay ken when tay leave somethin be.'

I nod, looking down at him.

Dad sighs and picks up the photos, an out-of-tune orchestra of faces.

'God, how did things get so fucked up?' And he gives a short laugh, scratching at his beard just like Derek.

'Dad?'

He looks up.

'Dad, dinnay go the same way as Mum. If ye do, I will hate ye. I will hate ye completely. And there'll be nay way back fay it.'

He holds my gaze, and it grows so icy and still that I feel the slightest motion from either of us will smash it to bits. He opens his mouth to reply, but I say, 'Do you understand?' and then leave

to disappear in Belinda with the Lads, Frannie keen to head out to Cally Park, 'tay check if the flowers are in bloom – nyuk nyuk!' his sex drive emerging like a bee from the winter, so we stop at Haddows for

181

Bacardi Breezers (where Dolby is asked for ID, haha) then cruise into the slow swarm of Callendar Park, relaxing our patter.

We get out and start walking. The Bacardi Breezers make ringing clinks as the sun flits across our faces. We climb the fence to the playground and lark about on the swings, pushing each other down the chutes. I feel like a kid. It's great.

A quartet of girls strolls past.

'Hey,' Frannie whispers, 'mind they girls I gave ma number tay?'

Wendy has clocked me, is smiling wickedly.

'Well, we made a wee arrangement . . .'

I wander over, trying to subdue a grin.

'Are you Ally Ferguson?' she gasps. 'Can I have your autograph?'

'Very funny,' I retort. 'Whaur did they dredge you up fay?'

She tuts, adopting Wounded Look #6. 'Never forget I've seen your willy, pal.'

They burgle our Bacardi Breezers, we colonise their ghetto blaster. It's all dance music, worse luck, save for one tape which is Brown Eyed Girl recorded twelve times (what is it with girls and that song?) and there's an easy feel to proceedings, vaguely expectant. The Lads are acting like Roman emperors being fed grapes by concubines, the girls preen like flowers contested by bumblebees. Each side thinks the other is doing all the running. Pointless chat fizzes like lemonade. Chilled-as-fuck lemonade.

'Whit song will be the first dance at yer wedding?' one of the girls asks, running her hand along the grass.

'In the Army Now by Status Quo,' Brian replies.

'Jump by Van Halen,' says Dolby.

The girls tut and ask them to think of their wives. Frannie does so. 'Wow, she's fuckin gorgeous.'

I just laze, getting drunk, watching a kid watching a beetle, thinking and thinking about the Stirling University prospectus which plopped on my doormat this morning.

'We Don't Need Another Hero by Tina Turner?'

'Hello, Hello, We are the Billy Boys?'

'The theme tune fay Only Fools an Horses?'

When I turn for a Breezer, Wendy is looking at me, her gaze heavy and true. Something clicks, a sort of tripwire deep in a primal place. Something shared and silent.

'Comin for a walk?' she says quickly.

We hold hands. Because of the trembling, I find I'm talking about Madonna albums louder than I should be. The ghetto blaster drones at Wendy's side.

'Let me get this straight,' she says. 'Ye've never listened tay Ray of Light?'

'Is it better than Like A Prayer?'

'Miles!'

'I dunno,' I shrug, 'Like A Prayer's quite a standard.'

'*Quite a standard*,' she repeats, posh.

'Less ay your cheek.'

She leads me into a shady bower, dappled with leaves and a quiet cool. I wave away a wasp. We sit, and she plays Ray of Light, lecturing me on its merits like a teacher, then she turns, puts her hand in my hair, and the weight of our eye contact drags us further down. 'Put your body close to my mind,' she murmurs. Or something. Her words seem to melt in the heat as she leans, kisses the space under my chin, and soon we are uncurling. Breathing. Our bodies, slightly slick, slide against each other. Birds are jabbering tiny sounds in the air and the sunlight is real and Wendy lies on top of me, her chin in her hand.

'Enjoy that?'

I nod thoughtfully. 'Yeah, it was good. Had a nice beat to it. I reckon it is better than Like A Prayer.'

She pauses.

'The sex, you idiot, not the album.'

'Oh,' I say. 'Um–'

She slaps me on the head, then does up her bra with an expertise which had totally eluded me ten minutes ago. She turns. Her back stretches, pocked here and there with tiny sticks, and I home in on the fine, red hairs which wisp at the base of her neck, the faint rouge tint in her skin, the tiny, bright mouths of sunlight which open in the green canopy above us. The scent of chlorophyll and sex. The distant, lazy drum of insect wings. The world seems to glisten with life, colour, choices. I think I'm in love.

Probably just hungry.

'Ken, Alvin,' Wendy muses, studying my face, 'you're actually no that bad lookin.'

'No that bad?' I repeat, aghast. 'Fuck's that supposed tay mean?'

'Well,' she says. 'Another couple ay years, fill oot a bit, decent hair-cut. You could be quite a catch.'

My skin is starting to redden. I look away, doing up buttons. 'Aye . . . well . . .'

I reach for a Coke and take a heavy, nonchalant slurp. Wendy stares at me, horrified.

'There was a wasp on the lip ay that can.'

Movement inside my mouth. A dull buzz. I freeze.

'Spit!' she urges.

184

A small body grazing the inside of my cheek. 'Spit!' she yells. 'Now!' and I spray the Coke from my mouth, panicked. The wasp lies fighting in a dark brown puddle, its stinger punching the air like a sewing needle. I stamp it to mush, howling and covering my mouth.

'Ye ken whit wid have happened if ye'd swall–'

'I ken,' I interrupt, raising my hand, 'I ken.'

Walking back to camp, we're laughing, but my nerves feel like they've been laced with acid. One wee sting and I would have been a goner.

Wendy asks if that was my first time.

'Naw,' I say. 'Well, aye. There was this false alarm before.'

'Ye mean like a pregnancy scare?'

'Naw. I thought I'd lost my virginity.'

'Aw,' she says: then, 'that's an alarm?'

We talk, daftly enough, about the Broons. I confess to her my secret fantasy for Maggie, she confesses hers for Joe.

'That waist!' I gasp.

'Those muscles!' Wendy marvels.

She asks what my favourite film is and I say Jaws, and she says – get this, nearly ruining the whole moment –

'Which one?'

'Whit d'ye mean, which one? There is only one.'

'No there's no. There's four Jaws movies.'

'Naw,' I stress. 'There is only one Jaws movie.'

She punches my arm – I let her, though she's clearly no Jaws purist – and it's fun and the world has a new and sudden brightness, but that wasp. Its tiny sting sliding into the walls of my throat. My throat swelling, choking. The closeness of death. The sharks, the giant sharks.

Wendy is pondering the shadows we cast, long and scrawled, in front of us, and then she is smiling at me.

185

'You've got a look,' she says. She has gorgeous eyelashes.

'A look? Like, whit sortay look?'

'Ye look–' she cocks her head, 'hungry.'

'I am hungry. I huvnay eaten since breakfast.'

'That's no whit I mean. Ye look like ye *want* somethin.'

'Have I no just had it?'

'No that. Naw, somethin bigger than that.'

'Hm. So, whit exactly dae I want?'

Wendy winks.

'Whit's comin tay ye.' Her hand snakes round my waist and stays there. 'Ye want whit's comin tay ye.'

and we split. Det

ach. Our fingers lingering. She fades across the green like a sunbeam as I bob back to the car with a helium grin. The grass makes a rustling noise and I am impressed, just convinced of nature's talent as a performing artist, the potential for life to outdo itself just when you'd given up on it.

and that night, drunkenly happy, that state in which things bubble and pop with life and you wonder how anything could ever be bad again, Derek and me go wandering round Hallglen. Terrain sharp with memories. Its labyrinthine streets. Its ancient satellite dishes, like barnacles on a sunken ship. The lock-ups we used to smash footballs against and the places where we made dens or played hide-and-seek and the doors we chapped and ran away from, shouting, booting garbage down the street.

I'm glad he's home.

But I still don't know why he's home.

The wind creeps between the houses. The boarded-up shell of one gutted by fire. I tell him about Wendy (but not her touch, not her scent, not her voice), and he nods, impressed but doesn't tell me about a single girl he met in London. We wander into a swing park where we both used to play, now desolate.

'Imagine you wiping your dick on your t-shirt,' he tuts.

'Whit else could I use?'

'The last of the great romantics,' Derek snorts and nudges an empty vodka bottle with his boot. Then he picks it up, weighs it, and hurls it against a nearby wall.

The smash rings round the scheme.

'I found her here once,' Derek gestures to the climbing frames, which rear against the dark like dinosaur skeletons. 'She was lying unconscious. Weans had put dog shit on her chest.'

I sit in one of the swings, rocking gently. The chain makes a comforting, nautical creak.

'Derek, why did ye come hame?'

He glances at me, then away, his eyes white marbles in the dark. He starts rolling a piece of the vodka bottle with his boot. 'She is alive, Alvin.'

He climbs onto the wee wall, gazes round at the unblinking lights of a place he once lived in, but never called home. Derek is the only one of us who followed his dream to see where it would lead. And where it led was straight back here. I swing despondently, my feet making random pushes against the rubber slab. The glass shards of the vodka bottle lie waiting for a kid's foot, so I sweep them to the wall. Then I climb up, stand next to Derek, listen to the howl of dogs' separated souls, while in the swing park phantom children laugh.

'She's out there somewhere. I can feel her.'

My older brother – who always took care of me, who always knew exactly what he was doing, why he was doing it, or so it seemed to me – grown up into an unwound ball of string, and I can't help but think:

Weren't we promised something?

Sitting in our primary schools (little chairs, little tables), listening open-mouthed to the magic sounds made by the teacher, we could see something, just past her shoulder, out there beyond the playground: a rough-draft of the world, an artist's impression. But it looked wonderful. Something true. Something good. Something to run towards.

'Ever get the feeling you've been cheated?' Derek murmurs, hopping down from the wall, wrapping his arms around himself as

we soar in and out of the badlands and Brian makes slurping noises with his Irn-Bru while music from gleaming vehicles veers close then away and Frannie, hollering, obscene with laugher, ignores the crap rap music on Belinda's stereo (Asian Pub Foundation?) to pose the question, 'So, if Batman wis a pop star, who wid he be?'

which is a tricky one, since you have to think about Batman's iceberg-cool image and it's pointless comparing him to, say, Robert Plant, the two just don't go together, silly even to consider it, and we pass a sign saying DON'T FALL ASLEEP AT THE WHEEL and I can't believe how many beautiful women Frannie has ignored tonight – forty-something trolley dollies with their Mrs Robinson maturity on show, carrying shopping bags, parked at traffic lights – he's totally possessed with the Batman question, and he should be, it's an important one, crucial, and I can't stop thinking that it's been seven years since the last Floyd album/tour (do they do weddings and ceilidhs for Richard Branson and Bill Gates now?) and Dolby is fighting with Brian to try and get some of the Irn-Bru but Brian's pulling it away, teasing him, bringing it closer, pulling it away, cackling, and the sky is mottled red-pink, the clouds ridged and quilted like herring-bone, and the Scotland game hisses on the radio (they're drawing 1–1!) and England were beaten 1–0 by Germany and this holds deep, almost mystical significance for everyone (Dolby gives the loudest cheer and he doesn't even like football) and I answer the Batman question:

'Surely he's cool enough tay be Bono?'

'Bono yer arse,' says Brian.

'Naw,' Dolby says, shaking his head seriously. 'Spider-Man's Bono. He's got the patter and the charisma. Batman's dark and tortured. Batman's Thom Yorke.'

'Aah,' everyone sighs in agreement, this flash of insight illuminating the whole car.

'But whit about Superman?' Frannie asks, concerned, plunging us into despair again, and mini-neds throw chips as we pass the Golden Bird and one of them hits Belinda's rear window, sliding greasily down its surface and we rack our brains, the four of us, to solve this problem somehow, and there are two girls in the car next to us, pointing and smiling (I'm guessing one of them is called Janice, since she has that Strathclyde look, and let's be honest, Janice is a Strathclyde name) but no lassies for us, not now, the Superman issue must be resolved and quickly, it's ruining the night. 'Elvis Presley!' shouts Brian, at the same time as Frannie shouts, 'Cliff Richard!' then they look at each other, incredulous, and Brian says, 'Cliff fuckin Richard?' at the same time as Frannie says 'Elvis fuckin Presley?'and as they argue we screech towards Grangemouth, the refinery lights like an enormous art installation around us, pollution spewing from a crystal carapace, God's own mad-scientist experiment, which we zip through as a chemical compound, as Brian goes, 'Naw. Superman is yer All American Hero. He is America. He's the King. He's tay super-heroes whit Elvis wis tay rock n roll.'

'Whit?' Frannie whines. 'Aw Brian, yer insane. Superman's yer typical straight-laced, squeaky clean, dae yer job wi the minimum ay fuss for fifty years, borin the tits aff everybody in the process sortay superhero. He's no cool, dark an edgy like Batman. He's no funny an smart like Spider-Man. He is a personality-free zone. If he didnay hae his job at the Daily Planet,

189

mark ma words, he wid be releasin Christmas records every year,' and the argument continues like this, even though Dolby tries to arrange another fishing trip to the Ness, even though Frannie's phone chirrups Shaggy's It Wasn't Me six times and even though I've got my baseball cap on back-to-front like a rapper and I'm making unconvincing Eminem noises and everyone laughs, with affection, and I tell Dolby I've reached the bit in Lord of the Rings again where Frodo meets Shelob the spider and we discuss this, excited, like kids swapping stickers.

'How dae you think they'll dae that scene in the film?' he asks, wiping his mouth, as if preventing himself from salivating, and Bruce Springsteen reminds us that it ain't no sin to be glad you're alive, and we honour him, raising our Irn-Bru in a toast, making plans to drive right across America when Brian emigrates, like Thelma and Louise, swapping these drizzly streets and Daily Record vendors and all of Scotland's crapness for wide-open desert landscapes, Belinda possessed by the spirits of Red Indians, as we drink Wild Turkey and get sunburnt and slam our glamorous Falkirk patter at yank chicks bored with Boston guys and we live on the road, forever the people, the ones who had a notion, a notion deep inside, and the Scotland game finishes 1–1 (a difficult away game to Croatia) and drunk on our own youth, speed, LedZepness, we roll down the windows and start singing

> Bonny Scotland, Bonny Scotland,
> We'll support you ever more,
> We'll support you ever mooooooore

as one single male beast of a chorus, as Dolby suggests that, 'we should go abroad, support the Tartan Army,' his face bright with patriotism, which is weird, since the only places I've ever seen him patriotic about are Narnia and Middle-Earth.

'Fuck that,' Brian spews, 'Rangers fans dinnay support Scotland abroad. Ye daft? We need oor money for the Champions League, man,' making me and Dolby shake heads, unimpressed by the suddenly Hun atmosphere, then Dolby's phone rings Start Me Up by the Rolling Stones, but he switches it off, whooping and slapping, why? for nothing really, no reason, just cos he can, just cos he can do things like wrench Belinda's wheel and practise handbrake skids in a deserted area of Bainsford, grannies peering worriedly from behind net curtains at the screeching sound, the tyre tracks imprinted in the road, our calling card, since we're off again, too fast for them, too fucking fast for anybody, and then it's a debate about our fantasy night out, our ideal drinking partners, and names like Gary Oldman, Lemmy, Keith Richards, Judd Nelson's character in The Breakfast Club and Homer Simpson are bandied about and Frannie narrates like David Attenborough, 'as Lemmy and Homer sink their twelfth pints, Brian Mann and Dolby sink to the floor and Alvin talks shite to a bored Keith Richards,' and Brian's mobile beeps the Top Gun theme and Dolby says, 'So who would be Wonder Woman?' and we all go, 'Madonna!' as another Irn-Bru is burst open and

The headlights become jewels in the flow of night. Our car is linked to them. We drape onwards, jewel after jewel, life after life, glittering in the distance. The road ahead is all that we know. The thrum of cat's eyes on tyres. The beckoning threat of darkness. We keep good company against it, building a close, comforting fire with our laughter.

on Friday night, after I slouch home from school, there is a doctor in the kitchen speaking to Dad and Derek. I fumble about, boiling the kettle, while she chats politely, hands folded across her lap. After she leaves I collar Derek upstairs, turning Top of the Pops up full so Dad won't hear.

191

'He's having a nervous breakdown,' Derek tells me, over the wail of Placebo's Slave to the Wage. 'He isn't mentally fit for work, but can apply for disability allowance.'

I sigh and place my forehead in my hand.

'And one of us can apply for a Carer's Allowance to stay home and watch him.'

I look at Derek. He looks back.

'Hey, it's no gonnay be me,' I say. 'Whit if I wantay go tay university?'

'I thought that was for poofs.'

'But whit if I decide I want tay go!'

'Well, you can't. Listen. I took my turn years ago.'

'Aye awright,' I say. 'You fuckin left. Who d'ye think's got him this far?'

'And a fine job you've made of it! He's had a nervous breakdown since I've been away. Oh, you are one selfish wee shite, Alvin.'

'. . .'

'Eh? Come on, Alvin, whit d'ye say?'

'. . .'

'Alvin?'

Frannie, in the backseat next to me, shakes my shoulder.

'Alvin, yer a million miles away, man.'

'Sorry. Just tired.'

'Aye, well. Whit d'ye say? Ye want tay go pickin oranges in California?'

'Oot Carmen Electra's bra,' says Brian filthily.

I look round the car. The three of them are staring, expectant. I scratch my nose, then eventually think I say something like, 'every night I dream I'm in Aliens. Fightin monsters wi, um, big teeth,' but they've started practising handbrake skids again and none of them hear me.

Dolby halts Belinda on the forecourt. Her brakes whine. We stumble out, almost bewildered, into Sunday morning, blinking like cats after our overnight fishing trip at Loch Ness. Last thing I remember before falling asleep was a particularly gruelling debate about which hairstyle Brian should adopt for the States when/if he goes. Frannie favours a classic mullet. I personally think he would look very dashing with Tom Cruise's greasy do in Magnolia. Dolby reckons he should go baldy, right down to the wood and be done with it.

'Why've we stopped?' Brian yawns. 'Whit's the story?'

'Morning glory.'

'Petrol,' Dolby grunts, wheel-fatigued. 'Belinda could dae wi a drink.'

'So the fuck could I.'

I stretch and look through the grey morning across the street, at toilet seats in the window of a bath showroom, their mouths gulping the cold air.

'Whit's yer favourite?' Frannie asks.

'That pink wan.'

'Whit? Naw. See that lilac wan. Lavender seat.'

'Frannie, yer insane,' I cry. 'A lavender seat?'

He shrugs, slaps a tempo on the car roof. 'Ach, it's aw shite anyway.'

On Friday, in class, I wrote a note to Tyra, telling her that I hope she is very happy with Connor. It took me fifteen minutes to write, probably missing valuable exam info. I wrote and wrote, my heart channelled through the pen onto the torn page of my homework diary, while she rested her flawless chin in her hand and gazed across the class at Connor, lovelorn. Then I folded the paper, wrote her name on it, and passed it across to her.

'It's aw shite!' Frannie hoots. 'Ye get it?'

She glanced up at me, took the note in her slim fingers and unfolded it.

'Alvin, ye get it? It's aw shite.'

As she read, her eyes gave little away. I watched them, sheathed in smooth lids, flicker along the lines. She seemed to hesitate over certain passages, pausing to re-read them, her brow furrowing gently. When she finished, she picked up her pen, scribbled, and slid the note back across the desk to me. It said

stay away from me, you fucking weirdo

We slam back into the car, Belinda refreshed and the rest of us waking. Fingers of light creep across the morning's corpse, Brian guzzling at the bottle of whisky and Irn-Bru left over from the fishing. His brain revolves with hangover.

'Guuuuh,' he manages. 'Fuckin Clapton solo in ma heid, man.'

'Nay hangovers like that in California,' I say.

'Tell me about it,' he says, brightening, 'the hangovers ower there are like orgasms!'

The next week, Brian is picking the empty glasses from in front of his arse-nosed customers. Not that the booze-hounds notice, jammed into their Sun, Record, racing papers or even (one of Brian's regulars, Terry, fancies himself as a bit of an intellectual, wears polo necks and everything) A History of Falkirk. Me, Frannie and Dolby are hunched over the bar like the Ochil Hills in miniature, Frannie watching Sportscene on the telly, Dolby talking to Brian about the Simpsons, while I read an interview with Bono in Q magazine (he looks very cool for 40). Orange streetlights simmer outside, Falkirk on fire. The pub is quietly beery. Decent jokes. Scrooge still trying to cadge a pound for Neil Diamond. Frannie peers at my copy of Q during the lull of a Motherwell feature.

194

'Imagine Bono was perched on the end ay the bar,' he beams. 'Whit would ye ask him?'

'I'd ask him whit the fuck he was daein in Fawkurt.'

'Naw,' Frannie shakes his head, Coisty-eyes glinting, 'cos he'd be oor guest. We'd have bumped intay him backstage an invited him on a pub crawl roon Fawkurt—'

'Aye right,' I say. 'Bono in Behind the Wall? Bono in the Newmarket? Bono in the Welly?'

'Hiy,' Frannie protests. 'Bono widnay be seen deid in the Welly.'

The interview with Celtic's new Latvian striker ends and Frannie resumes watching Sportscene as Terry clears his throat, officiously, wetting his finger and leafing through A History of Falkirk, just aching for one of us to say, 'Interesting book, Tel?'

'It is that, Brian,' Terry nods ponderously. 'Oor fair auld toon has quite the chequered past.'

'Whit, Fawkurt?' Frannie screws up his face. 'Whit ever happened in Fawkurt?'

'Ye'd be surprised,' Terry replies, appalled by the ignorance and arrogance of this generation. 'Youse boys should read aboot it some time. It's yer hame toon.'

'Ach, that's a lot ay shite,' Brian waves a dismissive hand. 'Nane ay that mettirs. The here an noo's whit counts, that's it.'

'Son,' Terry shakes his head wearily, 'ye're young. Ye've no been oan the planet that long. It's right that ye think like that. But ye'll learn soon enough that ye canny ignore the past.'

'Fuck that,' Brian dismisses him, wiping the bar aggressively. 'We're the fuckin history ay Fawkurt, eh boys? This is oor toon.'

His face shines with an almost fascist superiority, opposed by so much age and crapness, Brian Mann, king of the master race of youth. The three of us raise our glasses to him and he bows.

'Tay the history ay Fawkurt!'

'The history ay Fawkurt!'

and the front window shatters, spraying coloured glass across the tables. Shouts from outside – 'ya fuckin' – and Brian is out with the speed of a cheetah. We follow him, confused, into the street, in time to see car lights disappearing round the corner and before we can even realise what's happened Brian's hustled us into Belinda, handing Frannie a pint glass, 'At the next red light, get oot an chuck that at their fuckin winday,' then he runs back into Smith's and we're giving chase, like in a film, Dolby swearing uncontrollably.

'Who wis it, d'ye think?' I ask.

Frannie with the pint glass in his hand is like a statue of justice.

> finally
> you're paranoid
> but not an android

'Dunno.' He looks at Dolby. 'Cottsy?'

'Or them fuckers fay the races,' Dolby adds, screeching into the Cow Wynd and onto Comely Place, veering towards the traffic lights. Belinda roars righteously, and I want to be the one who throws the pint glass, feel it leave my hand, just like in the bottle fight at school, years ago –

But the streets are empty.

Even though we scour the roads like pirates for ten minutes they've gone. Dolby turns, sweating, and heads back to Smith's. Behind the bar, Brian stands like a Goliath.

'Yese get them?'

Dolby shakes his head, kicks a post, knowing he should have braked before he went over that boy's leg at the burnout.

196

'Right. The morra night,' Brian vows. 'We're gon doon the races to see these fuckin–'

cars revving, in heat, the howling of chromium dogs. Engines noise each other up. Belinda slinks between them, sleek, fish-like. Eyes follow her through windscreens. There is fake cheering on the chorus of a dance track. The Central Scotland boyracer circuit gathered, and beneath my Radiohead t-shirt I flex scrawny muscles.

We park, disembark. Our hands thrust into our pockets, we walk towards a gathering at the far end, where neds are standing with clipboards, the whole thing. One of them sees us coming and alerts Shiny.

'Ladies,' he says. 'Didnay expect tay see any birds here the night.'

'Why's that?' Brian asks.

Shiny points to a weapon in a stookie, hauling himself on crutches towards a thumping VW. 'No eftir yer GBH on Chas there. Broke a boy's leg, if I mind right.'

'Aye man,' says his pal, staring. 'Ye mind right.'

'That wis an accident,' Dolby stresses. 'He didnay get oot the way in time. Took his chances.'

'Aye?' Shiny shrugs, drawing himself nose-to-nose with Dolby. 'Maybe yer pal who works in the pub'll no get oot the way when we smash it tay fuckin bits. Wantay take yer chances there?'

Brian places a hand on Shiny's chest and replaces Dolby with himself. 'That's whit we're here tay talk tay yese aboot.' He eyeballs them. 'Wan race. Eftir that, nay mair squads uptay Smith's. Ye'll leave ma fuckin windays alane. Agreed?'

They consider this, huddled and swearing, inciting then calming each other while Fran sits protectively on Belinda's bonnet, eyeing up

197

neds. Brian's arms are muscled and tense. I try to hang near the front, my tendons expecting any second to spring.

    my tendons expecting any second to

    'Awright,' Shiny nods. 'We'll race ye fay there–' he points to the far end of the car park '– tay there.' The finishing line is a high brick factory wall

    'Okay,' says Dolby, reaching for his keys.

    'Naw,' Shiny grins, pointing to me. 'We want him tay drive it.'

    'Me?' I say.

    'He's no got a licence.'

    'He canny drive.'

    'Me?'

    'No take him long tay learn,' Shiny shrugs theatrically. 'Only goat tay accelerate and brake.'

    'Naw,' Brian says, 'he's no–'

    'I'll dae it,' I say.

    '– he's never had a lesson–'

    'I said I'll dae it.'

    '– no fair, come oantay–'

    'Brian,' I say, something new and determined rising inside me. 'Let me dae it.'

    Shiny nods. Car horns make ugly noises behind him. 'If he disnay, we kick yer fuckin heids in. Fair enough?'

        stay away from me, you fucking

so Dolby slopes Belinda to a clear corner to instruct me, like Mr Miagi in the Karate Kid, in the ways of the pedals, while Brian and Frannie kick gravel across the ground. My blood is rich with adrenaline. It sucks and breathes through my veins. I feel – actually – amazing.

198

'Feel that wee nudge? That's yer bitin point. Hold that an then–'

'Now lift the clutch, and ye'll need tay slam yer foot ontay the–'

'An as soon as ye get anywhere *near* that wall, hit the clutch, then the fuckin brake or–'

for twenty minutes I'm lifting and dropping pedals, testing biting points, practising emergency stops until I'm ready. Or ready enough to trail smoke for a few hundred yards then stop. Ready enough to prove something, as Bono, in U2's Rattle and Hum era, moans

> come on
> come *on*
> into the arms of america

the headlights blast along on the track, and we're revving, and though I don't glance at Shiny, I can feel his stare, and someone has turned a tape of UK garage way up, the tarmac pounding with off-time beats, and I am an anarchist, I am the antichrist, James Dean, John Travolta in Grease, ha ha, my trainers growling on the gas and Dolby is leaning in the window, reminding me of the pedal motions ('ye dinnay have tay dae this') but I'm not really listening. Can't. I'm on fire

isn't mentally fit for work but can apply for disability

and everything I've done, seen, fucked up at or obsessed upon, every time I wanted to talk to Tyra after English and that shimmering image of her kneeling before Connor, every time my Dark Side of the Moon CD sticks (on Money), everything I ever wanted to say to my parents, everyone I ever wanted to kill or fuck is now channelled through my rigid hands.

Shiny, in the next car to me, draws his finger along his neck and mouths *dead.*

A lassie raises the flag. The Lads are watching, as I flex the ball of my foot across the biting-point and we're

mum? mum, are you—

alive. Belinda roars outrage in my hands as the world slips past frighteningly fast, like fluid, and the wall is growing, a side-glance – Shiny's face, focused – then the wall approaching faster than I can

(–the brake?)

stab randomly at the pedals, panicked. A shout escapes then I'm

screeching

wailing

bricks rushing towards me and

Stop.

The world is still.

The world is very still.

Just ahead of me, a car (which car? what? where am I?) has met a wall and someone is hobbling from the front seat with blood on their face, and the slow, still world – so beautiful and within my reach – suddenly whirrs back to speed, noise, screams, the face near me, hammering a bloody fist on the windscreen and leaving marks. I stay locked in my seatbelt, watching him. Nearly fascinated. After what seems like a year of his hammering and shouting, people swarm the car. I am in a bubble. Their cries are dull. I start to shiver. Sirens are wailing and there are yells and in the rear-view mirror cars are exiting, blue light splashing, as Belinda's door is wrenched open and Dolby is pulling me out – 'move it, Alvin!' – into the back seat with Fran and Brian, taking off, hissing, hauling at the wheel, the world sliding to the side as noddies scatter like marbles and the police grab at

Stirling University is gorgeous. Green on every side. There's a loch shimmering in the middle and students coming and going across the bridge with folders and important-looking books with mind-boggling titles and they wear baseball caps and yak into mobile phones without – I stress this – without looking like boyracers.

Fuck Derek and his 'carer' plans for me. I want to see what this place looks like.

The four of us are led by a bubbly young guide in a Stirling Uni tracksuit who keeps yelping 'Great!' and 'Good question!' but she's nice. She looks like she'd be fun in Smith's after a couple of Aftershocks, Frank Sinatra playing in the background.

'Fuckin students,' Frannie mutters, 'why don't they get a real fuckin job?'

Ducks splash oddly in the water and sprays of violet flowers leap like effete muggers from the lochside, while canoes slink and young couples walk hand in hand, stop, read books, walk on again, and our guide tells us that classes are suspended on Wednesdays for sports and bees buzz and the Lads are just about impressed. Dolby nods at everything she says, asks a question, nods again. Brian checks out the girls gliding past like swans. Frannie wants to go to the sports union to see the swimming pool, lithe bodies cutting its blue skin, and then Dolby takes us to the MacRobert Arts Centre (tonight showing a reissue of Hellraiser) where a stall nearby sells posters of Kurt Cobain, Moulin Rouge, Eminem, Christian Bale in American Psycho, the Beatles recording Sgt Pepper and students amass and muse and laugh and talk about maybe going to the pub and the posters advertise a Traffic Light Disco in the Fubar and the Star Wars trilogy at the Sci-Fi Club. They have a Sci-Fi *Club*? We visit the library: three floors of books! I go to a terminal, type in Stephen King and see

Different Seasons	IN STOCK
Carrie	IN STOCK
The Shining	Due 30th June
Skeleton Crew	IN STOCK

and that one student who has taken The Shining out fascinates me. I fantasise about meeting her on the first day of term over a peach schnapps, talking about Kubrick's film adaptation, its strengths and its flaws, in the Student Union where our tour party is soon taken and where beardy intellectuals sup ale and trendy young things touch their lips against crystal-clear drinks and rugger boys slam tequilas and people are brought toasties and hot-pots on steaming plates and a birthday party for a girl called Claire kicks off in the corner and

We sit by the lochside, overwhelmed.

A group of tanned students roll a football across the grass, their shadows long on the ground.

'Christ,' Brian remarks between mouthfuls of sandwich, 'this place is a fuckin holiday camp.'

In the Falkirk Herald this week there was a story which went

INJURY AT UNDERGROUND CAR RACE

Police disrupted an illegal car race in Camelon last week, just seconds after a youth had been injured. Arrests were made. There have been several similar races in the Falkirk area recently and police are growing concerned. Mark Baxter (17) was taken to hospital with a fractured skull after his car collided with a factory wall. Although several of the participants eluded the police, Constable Eric Richards has promised that there will be a crackdown on this sort of dangerous activity. 'These youngsters think they'll be able to carry on like this forever but we're

taking shots at an imaginary goal. Hip hop stutters from their ghetto blaster. Girls lounge in the afternoon next to half-open books and silver phones and a light veil settles over everything: the bridge, dotted with French accents, the loch speckled with white birds, the Wallace Monument standing like a dazed sentry, the lulling spell of an American woman reading a fairytale to her child. There is a vague, Spring work ethic. From an open window I can hear a chiming waterfall of guitar notes and someone sing

> looks like we might have made it
> yes it
> looks like we've made it to the end

and I feel like I might belong somewhere.

Everything is beautiful and vibrant. The campus rings with tantalising laughter. Nobody looks like they might want to kick my head in. Myriad windows, where students lean, chatting, smoking, so many people to meet. I keep the desire to explore close to my chest – while the Lads yak about the Rangers game and a new clutch for Belinda – until eventually it churns in me, burns, aching for them to be gone.

Frannie's patter. Brian's disaffected grunt-language. Dolby's pop-philosophy. My wide-eyed naivety. The rightness of our being together.

But for the first time ever, *they* seem a burden to *me*, not the reverse, and though the shame of this goes deep, the louder they talk – the more fucks and fenians – the greater is my need to be rid of them, although I don't know what they have done to deserve this. On the way home I will remember the translucent laughter that drapes the campus, will close my eyes as Belinda chugs and splutters into the concrete jungle of Hallglen and a shoplifter tears from the corner shop with a bottle of Buckie screaming, 'Paki bastaaaard!'

'Student poofs,' says Frannie, untouched by it all. 'Look at them. These arenay real people. Aw the guys are nancy boys and the girls are up themsels.'

'Just as well,' Brian says, 'cos you'll no be up them.'

Dolby shrugs. 'Dunno, man. The Runt could dae worse.'

'Ye'd come up an visit me, though?' I ask, a chill thought passing through.

'Wid we no just,' Brian says. 'Fuckin Butlins here, man.'

Dusk floats in. The sun settles orange petals on the water. But the Lads seem sad, darkening like shadow, ageing right before my eyes.

'Hey, whit's the coolest thing ye've ever seen?' I ask, quickly, fearful they'll grey and collapse if I don't divert them.

'Brian's nipples,' Frannie clucks with revenge.

'Dinnay be a dick. Whit's the coolest thing ye've ever seen?'

'That girl's arse.'

'Gonnay take this seriously.'

'Gonnay take this seriously? "Whit's the coolest thing ye've ever seen?"'

'Coolest thing I've ever seen,' Brian begins, surprising us all, 'was when I was walking through Dollar Park wan night as a bairn. The sun wis gon doon, the sky wis lit-up aw different colours, just like this. And I mind there was this guy, this auld guy, an he was jist sittin under a tree, an he was–' he blinks, as if the guy is flitting before him just now '– playin the saxophone.'

He swallows his Irn-Bru, burps, hurls the can. I see it spin, the drop-lets falling like parachutists.

'An that's it. That's the coolest thing I've ever seen.'

There's silence for a while.

Imaginary saxophone notes curl between the student halls, the old guy treading carefully, lest he tread on our dreams. My hands have grown cold, the fingertips numb, and my favourite episode of the Simpsons is still the one where Homer tries to join the Stonecutters. The fizz of the beer on the rim of Frannie's bottle, and the two of us leaning against his bed, laughing so hard that his Mum banged upstairs.

Dolby turns to me suddenly. 'Sam Raimi's directin the Spider-Man movie.'

'Sam Raimi?' I gasp, shocked.

'He did the Evil Dead.'

'Whaaaat?' I whine. 'Whatever happened tay James Cameron?'

Dolby shrugs. 'Jumped ship.'

'Ha-fuckin-ha.'

The old guy shedding languid notes in the dark and I know this:

I can't connect with the people I love.

'I hate that,' Brian mutters. 'I hate when yer lookin forward tay somethin and it turns oot tay be crap.'

We all grunt agreement.

'Anybody want tay know the coolest thing I've ever seen?' I ask, but Frannie snorts, shoving a crisp packet down my back.

'Alvin. Two ay your heroes are called *Brett.*' (Anderson and Easton Ellis) 'Nothin you've seen is cool.'

Everything must go.

Events are slowing down, speeding up, slowing down. Hour after hour spent cruising Polmont, Bo'ness, Dennyloanhead, stopping for petrol and Loaded magazine, schmoozing half-heartedly with girls behind the counter, playing the soundtrack to Fight Club. Patter is flat. Belinda has the feel of a once-beautiful film star long past her prime. The streets hold all the fascination of an empty paper bag rotating in a slight breeze. Frannie tells a joke; only one of us laughs. Dolby mentions that Whirlpools Direct might be shutting down. Brian reassures him that he'll get him work in Smith's, but this is forgotten in a debate about Al Pacino (does he over-act?) which also expires, uncertain of itself, unresolved. We whistle at girls – shining white in GAP – and for a second the sky has all the brilliance of a summer's day, until grey clouds make everything concrete, dead, and nobody expresses disappointment at this, its predictability.

Brian says, 'California's takin longer than I thought. Havenay heard yet about ma visa.'

Dolby says, 'I'm thinkin of takin an evenin degree in Philosophy.'

Frannie sings, 'If you steal my sunshine.'

I say, 'Is anybody listening to me?'

while anti-capitalist demonstrators in London break the windows of McDonalds, defacing a statue of Winston Churchill, spray graffiti across banks and building societies, and William McIlvanney is on the radio saying that 'the event has reminded us of the rights of the young to be subversive. But there is a question of how immature protestors can be and still claim to be expressing more than their own petulance. These caperings carried as much threat to capitalism as a kindergarten sit-in. If you–'

steal my sunshine

'– don't pay attention to us then we'll break our toys. Meanwhile, the protestors were distressed by the violence of the anarchists, the anarchists were distressed by the passivity of the protest, the right-wing papers where distressed by anyone who wasn't a statue, Tony Blair was distressed that Britannia had lost her cool. If you–'

steal my sunshine!

'– want to think of this event as a sort of cultural compass, then we are headed into a perpetual and vacuous present.'

Brian starts drumming his fingers on his knee and talks about franchising his own chain of pubs. I compose silent poems about graves. Frannie tells us that Elaine Section Manager was looking 'miiigthy fiiiine' today. Dolby changes the music, constantly.

How would we do it, if we were ever famous? Would we be media-hugging icons like Robbie Williams, describing on chat shows our years cutting the Falkirk tarmac, before confessing our alcohol addictions? Or would we be interview-shunning enigmas like the Floyd, emerging from our ivory towers once every decade to a world that has mourned our absence?

I'm never sure how we are expected to reach this level of stardom, since we won't become famous for quoting Raiders of the Lost Ark, but hey it's Saturday and

Snakes.

Why'd it have to be snakes?

we're at this guitar exhibition at the SECC in Glasgow, with Dolby's
Dad (who really does resemble Lee Van Cleef). Guitars mounted all
over like hunting trophies and I touch the strings of one. Gruff trolls in
denim spring immediately from behind amps to challenge my un-Def
Leppardness.

'Wow,' Frannie remarks. 'Nice armpits.'

Dolby's Dad has paused at a stall where some poodle-haired rocker
is lost in playing the guitar solo from the Cream song White Room, his
fingers performing frottage on the fret. Dolby's Dad turns to us, nods
seriously, and says, 'That's fuckin good music.'

Funny how overweight the world can seem sometimes, how if you
pause and concentrate for long enough you can hear it groaning.

it is the sound of Derek coming into my bedroom, as he is now, sitting,
his face tight and troubled. He passes me a tray of bourbon creams. Bad
start. They're the biscuits we devoured by the barrel-load when we
were kids. Why does he think I need comfort food?

'Eat them,' he instructs. 'I've went right off them.' He goes to my
CD rack and draws out OK Computer, puts it in the CD player,
presses play, then watches the lights and sits down. 'Good album,' he
nods, 'but no the best ever made,' and he seems to have shrunk in the
time since he's been gone to London. Outside it decides to rain

down, rain down
come on rain down on me
from a great height, from

208

Derek says 'Ken, Alvin, when I lived in this house, I wanted to do almost anything to get away. As far away as possible. There was a whole world out there full of excitement. So I went to London, where the money is. Like Dick Whittington or something. Thought if I had enough money they'd let me in.'

He shrugs.

'Didn't even know who "they" were. Didn't know where it was I was trying to get into . . .'

He tails off, examines the six holes in a bourbon cream.

'Got the job in the bank. Ya dancer. Still couldn't bring in enough money to pay the rent. Moved to a bedsit. Could afford the bedsit, but it barely left me any money to go out or see a film or hire a video, never mind go to a club. My landlady didnay allow me to have visitors over, and I didn't complain cause the rent was so cheap, but if I wanted to see anybody I had to wait for them to invite me over, which they never did, and I couldnay get a better job cause my CV only had on it this crappy post at the bank, and I couldn't get promoted cos there's millions of young folk down there with a better CV than you. They're like a pack of snarling dogs down there, these young guys. Every day all these rich folk are handing over their cash, giving me all the attention they'd give a hole-in-the-wall, griping about their mortgages and the rates on their savings while I'm thinking, Do you know what a luxury a mortgage is? Do you know how few people have savings? You don't have a clue, do you?'

Chapter VIII of The Great Gatsby, open, unrevised, in my lap, is beginning

> I couldn't sleep all night; a fog-horn was groaning incessantly on the Sound and I tossed half-sick between grotesque reality and savage, frightening dreams

Derek breathes in and places his hands on his knees.

'Then I started seeing Mum. I saw customers who looked like her. Beggars who looked like her. Prostitutes who looked like her. She was everywhere. One morning I chased her down the street. I chased her, shouting, and she screamed and ran into a police station, so I thought I'd better leave her alone, ha ha.'

He leans back in his chair and folds his hands behind his head.

'Later that day, this woman came in. Middle-aged, middle class. I was trying to count her money, but I couldn't do it. I was thinking about Mum. And Dad. And you. And what was I doing there, alone, scraping out a living, roaming the streets in boredom every night, looking in the shop windows at things I couldn't afford. This wasn't what it was supposed to be like. This wasn't what I was promised. And this woman starts shouting at me to hurry up. And I looked at her. And she looked at me. And there was nothing in her eyes. They were just like steel. She had so much money she'd just become a robot, and I realised she could never connect with me, that it just wasn't possible, that there was nothing out there for me in the whole, wide world, it had all been an illusion, and I'd fallen for it. Something snapped. I was just standing there, counting her cash, listening to her hissing at me to hurry up like I was some kind of servant. Then I picked up her money, hurled it at the glass partition and told her to go take a fuck to herself. It was all I could think of to do as a protest. Silly, really. But it was so funny.'

He smiles, cheeky, like the daredevil wee boy I remember playing chap-door-run, and as I picture some rich old bat watching her money swirl and flap through the air, while Derek picks up his copy of the NME and leaves, right there, everyone watching. I'm proud of him. For feeling it enough.

'So,' I say eventually, 'ye lost yer job.'

He raises an eyebrow, dabs with his tongue at a roll-up.

210

'The job, the bedsit, ma mind.' The roll-up is finished expertly and waves in his mouth as he talks. He searches his pockets for a light. 'All that's out there, Alvin, ma man, is the Withs and the Withouts. An it's worse bein a Without among the Withs, let me tell ye.'

The fag is lit. 'That's why I came hame.'

His eyes pinch as he draws at the fag. Tiny orange brightness.

'Dae ye really think she's alive?' I ask, my voice small in the room, but Derek stands up, having said enough, and we hold each other's gaze while Norman Bates twitches nervously in Psycho in my mind.

'I'll watch Dad,' he says, 'if you can prove tay me staying away's no impossible.'

'Whit d'ye mean?'

'It's your turn to go.'

I nod, then we smile against the memories, somehow defeating them, and he shuffles off back to his own room in a hash-haze, quietly, as though

we're all in our private traps. clamped in them, we scratch and claw, but only at the air, only at each other. and for all of it . . . we never budge an inch.

his appearance had been that of a ghost.

Belinda pulls up outside the house, her horn calling, insistent. From the window I see Frannie bounding from the driver's seat (driver's seat?), his steps athletic and his grin like fresh cheesecake.

'Guess whit?' he beams, when I open the door.

'The Martians have landed?'

'Nut.'

'There's nothing the psychiatrist can dae for ye?'

'Nut.'

'Ye've shagged Ally McCoist?'

'Nut!'

'Whit is it, man? I'm studyin.'

Frannie pulls out a plastic wallet and at first I think he's joined the police or something. Then I notice the letters DVLA, the name Colin Franton printed beneath and I realise it's a driving licence.

'Franman!' Our hands slap in mid-air. 'I didnay even ken ye were takin lessons.'

'Well, I didnay want yese tay ken,' he shrugs. 'In case I arsed it up. Comin oot for a run?'

'I dunno, man. Loads ay studyin tay dae. Big exams soon.'

Frannie is too cheery to accept this. 'Aw the mair reason. Ye stressed?'

'Aye.'

'Shitein yersel?'

'Aye.'

'Ye should be. Cos if ye dinnay come oot, I'll kick yer fuckin heid in.'

so we go on a maiden run to Cumbernauld and Frannie's sky-high, gripping the wheel like a kid in a go-kart, actually going 'Wheee!' as the evening roars dramatically past and I feel sick/exhilarated/stressed/ chilled all at the same time and at this speed something feels ending – this Robbie Williams song? My tether? the world as we know it? – Brian winks and passes me a Becks, which I struggle with (beer, to me, still tastes horribly like beer), Fran guided through motorway lanes by the wise Dolby-Wan Kenobi. He has a grin glued to his face, still going 'Wheee!' and I decide to play that Pink Floyd song called Several Species Of Small Furry Animals Gathered Together And Grooving

212

With A Pict (yes, it actually exists) but Dolby slaps the CD away as if it's an amorous advance.

'Gie me one good reason why *you* should pick the music.'

'I'll gie you three. Robbie fuckin Williams.'

Frannie tells us about something weird that happened to Ace of Spads, the guy he knows in Tesco's: 'He's drivin up north, right, on this back road, an the mist's comin right at him, thick as, when he sees this thing runnin towards him through the fog.'

'Whit? A dug?'

'Well, that's whit he thought. Then he realised it wis too big for a dug. Far too big. It's as big as a horse, except it looks nothin like a horse, an it's chargin right at him.'

'Whit was it?' I ask.

'An ostrich.'

'Whit?'

'Get tay fuck!'

'Tellin ye. He must have been near wan ay they ostrich farms or somethin. But this fuckin thing strides right up tay him, heid gon like that . . . an then it just veers away. Meep meep, ya bas.'

'That wis the Road Runner.'

'Aw Frannie, away,' scoffs Brian.

'I'm tellin ye,' says Frannie. 'Ask anybody in Tesco's.'

'Aye, right,' says Dolby. 'The same reliable sources that said the floodlights at Ibrox are hotter than the sun?'

'Hiy,' Frannie notes, 'the *surface* ay the sun.'

'I bet there isnay even an Ace ay Spads,' Brian complains, knocking the back of the plastic Han Solo off the dash. 'I bet you've been makin it aw up.'

'Like Frannie's got that much imagination.'

'Well,' Frannie shrugs, smoothing his hands down the steering wheel, 'I'm the one wi the drivin licence, Mr Mann. You couldnay get a licence tay have a *pish.*'

I'm listening, laughing, staring at the Irn-Bru can on the dashboard, the mystery which has evaded me all this time (if it's not attached to the car, why does it drop in a straight line? whywhywhy?) and realise

How little everything's changed.

How much everything's changed.

We're still in the same car on the same roads, inflicting the same patter on each other, lusting after vague girls, trapped in an endless cycle of stadium choruses, FHM articles, arguments about what the best Superman movie was (the second, obviously).

Except we're different. There's a hollowness to Dolby's Star Trek soliloquies, as if he's sensed at last they're lost on the other two. Brian is spending more and more time on his phone, trying to organise his emigration while keeping Smith's from being a hang-out for the cast of Deliverance. Frannie seems jaded, energy-less, like Coisty after he moved from Rangers to Kilmarnock.

And me?

I hate myself and I want to die.

as the argument over who has the biggest disc spirals out of control, and Bono yips

it's a beautiful day!

and Frannie accelerates, whooping, Belinda complaining deep in her intestines and the sky over Scotland is a cool vermillion and I appeal, 'Guys? Whit does it matter who's got the biggest disc? I dinnay even own a computer.'

'Dick,' Brian explains, 'we're arguing ower who's got the biggest dick.'

It's then I notice Frannie glancing in the mirror, glancing again. His brow furrows as a car draws up beside us and Cottsy leans from the open window. When he smiles, I notice the gap in his teeth made by Brian's fist at the Hollywood Bowl.

'Awright gents,' he says, as the car veers close, making Frannie swerve and Dolby shout, gripping the wheel: 'Fucksake, Fran!'

'Shit, Dolby. You'd better take ower. The fucker's gonnay ram me aff the road!'

'Forget it,' Brian barks. 'Stop the car an we'll take these cunts.'

Cottsy is holding up a knife.

'Mibbe no,' says Brian. 'Keep drivin.'

Cottsy's squad are crammed into their Fiat Uno, HARDCORE sprayed down the side. Dance choons blasting. His noddies crack themselves up at Frannie's nervy swerving and my stomach goes that floppy way again and the muscles in my arms solidify for battle.

'Take the fuckin wheel, man!'

'I canny, you're in the drivin seat!'

Cottsy's car pulls close in, almost close enough for him to grab Belinda's wheel himself.

'You boys fancy pullin ower for a chat?'

Frannie hits the pedal and roars away. We must be doing ninety. I look back to see Cottsy weaving in our wake. Frannie is accelerating like a madman. 'Slow doon, fer fuck's sake,' Dolby commands. 'It's yer first time on the motorway.' Belinda starts a violent shuddering. The gauges strain and bob.

'Slow the fuck doon!'

My heart retches. The four of us shout at once, then this happens in crystal stages frannie clips someone's wing-mirror

cottsy edges up behind us.

   smoke erupts from belinda's bonnet

        dolby shouts 'get aff the road! get aff the road! get aff the
        fuckin road!'

                                         then

things hurtle back to speed as our voices are lost in a prolonged moan
from belinda's engine and shaking starts in the car's frame and our
speed starts to

                drop

                and
we skim between two juggernauts
                        off the road

    plough up the grass at the side of the motorway and

cottsy shoots by, a jeering blur.

There is silence for a whole ten seconds.

We get out, slamming doors. The sounds of cars whizzing past and a hissing radiator. Frannie tries Belinda's engine, but she struggles for breath, making gasping noises.

'How long will it take them tay come back?' I ask.

Dolby shrugs, gazing up the motorway.

'Ten minutes?' he says. 'Fifteen?'

Then he turns decisively and tells us what to do.

'Are ye stupit?' Frannie argues, holding Belinda's wheel protectively. 'That's the worst idea I've ever heard.'

'Dae you want tay be here when they get back?' Dolby asks.

The A80 is bordered by a wire fence, which bars access to a steep slope. We kick at three of the stakes like punk rockers, stamping the wire to create a hole just big enough for a car. We laugh and make jokes. It begins to feel like playing.

Frannie is posted in the front, while we push and grunt against the rear.

'Bit more,' he encourages. 'Bit more. Bit more. Bit mooooooaaaaa–'

Belinda disappears from our palms, trailing a scream, and we realise we've misjudged the gradient. She hits the bottom with a tinkling thud.

We charge down to see Frannie's teeth gritted, his face a terrified rictus.

Belinda cools and gives up her life, while we just stand biting our nails and the evening edges towards darkness.

'Fuck!' Dolby yells, hammering her bonnet. 'Fuck! Fuck! Fuck!'

Then he stands. Stares at her. Starts tearing off the licence plates.

'Whit are ye daein?' I say, baffled.

He cuts me a look. 'We're leavin her,' he explains. 'Look at her, she's a write-aff. Gie us the papers fay the glove compartment.'

We watch him, stunned.

'Come an help, then,' he commands. 'It's startin tay fuckin rain.'

So there Belinda is left, her bonnet crushed and curled like petals, her windows cracked, her headlights drawing slowly down on the world.

We stand there for a while. Just looking at her.

Then Dolby utters, monotone, 'Let's go afore somebody calls the polis.'

We head into the night, boxing our shoulders. Only once do I glance back at Belinda, to see her broken, alone. Dolby's hands are tight in his pockets, his face giving nothing, but I can feel him shutting down, some part of him dying with Belinda. Rain patters on my brow. Sodium light stretches on the surface of the road. I've started to shiver and feel cold. The four of us trudge in stark silence.

This – as David Bowie said at the Freddie Mercury tribute concert – is where the fun stops.

We have no place left to go.

And we have no place left to go.

when I traipse into my house, freezing, the phone is ringing. Derek answers it, as I shuck off my wet clothes, and as he says, 'Alvin? Aye, he's just walked in the door–' he's seeing the state I'm in, seeing my clothes hitting the floorboards with a dull slap.

He hands me the phone. The room seems to sway. 'Hello,' I mumble.

There is laughter from the other end of the line.

'Hello?' I say again.

'Hello,' someone repeats in a silly voice.

'Who is this?'

'It's a friend,' the voice answers. There is a host of giggles. 'Just wanted to, you know, ask if you enjoyed the party?'

Things are starting to swirl gently. I clutch the kitchen door to make them stop.

'Whit party? Whit ye talkin about? Who are you?'

'What party?' he says, a polite, clean voice. 'Have you forgotten already? Tyra's party. Your big night out.'

'Whit big night out?'

'The one you weren't fucking invited to.'

'Tell him, for fuck's sake–' people snigger in the background. 'Put the mink out of his misery.'

'Whit d'ye mean? Of course I wis invited.'

My hand is starting to tremble, rage or nerves or something else.

'Du-uh! Do you not know a fake invite when you see one? Sorry I couldn't catch you at school, Alvin,' the caller repeats, sarcastically. 'Would love it if you ca-ame! Sound familiar?'

My legs are weakening. Someone drives bolts into the base of my skull.

'As if Tyra would invite y–'

I hang up, shaking, my teeth chattering in my head. Derek's crossing the room to me, but all I can focus on is an advert on telly, which is trying to sell me a car using a voiceover from On The Road.

'Alvin?' Derek's peering at me. 'You alright?'

'There's too much,' I think I say and

that night I am caught between fire and ice. Curled, foetal, shivering. For well-on five hours I am packed in my own sweat and carbon dioxide. The room pulses in and out of view. My breathing shifts up and down gear. The curtains are not billowing, but somehow it seems they should be. So hot. So cold. Between the hours of 3am and 4am I discover Mum at the end of my bed. She is wearing a floral dress and her blonde hair is flowing. I keep asking her why she's crying and tell her I'm sorry, we should have been better kids, it's all our fault, but she says, 'It was nothin tay do wi you, son,' then becomes Dave Gilmour from Pink Floyd. I interview him about the making of The Wall and he gives full, polite, elaborate answers and some time later I wake making tea for the writer Iain Banks, and Dad comes into the kitchen to find me naked and chatting to an empty chair, a stream of day-old tea spattering onto the floor and

calls the doctor. I feel tiny and huge in the corner of the room, watching him, watching the nation start to yawn and stretch on television. A Royal Variety performance. A bomb going off somewhere in Ireland. Brad Pitt. Jennifer Aniston. My teeth chitter like ice cubes in a drink. I am fucked. Exhausted. It's over, I repeat to myself. It's all over. I'm dying. Dad's eyebrows furrow, the phone gripped in his palm, his mouth not moving in time with the words, 'No, he doesn't take drugs. There is paracetamol in the house, but . . . well, he's been under a lot of stress recently with his exams, and there's been some family trouble,' and I start singing, badly, aware of how badly I'm singing God Bless Hookey Street, the end-credits theme from Only Fools and Horses, and Dad glances at me, repeats his urgency to the doctor. He starts to get me dressed and I try to stop myself laughing, hopping into the legs of my jeans, my chest cold and burning and exposed, then I'm in the back of a taxi, Dad asking me questions, and I'm trying to answer them but the causeway between my mouth and my brain is too wide and all that comes out is, 'I'm fine, Dad. I'm actually fine. Dad. Stay with me. I feel terrible,' and the stars are silvery and wintry, making me think I'm ascending, like ET. My back hurts. My joints move like they're full of broken glass. Words dissolving on my tongue. The doctor feels my head and frowns, 'No drugs at all?' and I sing now the drugs don't work, they just make you worse, and laugh, but he doesn't seem to find it funny. No, not at all. A woman haunting the fringes of my vision. A vase of white flowers, the heads drained and tired like people at the end of a long, traumatic day in which their lives had felt ill-fitting. One of the nurses looks like Gwyneth Paltrow, a babe, and how annoying that she has to see me like this, as she withdraws the blood slowly, carefully, from my pendulous arm and I try to explain to her that I'm not a junkie or anything, I just have a head like a zeppelin on fire and the ghost of a wedding dress pulsing at the corner of my eye telling me something about misery and the wind and I turn to look but it is

gone

Rain falling against the window. Hospital radio playing the Foo Fighters. Those two things just not going together at all.

This is the infirmary where I was born. Falkirk Royal. Being here again makes me feel tiny, acorn-small. Nurses coming and going and doctors coming and going and me smiling like the professional patient.

While I'm here, I read the whole of Moby Dick, the only book lying around the ward, which is totally boring, since the whale doesn't appear until the second last chapter. Eight hundred pages of talking about the whale and no fucking whale. There's a message there, which is probably crucial to life or something, but I'm just too tired to figure it out.

I feel like I've been running for a long, long time.

My head feels compressed with the relationship between Barrett-era Floyd and Parklife-era Blur (more similar than critics realise, I could go into this), my body numb to everything but my own inadequacy, and that long, awful walk after we jettisoned Belinda.

Mum has been drifting at the end of the corridor, glancing in my direction. Her smile is weak and sad. When Derek and Dad arrive it is a family reunion of sorts. The faces are drizzly and faded, like a photo left out in the rain.

'Looking good, Billy Ray,' Derek says.

'Feeling good Lewis,' I manage.

There is hand patting from Dad.

The Lads turn up just as Ahab spots the fucking whale!

I like Brian's new puffa jacket. Frannie is wearing a Rangers baseball cap. Dolby is dressed like Chris Martin from Coldplay. They look more like boyracers than they ever have. They warm the room as soon as they enter it, and to ease things along – me, the still centre of their swirling banter – Frannie and Brian start slagging Dolby. Uriel, what the fuck was he thinking about, what a woofter. But he grimaces, holds his hands up. 'I'll come clean, boys. I've changed ma name back tay Martin.'

'Whit?' we all gasp. 'Why?'

'Naybody ever called me Uriel,' he shrugs. 'It wis a silly idea in the first place.'

We shake our heads, tutting, and nobody mentions the coincidence of it, that Uriel died with Belinda. And Dolby, trying to laugh along, but out of sorts, mourning, looks like it's a double suicide he won't recover from. Some tragic part of him out there on the road with Belinda forever, fluttering his wings.

They shuffle about the room, checking out the nurses' arses as they pass in the corridor. None of them ask, but I want to tell them anyway. I raise myself up in bed, finger the new Radiohead CD, Amnesiac, which Dolby has bought me, which has a weird cover, then put it down and say:

'I know yer aw wonderin whit happened tay me. But I'm . . . no really sure. This last year, I've been fightin against somethin, somethin horrible. There's been things gon on inside me that I don't understand at aw. I even thought about–' the sheets are scrunched up in my fist, '– but, ehm, I didnay. And I want yese tay know that if it wisnay fir youse guys, I wouldnay be here. I want yese to know that. I wid have–'

I pause, it's rising.

'But I didnay dae it. I'm here. We made it. The four ay us. Tay the end.'

Frannie turns and faces the wall. Dolby looks at the floor and murmurs, 'The new Radiohead album's awright. No as good as Kid A.'

Brian coughs, and when his voice emerges it is new and certain, ringing out.

'Next year for California, boys. Next year it'll happen. For sure.'

and I realise that I haven't said these things at all, just thought I had

and that now I never will

and that's that

The summer has wound down like an old clock. The mornings are tinged with a bright, sharp cold. Dolby and Brian's twentieth birthdays came and went. We did nothing special to celebrate them.

Dad helps pack the car. There's a battered typewriter he's fished from the loft for my essays, plenty socks and underwear, the copies of Kerouac and Kelman and rubbish critical books with names like In Defence of Realism which Mrs Gibson gave me, shining with pride, when I told her I'd made it onto the English degree course at Stirling University. Her notes in the margins, her pencilled thoughts forever adrift in the world. I open one at random and find a line which says

as if there could ever be any such things as true stories

and in my pockets I have a dozen photographs to stick on the walls of my new room: the Lads in jubilant poses, me and Derek sharing cocktails on the back slabs, Dad glancing over the top of the Daily Record in his old Clash t-shirt, and

Mum.

We heave the stuff out from the house – me, Derek, Dad, the Lads – grunting and joking like workers, like men. Afterwards we stand about, sort of chatting pointlessly. When I ask what they've been up to recently, Brian shrugs.

Through a heat-blanketed summer, I've met with them rarely. Since we've no car, our reasons for meeting up are few, though there's been the odd drunken phone call, boasting about some shag (not many of those, actually) or raving about some film. Generally, I've been relieved when Frannie's said, 'Does your phone dae this?' and the receiver's clicked down. Mostly, I've stayed in with Dad, listened to the clock's tick and the birds' chirpy nonsense, read books for my new course, watched The Godfather Parts I and II (never III).

'Got everythin?' Dad asks, closing the boot.

'Aye. Ready to heddy.'

We all stand silently, absorbing the moment. Cars shoot past on the main road. Our hands are in our pockets. It's as if we've just been introduced to each other and are desperately forming excuses to escape.

'Oh,' Dolby says, reaching into his jacket. 'Before I forget. We got ye a present for yer new room.' He hands me the plastic Han Solo from Belinda's dashboard. I stare at it, its wee arms and legs askew, blasting an invisible Greedo.

'Before we left her,' he says, 'I managed tay salvage Han.'

'An this,' Brian beams, handing me a can of Irn-Bru. 'Fir the back seat ay yer first car.'

'Front seat,' I remind him. Never did work that one out.

We shake hands. Each of them wishes me well, promises to come up to Stirling to visit. Brian asks me to set aside any tasty nursing students. The wind whistles the approach of winter and we huddle our hands further into our pockets, and standing there with them, I feel older, almost the same age as them.

I have to leave them. But every second heartbeat is a scream to stay.

'Aw the best.'

'Heddy haw.'

'See ye in the Hotel California.'

Just before I go, the mobile in Frannie's pocket beeps (the theme from

The Magnificent Seven) and he draws it out to check his text message.

'Alvin, it's for you,' he smirks, passing me the phone.

'For me?'

'She still has ma number . . .'

> Sorry I missed Ally Fergusons last match
> Give me a text sometime? Wendy.x

'How dae I text her back?' I panic, fiddling with the buttons. 'Whit dae I–'

'Well, ye'll need tay get a phone then.'

'Ye canny be a student if ye've no got a mobile phone,' Dolby points out.

'Fuck naw,' says Brian. 'How else are we gonnay get near they wee posh tarts?'

'Okay,' I say, 'I will.'

I move towards the car slowly. Things feel a bit like the end of The Breakfast Club. Simple Minds should be playing Don't You Forget About Me in the background, highlighting the excellent crapness of the moment. As I clamber into the front seat, Derek shuts the door behind me. He seems to want to say something, struggling with it.

'Looking good Billy Ra–' he says, but I cut him off.

'If there is anythin oot there,' I say, 'I'll find it.'

He smiles, ruffling my hair, and it's such a corny gesture, like something a brother would do.

It's time.

Me and Dad pull away, and they're all in a line, everyone I've ever cared about, waving, smiling, flicking me the Vs, and as the car gathers speed, it's too painful to watch them disappear behind me, so I don't.

Ahead, the sun glows pink/orange/lime, like Bacardi Breezers, like a champagne supernova in the sky, and all the last songs on albums and all the closing scenes from films merge then part on a motorway in my mind, and everything under the sun is in tune, as I fiddle with the radio, settling on some crackling Highland channel with its comforting hills, heather and lochs and

> you'll tak the high road
> an i'll tak the low road
> an i'll be in scotland afore ye

and the Lads and me watching drunken Rangers matches, and I think about Wendy's text. I'm not sure that it matters if I text her back or not, but I really think I will. I'm buying a mobile phone. This decision is made. I stand Han Solo up on the dashboard and he carries the world on tiny shoulders.

Dad says, 'Did I ever tell ye I saw Elvis Costello at the Maniqui?'

He winks, and there's a grin there that I thought had died from his face quite some time ago.

'Naw, ye've never telt me that, Dad,' I smile.

ROLL CREDITS. VOICEOVER. We are a generation who awoke to find all gods dead, all wars fought, only delusions to believe in, hope for, which we spend our whole lives racing towards, bright, shimmering on the horizon, but then

We glance back. And the way we've come has gone. And we didn't stop, breathe, absorb any of it. It all zapped past. Like Grand Prix adverts. Like a sitcom double bill.

where me and ma true love
will never meet again
on the bonny bonny banks of Loch Lomond

planet Earth, scorched with the touch of the sun, its rays appearing/
disappearing/appearing again and happiness becomes – *is* – attainable.
It isn't *this*, but I know it's coming, making me chase it, frantic, like a
greyhound after a rabbit, and who knows, maybe I've shot past without
even noticing, but till the day when all makes sense there is this. This
feeling.

'You and Derek are awright, Dad? I ask. 'I mean, yer on the right
track? Stirling's no far away if ye want tay–'

'We'll be fine, son,' he says, squeezing my hand. 'Ye're brother's goat
that carer's allowance. He's gonnay stay for a while. We'll take care of
each other.'

The road stretching out ahead. Cars firing towards mystery destina-
tions. Those simple words, 'We'll take care of each other,' and what
they mean, what they do, and the world, I've decided, is a good place
to be, still fascinating. I have not exhausted its possibilities. It ain't no
sin to be glad you're alive, and above all else it's this I realise, suddenly,
like an epiphany, like the sun glowing through the clouds or the heady
feeling we had in Belinda, racing through all those nights together,
together, so I roll down my window, turn up the music, then just roar
something triumphant at the sign rushing past which says

YOU ARE NOW LEAVING FALKIRK

Boyracers: Resprayed

If you've just finished this book, you might have guessed that I was a big Stephen King fan when I was younger. His novels and stories alone, replete with good old Americans battling some supernatural threat, were thrilling enough (or most of them anyway, as I've never felt the need to go back to *Rose Madder*), but what I also loved were King's introductory essays to his books, in which he'd explain, face to face, how he came to be a writer, how he typed away in a trailer, he and his wife doing about six jobs between them, a baby on the way, how his wife fished his abandoned manuscript *Carrie* out of the bin and made him look at it again. The rest, as they say, is bloody, ghost-ravaged, nightmarish history. King would be telling you this, with all the down-home straightness of someone sliding a pint down the bar to you. It all had this glow about it. Yet what difference did it make how the books came to be written? Why do we care about the particular context a novel came to exist in, whether it's Orwell holed up on Jura with tuber-culosis, feverish with *Nineteen Eighty-Four*, or the furore surrounding the publication of Bret Easton Ellis's *American Psycho*? Sometimes, say, with Ted Hughes's *Birthday Letters*, the artwork and the real life are so enmeshed that either only makes half as much sense without the other.

Now, I'm not Stephen King, and I'm certainly not Orwell, Ellis or Hughes, but even your friendly neighbourhood Falkirk novelist has been asked often enough at readings variations on the following: 'How did you become a writer?' 'Who were your influences' 'Is your work autobiographical?' 'Where do you get your ideas from?' (all-time classic, as any writer will tell you) and even the cracker: 'How did someone from a housing scheme manage to write a book?' That one always makes me smile. So I'm well aware that people do sometimes like to see behind the veil, to see what the Wizard of Oz looks like, even if like Dorothy, they're frequently disappointed to find that we're made up of the same boring bits and bobs as everyone else.

I figured I'd save us a wee bit of time in future and give answers to them all at once, and the Afterword to the Tenth Anniversary edition of my first published novel feels like the most obvious place to indulge that, since we've been talking to each other anyway, you and I. So if those questions mean anything at all to you, you'll get the answers here. If not – if you want to believe in the Wizard of Oz, don't like hearing writers prattle on about their 'struggle', or just hate people with pop-culture Tourettes – then move along, please. These aren't the droids you're looking for. Seriously, the next sentence alone will be enough to put you off.

To paraphrase Ray Liotta's opening shot in *Goodfellas*, 'As far back as I can remember I always wanted to be a writer.'

My family – who, it's worth saying, are nothing like Alvin's in this novel – still have no idea where it came from. Neither of my parents were avid readers, my siblings haven't turned out to be, and the few books I can remember lying around our house were mainly my mum's *Flowers in the Attic* series and my dad's books about the Glasgow razor gangs. I was drawn to their copies of Peter Benchley's *Jaws* and the novelisation of *King Kong*, because they were the only 'grown-up' books in the house which had actual monsters in them. These books had a feel and smell which I can loosely describe as adult: the paper was thicker, grainier than I was used to, the type was tiny and there was so much of it. Worst of all – no pictures! Nonetheless, when I was maybe seven or eight, I tried to read *Jaws*. My mind strained at the length of the sentences and I couldn't hold on to their sense for very long, but neither could I remove from my head the eerie image in that opening line: 'The great fish moved silently through the night water, propelled by short sweeps of its crescent tail.'

The hugeness of that fish in my mind. Death itself.

Ours, like almost every other working-class family's in Scotland, was very much a household of quiz shows, soap operas, murder mysteries, football, horse racing, Sixties hits, the Corries and Kenny Rogers. My mum claims she initially bought me books because they were cheaper than toys, and was pleased when I took up with them, as they kept me very quiet. Importantly, built into every schoolday at Hallglen Primary for seven years was half an hour of the teacher reading stories to us. Roald Dahl, *The Chronicles of Narnia*, the Famous Five and *Charlotte's Web* cast a spell which kept us silently glowing with excitement each day at three o'clock. They were the only times when our class, in all its variation, felt united.

Little boys who aren't good at football or fighting have to find self-worth in their own imaginations, and so mine was concerned chiefly with writing and drawing. A *Beano*-style comic strip about my mischievous little cousin Scott was a hit with my extended family. I'd imitate *Oor Wullie* and *The Broons,* my first attempt to write in Scots, and design choose-your-own-adventure novels like the Fighting Fantasy books by Steve Jackson and Ian Livingstone. I wrote a whole series of superhero comics based on me and my friends, with myself as the ninja-like Biscuit Boy, who could mentally control digestives. Writing stories was something I did whenever we were given free play in class, or when rain meant we couldn't go outside. It was the thing I did when

233

I went home. It was what I was praised most for by teachers. In Primary Three I won first prize as part of the school's Robert Burns celebration, with a recital of J.K. Annand's 'The Crocodile', which I can still remember word for word to this day. A writer, I'd decided, was what I was going to *be*.

In Primary Six I had my first ever encounter with another writer. We met like two lizards with florid throat displays. The top brains of our year group were placed in a composite class with some Primary Sevens, who generally wouldn't talk to us, so of course exuded a faint glamour. One day, our teacher, Alison Shanks, set us the task of coming up with a ghost story, which naturally I threw myself into, concocting a tale about a spooky river which flowed up the side of a mountain. Mrs Shanks read it to the class, who clapped approval, before she read out a story by Lindsay Gardner, a Primary Seven. It was about a girl home alone, whose doorbell was rung again and again by a man selling jade figurines. We held our breath each time the girl went back to the door. It was atmospheric, ambiguous, creepy and stylish. I didn't know what the hell a 'jade figurine' was but it sounded great! When the teacher had finished, when the story released us, the class went wild, whooping and cheering. Lindsay blushed and looked at her desk, and I regarded for the first time someone who was better at me than the thing I was best at. Since I can't find her on Amazon, I like to think that Lindsay – my first 'influence' – is now writing superb murder mysteries under a pseudonym.

Let's make no bones about this, at Falkirk High School I was geeky. The very things that make you stand out in a good way at primary school – intellect, imagination – make you stand out in a bad way at secondary school. The conformity, the sudden obsession with who to be seen with and what clothes to wear, is crushing to the spirit of those who can't keep up. This was terrible for my self-esteem but great for my writing, and I cast myself in the role of the romantic outsider, cut adrift from society, as revenge for upbraidings on the football pitch. *Yes*, I have read *Catcher in the Rye*.

In Fourth Year I wrote a story called 'The End of the World', a short, simple piece produced very quickly that used only dialogue and sparse description. It was about two five year-old children, Marshall and Jenny, sitting on a wall at a swing park. Jenny looks up to Marshall because he's a few months older, but Marshall abuses this privilege, trying to impress her with a fib about how he's visited 'the end of the world' which lies beyond the line where the sky and the ground meet. It has monsters and lions, he tells her, and a man called Arthur Haveabanana, who gives you a banana. Excited, she begs him to take her, but he refuses, for her own safety, not wanting to tell her that the real reason they can't go is because he's not allowed to cross the road. 'Another time,' says Jenny, before they run back to the house. 'Yes,' sighs Marshall, 'another time.'

The story seemed to me, at fourteen, a little juvenile, and was written as an experiment, a sideshow to the epic, Tolkien-esque novel I was planning in my head. My English teacher, Georgina Young, however, loved it, and read it out to the whole class. They listened and kept listening, then at the end went wild the way my Primary Six class had for Lindsay Gardner's jade figurines. I can still remember them all looking at me for the first time as though I wasn't a nothing any more. I wanted to feel that again, and again, and again, but couldn't quite understand why this particular story had enjoyed such an effect. So I went back to writing about vampires.

Now that I look back on 'The End of the World', with two decades' worth of experience, I can recognise certain elements that weren't in my horror stories: realistic dialogue (for two five-year-olds anyway), characters properly differentiated from each other, a power dynamic in

235

flux, the lack of genre clichés, an organic twist in the plot, and an atmosphere of sadness that avoided being maudlin. Mrs Young told me that she'd started to read it out to all of her classes, even the Fifth and Sixth Years – mainstream success! – but the school environment can take back as quickly as it gives and before long my head was back under the parapet.

It was a quiet wee triumph, though. A step.

Round about then, what it meant to be a teenager really kicked in. In May of 1990 I met Allan, Moonie and Toby, who were a good three years older than me and had all left school. We lived near each other in Hallglen, a scheme in Falkirk built in the mid-Seventies, set on a hill, where each box of a house is of the same white pebbledash as the next. You can see it clearly from the window of the Edinburgh–Glasgow train, just before Falkirk High station. 'The Lads', as they called themselves, took me under their wing, in the pitying, brotherly way that older teens sometimes do. As thanks for this patronage, I worshipped them. They all had jobs and disposable income, they drank alcohol, and they'd had actual sex with actual girls, all unknown concepts to me. I listened to their stories about work and fights and club nights with rapt fascination. Each evening, at six on the dot (after *Neighbours*), I'd change out of my school clothes and charge straight down to Toby's, and we'd hang about in his bedroom or Allan's living room and spend our time on a general ripping of the pish, to a soundtrack of classic rock, maybe a Bruce Lee, Clint Eastwood or Arnold Schwarznegger film to round the night off.

Then Toby passed his driving test, bought a car, and suddenly the whole of Scotland was open to us.

I remember those nights as being some of the most exciting of my life, even if, as youngest, I was the designated runt. Everything moved so fast. There was something new to see every day. We were loyal and we believed in each other. Together, our world felt limitless. Moonie introduced me to *The Simpsons* and David Bowie; Allan to Subbuteo and spaghetti westerns; Toby to Pink Floyd and Clive Barker, who became my first obsessive literary crush and who dictated my subsequent reading of Stephen King, Thomas Harris, H.P. Lovecraft, James Herbert and Edgar Allan Poe. The inside of my head grew strange and dark, all sorts of ghosts and madmen drifting through its purple drapes. I started to dress all in black and grow my hair long and think of myself as a creature of the night. If you are a teenage boy in this stage at the moment, my message is this: don't worry, you're going to be fine, but only once you realise that women aren't the enemy, Jim Morrison's poetry is rubbish, and that colours are nothing to be scared of.

In Fifth and Sixth Year my writing started to move, thanks to two hugely influential English teachers, Eileen Gibson and Mollie Skehal, who believed in young people, encouraged free thinking and offered the sort of purely literary pleasure which most kids avoid because 'it's boring'. I was no exception, and resisted what they called Good Books, but a great teacher can unlock any text for anyone, and this is how I was introduced to Arthur Miller, Norman MacCaig, Thomas Hardy, Tennessee Williams and F. Scott Fitzgerald. Thanks are also due to Georgina Young for Shakespeare, John Graham for Chaucer (and Joyce Lidgertwood for telling me in First Year that I was 'being silly' for putting a used condom into a story just because Stevie Miller had dared me to). What came at me from all of these writers, as my mind was trained in how to read and talk about Good Books, was a sense of realism, of the natural complexity and drama of human emotion. No demons were to be found except those of a character's own making. This, in its own way, made things more exciting because I could sense more truth about the world being presented to me. The danger the characters were in was more human, more tangible.

But I still liked things with fangs.

In 1993, in my final year of school, a supply teacher called Alison Armstrong, herself an eminently published writer of short stories, formed a Creative Writing group with Mollie Skehal. Our Sixth Year English class jumped on it, and, sensing my appetite for writing, Alison gave me a copy of *Rebel Inc.* magazine, published in Edinburgh by Kevin Williamson and featuring stories by then-unknowns Irvine Welsh, Alan Warner, Duncan McLean and Laura Hird. The cover showed Malcolm X holding a rifle. The stories all had swearing in them and were set in Scotland. This was a brew of a different order, dirty and provocative. I had absolutely no reference points for this kind of thing. Two of the writers in *Rebel Inc*, Gordon Legge and Shug Hanlan, were even from the Falkirk area. Alison encouraged me along to a poetry and pints night upstairs in Behind the Wall, where the main reader was the poet Janet Paisley. She lived in the village right next to Hallglen! A real poet! Alison introduced me to people by saying, 'keep an eye out for this boy in the future', which felt like huge praise to my shy seventeen-year-old self. She took me to an open mic night in Edinburgh – Edinburgh! – and I stepped onstage just the once, just to see what it felt like, told a joke about a guy going into a shop to ask for a wasp then sat back down to amused applause, a brief whiff of affirmation, before the actual poets went back to the mic.

On the scene, all the talk was about one particular writer starting to pull ahead of the pack: Irvine Welsh. The name seemed to float in and out of the smoke. Long before *Trainspotting* became a film classic, I was energised by the novel, as well as *The Acid House* and *Marabou Stork Nightmares*, which were about a Scotland I recognised, one that wasn't

238

the Broons or tartan but which spoke in the natural voice of the working-class. *My* voice. I'd presumed before that this kind of writing wasn't even allowed, given that teachers had always marked my essays with 'colloquial' each time an informality crept in. I started sketching stories about some of the guys in Hallglen, the hard guys and shaggers, but the characters would always end up falling into another dimension. Couldn't keep those pesky alternate worlds out of Hallglen.

My final two years at school were ones of uncertainty about my future, exam stress and acute emotional confusion. I had a bright, creative mind, but was not a diligent student, and the romantic outsider role had become subsumed by that of the adolescent depressive. This was especially acute given I'd stayed on at school to the point where only the university-bound sons and daughters of the middle class remained, all of whom seemed so assured and confident. I liked many of them but I wasn't one of them, and couldn't share the faith they had in their own destiny. No one in my family had ever gone to university. I didn't even know that sentence was a cliché at the time, it was just a fact. Sure, I wanted to be a writer one day but I hadn't a clue how to go about it. My dilemma was this: should I leave school and get a labouring job in Falkirk, as the Lads had, or head off, terrified, into the unknown? Everything in Hallglen was reassuringly familiar, but I could sense that the Lads all hated their jobs and that this would become my inevitable fate. Life for a working-class teenage boy, furthermore, is tinged with the very real possibility of violence, and I'd started to feel Falkirk pushing in at me from all sides, sharply.

Seeing as you've just finished *Boyracers*, you'll recognise this situation. For the record, I really was nicknamed Alvin back then (the Lads already had one Allan and didn't need another).

In 1993 I *just* scraped my way on to an undergraduate degree course in English at Stirling University. It was only twenty miles from Falkirk but an entirely different world. There I was, fully absorbed by the middle classes, whose voices and mores and codes were quite alien to me, with no Plan B and only the fear of going back to Falkirk to spur me on. I figured that, like Steve Guttenburg's character in *Police Academy*, I'd just stay until they kicked me out.

I loved it. Of course I did. Just as Steve Guttenburg's character, once he gives it time, loves the police academy. Four years later, to my shock, I'd achieved a First Class Honours degree in English and Education and my self-confidence was burgeoning, all the insecurities of school banished, and before I knew it, I was out into the real world.

For the first half of 1998, when I was twenty-two, I worked as an English teacher at Elgin Academy in the North East of Scotland. The work was enjoyable but the volume of it crippling. Rejection letters for my stories were coming thick and fast, and I soon realised that if I was to remain a teacher, I would never improve as a writer. For this reason, in the second half of the year, I started a PhD thesis back at Stirling University to give my mind a good workout.

My mind, however, turned out not to be the Goliath I'd presumed it to be and working it out, unfortunately, was among the most disheartening experiences of my life. That's no comment on the teaching staff at Stirling Uni, who'd always conveyed excitement, and were thus exciting (the stars in this regard were David Punter, Rory Watson, Glennis Byron, Jackie Tasioulas, Judy Delin, and Angela and Grahame Smith) but there I was, aged twenty-three, facing three long years stuck in Room 101,[1] lost in a thicket of critical theory, surrounded by people

---

1 It actually was Room A.101 of the Pathfoot Building, Stirling University.

who were all much, much cleverer than me. I was living on next to no money, working in Waterstone's every Saturday and Sunday to meet the bills, which, of course, kills a weekend life for someone in their early twenties. I could feel my confidence ebb again. I'd decided I didn't want to be an academic but I was training myself to be nothing else. The rejection letters were even more plentiful now. As Ray Liotta also says in *Goodfellas*, 'This was the bad time'.

A survival instinct kicked in. In early 1999 I started attending Stirling Writers Group, who met in the Cowane Centre, to see if I could revive my moribund ambitions. The tutor there, the poet Magi Gibson, saw enough potential to start hot-housing me, and within a few months the group had become a well-functioning unit of strong, ambitious writers, feeding off a shared energy and critiquing each other's work. We improved rapidly. Above us, Scottish Literature was undergoing a renaissance. The Rebel Inc. generation had come of age: *Trainspotting*'s huge success had meant international exposure for a whole host of Scottish writers. The cultural moment was palpable and vibrant. In the library of Stirling University, when I was supposed to be researching my PhD, I went to the Scottish Literature section and devoured James Kelman, Alasdair Gray, Janice Galloway, Ali Smith, Iain Banks, Des Dillon, Tom Leonard, Edwin Morgan, Jackie Kay, Alan Spence, William McIlvanney, Ron Butlin and A.L. Kennedy. The range of their experiments, the array of very real Scotlands which they presented, the sense of identity, the force of their language, the truth of their politics – all of it converged with a new momentum I'd started to achieve in my own writing. Under Magi's tutelage I abandoned fantasy and horror altogether to tell stories about the very thing I'd struggled to get away from: my class.

It released something in me. Things gathered speed. I was suddenly shortlisted for competitions, published in magazines, read out on the radio. I was still only twenty-four. Magi took me on tours of the Scottish live literature scene with her – to the Borders, Aberdeenshire, Glasgow. I became her secret weapon, and I started to enjoy the experience of performing, of encapturing an audience from a whole other part of the country and playing about with them. My work grew more verbal, stronger, conscious. I was on the move.

All or nothing: it was time to seize my chance. A bored postgrad, I had both the time and the motivation, and was aching again for that freedom and fun I'd felt tearing around Falkirk with my best friends, nothing else to do but talk about bands and chuck film quotes at each other. The point of innocence was disappearing in adulthood. I'd soon be too old to even remember those years with any clarity. Falkirk, a place I'd thought I'd finished with, had decided it had not finished with me. All things needed was a catalyst, a spark, for things to really take flight. That spark was a short story called 'Boyracers'.

In 2000 Magi and I had started to organise a regular poem and pints night in Stirling called Growwl. It's worth saying to anyone who laments the absence of a creative scene where they are: make one. We found a venue, the backroom of a bar whose name I can no longer remember, advertised to other writing groups, and were besieged by the initial turnout. Our star reader, the novelist Des Dillon, was someone whose work I very much admired for the way it reflected the energy, and not the deprivation, of working-class life. I wanted to read something that would really impress him. I sat down and wrote a story of perhaps 1,500 words about some of the stuff which Toby, Moonie, Allan and myself had got up to back in the day, gave it the title 'Boyracers', and when my time came I stood on a chair and read

242

the thing aloud with all the belief I could muster. I've never forgotten the volume of the reaction. After years of dreaming, it was finally happening, I could sense it: *I was becoming an actual writer.*

Des took the story away and published it in *Cutting Teeth*, a magazine he was editing at the time, and both Magi and my then-wife Caroline told me that they suspected there was more material to come, if I just pulled the thread . . .

And so, buoyed with enough youthful confidence to power a small town, I opened up my memory and *Boyracers* came roaring out with all the force of a debut album by a Northern rock n roll band.

The novel was published by Polygon in September 2001, coincidentally the same month my PhD thesis failed. I was twenty-five, the age at which Stephen King had published his first novel, *Carrie*, which pleased me no end. *Boyracers* has never been out of print, a remarkable achievement for a release by a first novelist from a Scottish independent publisher. It rode on what was perhaps the last wave of the spirit of Rebel Inc., just before centralised bookselling and the default middle-class setting of British literature made novels about the Scottish working class unfashionable again. That it has reached its tenth anniversary, given these conditions, delights me.

Ten years. Enough for me to come at the book with some objectivity. I was a very young man when I wrote it. I still love its fizziness and charm, but it's obviously written by someone who had no idea what he was doing. It's all heart and no shape, all energy and no definition.

So, for this edition, and in order to mesh the story with its imminent sequel, *Pack Men*, I typed the whole thing back out again. I mean, I retyped *every single sentence*.[2] It seemed like the only logical thing to do in order to understand it again. What occurred was a weird time travel experience, whereby thirty-five-year-old me became twenty-four-year-old me being sixteen-year-old me. I liked revisiting these past selves, clothing myself in their naive thoughts, but it was immediately clear that the book had been written and edited too quickly. It had perhaps too much youthful *whoosh*! and *gasp*!, and not enough discipline or craft. Errors of plotting and chronology had slipped through and terrible decisions of formatting and punctuation had been made in the name of experimentation. I'm very much in favour of the free play of words on the page, but, as Norman MacCaig once said, 'The real journey of any writer is towards lucidity.' For these reasons I have tidied up the prose somewhat in this edition, put it through a car wash. The material itself remains almost exactly the same, but it's been given a good edit, with a clearer eye than I had then. Think of this as a digitally remastered version, if you like, of that debut album by a Northern rock n roll band.

After all, the world of *Boyracers is* a digital one. Theirs is, as I'm sure yours was, an attention span battered by MTV, sitcoms, computer games, song lyrics, film quotes and advertising jingles. The story finishes – by coincidence, not by design – the day before 9/11, in Scotland as it was at the start of the new millennium, before the invasions of Afghanistan and Iraq, before the election of a SNP government in Holyrood, before *Lord of the Rings* and vast superhero franchises, 3D cinema, the financial crash, the iPod, the iPhone, the iPad, the e-reader, George Bush, Barack Obama, David Cameron and Nick Clegg, the hollowing-out of the public sector (and Scottish football), and the mass

---

2   Actually, I only typed the first half. My girlfriend, Kirstin, typed the rest of it and contributed wise editorial suggestions.

spell cast by the internet. What a huge ten years it has been. *Boyracers* is an artefact from an era when mobile phones, text-messaging and online communication had only *just* come into widespread usage, but in its pages we can see the world speeding up and becoming illusory, less in tangent with real emotion and deep connections between people. The book betrays a sense of trying to hold on to a world that will inevitably flash into the past.

And so it has. The turn of the millennium in Britain was buoyed by an expanding property market, employment, widespread university access, rising living standards, the demise of the Tories (oh, the irony) and Scottish football clubs who could actually compete with the best in Europe. The masters of the universe have since found ways to take it all from us again. Let's admit it, we fell for their pish. It was a hallucination based on financial sector greed, phantom money and insatiable consumerism. It would be impossible to write, for example, a sentence like 'We are a generation who awoke to find all gods dead, all wars fought' with a straight face now, given *Boyracers* was published at virtually the same moment the planes struck the Twin Towers.

This is why, despite its flaws, I still love this book. It represents good times, that I lived through and created in. It's not only written by and about a person I'm not any more, but describes a Britain we might not see the likes of again for a while. For sure, it's going to be a hard winter under modern capitalism, but if there's any message in *Boyracers* that still comes through, it's that there's always a road leading out. We just have to trust ourselves to follow it.

Alan Bissett
March 2011

Acknowledgements

Thanks again to everyone who was thanked first time around, but especially Thomas Tobias, Victoria Hobbs, Mollie Skehal, Magi Gibson, the members of Stirling Writers Group circa 2000, Caroline Waddell and the late Eileen Gibson.

Thanks for her diligent labour on this edition, and for her insights into the novel then and now, to my partner, Kirstin. You walked these lines with me.

Thanks to Alison Rae, Neville Moir, Jan Rutherford and Vikki O'Reilly at Polygon for their support with this edition.

Heddy Haw